KU-481-324

CAPTURED COUNTESS

Ann Lethbridge

All rights reserved including the right of reproduction in whole
or in part in any form. This edition is published by arrangement with
Harlequin Books S.A.

This is a work of fiction. Names, characters, places, locations and
incidents are purely fictional and bear no relationship to any real
life individuals, living or dead, or to any actual places, business
establishments, locations, events or incidents. Any resemblance is
entirely coincidental.

This book is sold subject to the condition that it shall not, by way of
trade or otherwise, be lent, resold, hired out or otherwise circulated
without the prior consent of the publisher in any form of binding or
cover other than that in which it is published and without a similar
condition including this condition being imposed on the subsequent
purchaser.

® and TM are trademarks owned and used by the trademark owner
and/or its licensee. Trademarks marked with ® are registered with the
United Kingdom Patent Office and/or the Office for Harmonisation in
the Internal Market and in other countries.

First published in Great Britain 2014
by Mills & Boon, an imprint of Harlequin (UK) Limited,
Large Print edition 2015
Harlequin (UK) Limited, Eton House, 18-24 Paradise Road,
Richmond, Surrey TW9 1SR

© 2014 Michèle Ann Young

ISBN: 978-0-263-25538-6

Harlequin (UK) Limited's policy is to use papers that are natural,
renewable and recyclable products and made from wood grown in
sustainable forests. The logging and manufacturing processes conform
to the legal environmental regulations of the country of origin.

Printed and bound in Great Britain
by CPI Antony Rowe, Chippenham, Wiltshire

LIBRARIES NI	
C901394894	
MAG	12.02.16
AF	£14.99
AHS	

He grinned at Nicky. 'I've been on the Town a long time, Countess. I have not failed to learn how to make the most of the company of a lovely and enticing woman.'

She settled herself more comfortably on the seat. 'I do not respond well to flattery.'

'And if it is the truth, Countess?'
She shook her head. *Incorrigible.*

LIBRARIES NI
WITHDRAWN FROM STOCK

She said it the French way and the caress in her voice was unmistakable. Velvet and honey and fine old brandy wrapped up in one word.

'But you should know, Milor' Mooreshead,' she continued as he wove between the slow traffic of carters and tradesmen about their business, 'your reputation precedes you. I have been warned that there isn't a lady in London who does not fear for her virtue when you smile her way.'

LIBRARIES NI
WITHDRAWN FROM STOCK

AUTHOR NOTE

Have you ever wondered what it would be like to live in another time—to be the heroine of some grand adventure? I know how fortunate I am to get to do that on a daily basis. It doesn't always go as smoothly as I would like, or exactly to plan, as characters have a way of twisting things to suit themselves. On the other hand, I must say I have a lot of fun discovering their stories. This time we are revisiting Beresford Abbey, which you may recall from HAUNTED BY THE EARL'S TOUCH. The ghost is being her usual helpful self—or is she? And the French are massing across the Channel.

Without a doubt the Regency era is one of my all-time favourite periods of history. However, it can easily be forgotten, in the glitz and glamour of London's ballrooms, that it was a time of war as well as a time of great change—the dawn of our modern age. I touch on these matters as we follow Nicky and Gabe's adventure.

If you want the latest news on my books, go to my website, www.annlethbridge.com, where you will have a chance to win my newest book and sign up for my newsletter, 'like' me on Facebook, AnnLethbridgeAuthor, or follow me on Twitter @AnnLethbridge.

Ann Lethbridge has been reading Regency novels for as long as she can remember. She always imagined herself as Lizzie Bennet, or one of Georgette Heyer's heroines, and would often recreate the stories in her head with different outcomes or scenes. When she sat down to write her own novel it was no wonder that she returned to her first love: the Regency.

Ann grew up roaming Britain with her military father. Her family lived in many towns and villages across the country, from the Outer Hebrides to Hampshire. She spent memorable family holidays in the West Country and in Dover, where her father was born. She now lives in Canada, with her husband, two beautiful daughters, and a Maltese terrier named Teaser, who spends his days on a chair beside the computer, making sure she doesn't slack off.

Ann visits Britain every year, to undertake research and also to visit family members who are very understanding about her need to poke around old buildings and visit every antiquity within a hundred miles. If you would like to know more about Ann and her research, or to contact her, visit her website at www.annlethbridge.com. She loves to hear from readers.

Previous novels by this author:

THE RAKE'S INHERITED COURTESAN†
WICKED RAKE, DEFIANT MISTRESS
CAPTURED FOR THE CAPTAIN'S PLEASURE
THE GOVERNESS AND THE EARL
  (part of *Mills & Boon New Voices...* anthology)
THE GAMEKEEPER'S LADY*
MORE THAN A MISTRESS*
LADY ROSABELLA'S RUSE†
THE LAIRD'S FORBIDDEN LADY**
HAUNTED BY THE EARL'S TOUCH
HER HIGHLAND PROTECTOR**
FALLING FOR THE HIGHLAND ROGUE**
RETURN OF THE PRODIGAL GILVRY**

and recent books in the Mills & Boon® Historical *Undone!* series:

DELICIOUSLY DEBAUCHED BY THE RAKE
A RAKE FOR CHRISTMAS
IN BED WITH THE HIGHLANDER
ONE NIGHT WITH THE HIGHLANDER **

And in Mills & Boon® Historical eBooks:

PRINCESS CHARLOTTE'S CHOICE
  (part of *Royal Weddings Through the Ages* anthology)

And in M&B:

LADY OF SHAME
  (part of *Castonbury Park* Regency mini-series)

†linked by character
*linked by character
**The Gilvrys of Dunross*

Did you know that some of these novels are also available as eBooks? Visit www.millsandboon.co.uk

DEDICATION

It isn't often an author has the privilege of
working with two editors, but for this book
I have been fortunate to have the advice of
Joanne Grant and Anne Marie Ryan, so I am
doubly blessed. Thank you, ladies, for your
help in bringing this story to fruition.

I would also like to dedicate this book
to my sister-in-law, Diane Jones, a courageous
woman who loved family above all else.

Chapter One

August 1804

When Napoleon amassed an army twenty-two miles away on the other side of the English Channel, what should an English peer of the realm do? Attend Lady Heatherfield's summer ball, naturally. Gabe D'Arcy, the recently gazetted Marquess of Mooreshead, eyed the occupants in the over-hot marble-columned ballroom with a sense of despair. Did they have no idea of the danger facing their country? Did they not see the disillusion of the common man on their estates, in their cities and towns? If they did, they didn't show it. Or seem to care.

The myriad candles reflected in gilt-edged mirrors threatened blindness as he gazed at his fellow peers. How would these carefully coiffed heads look in the basket at the foot of a guillotine? It was where they would end up if Britain became a satellite republic of France.

It wouldn't happen. Not if he had anything to say about it. He'd given up everything he had to make sure it did not. His principles. His honour. Not to mention his rightful inheritance. Damn his father.

He and his father had never seen eye to eye about a great many things—politics, the treatment of tenants, the bullying of his mother—but Gabe never expected his father's outright mistrust. Had been shocked when he understood how deep their differences of opinion had gone, to the point where his father considered him a traitor to the family name and to his country. But that was all water under the bridge. His father was dead and Gabe's rebellion against his father's autocratic rule had made him who he was now. A penniless marquess and a spy.

He did not let his impatience or frustration show. A worried countenance fuelled gossip. He'd suffered enough of that when details of his father's will had surfaced. The first to turn their backs had been the matchmaking mamas who had plagued his early years. A poverty-stricken marquess wasn't worth the time of day. Not that he'd cared, since he had no intention of marrying for years. If ever.

The hearsay about the unsavoury source of his income to support his privileged and idle bachelor life, whispers of him gulling green 'uns at the gambling tables or, worse, cheating, rolled off his shoulders. They were conjectures he'd encouraged.

The rumours about why he'd been denied the income from his estates cut pretty deep. Gossip about his support of the French revolution. The doubts about his loyalty to his country. Unfortunately for his pride, those rumours were also to be encouraged. They served a higher purpose.

Worse would be the revulsion of his fellows if the truth of his real activities came to light. A man could seduce innocents, kill a man in a duel or cheat on his wife, as long as it was all open and above board. It was the kind of underhanded dealings Gabe engaged in that would make him *persona non grata* in the world of the *ton*.

So he let them think what they would while he risked life and limb to save theirs. Given his preference, he would never visit London at all, but since he kept his base of operations secret, and since his French contacts demanded the occasional face-to-face interaction, he'd had no choice but to don the guise of charming philanderer and inveterate gambler and mingle with his fellows.

Hence his appearance at Lady Heatherfield's ball.

A passing gentleman lurched into Gabe, who put out a hand to minimise the clumsily executed *accident*.

'I beg your pardon, *m'sieur*,' the florid-faced, rotund gentleman murmured, bowing low. 'M'sieur Armande, *à votre service*.'

The contact he'd been expecting. 'Mooreshead. You suffer from the heat, no doubt.' Code words of recognition, even though they needed none. Armande, a supposed *émigré*, used his position to gain information for money. They had come into contact more than once over the years.

The man bowed again. 'Indeed. Fortunately, the winds are strengthening and should bring a change in the weather.'

The winds that would bring the French from France, but there had been a change in plans. What change? 'Let us hope it occurs soon, sir.'

'Indeed. I have been almost prostrate these last five days.'

Five days? He had not anticipated they would make their move so soon. He had to get back to Cornwall and prepare. But what was the change in plan? 'We will all welcome a change in the weather, even if it brings storms.'

'The captain of your yacht, the *Phoenix*, I believe, would likely be interested.'

His orders were being sent to his ship. Why drag him all the way to London to tell him that? 'I shall be sure to let him know.'

Armande dug out his snuff-box and offered it to Gabe. He lowered his voice. 'You are in danger, *mon ami*. They do not trust you. Someone has been sent.' He smiled blandly and raised his voice to normal tones. 'No one but the English would fill their rooms so full on such a warm summer evening.'

A spurt of anger surged hot in Gabe's chest. He controlled it. He'd spent years trying to win the trust of both sides in this war—any chink in the walls he'd built could prove disastrous. 'Who?' he asked in an undertone. A double-edged question. Who had been sent? And by whom? Armande had loyalty to neither side. He glanced around as if considering the man's earlier words. 'Personally, I am surprised anyone is in town at all at this time of year.'

Armande shook his head, his eyes regretful. He did not know the answer to either of Gabe's questions. 'A debt paid.'

Gabe had saved Armande from being picked up by a British coastguard one dark night. All part of the job, but even men like Armande, a man who profited from war, had a code of honour and paid his debts.

The Frenchman once more raised his voice. 'No doubt refreshment is in order.'

'Over there, *m'sieur*. Enjoy your evening.' Gabe indicated the direction of the alcove where a footman guarded a table groaning beneath the weight of punchbowls. The Frenchman bowed and moved on.

Who didn't trust him, Gabe pondered. The French? Or the British?

Either was possible. Or was it speculation without substance? In the world of espionage rumours ran riot.

'How was Norfolk?' a voice behind him asked as a heavy hand fell on his shoulder.

He turned to meet the stern, harsh face of one of his oldest friends. Bane, Earl Beresford. One of only a handful of people Gabe would trust with his misbegotten life. A captain of industry, Bane owned mines and factories that fed the British war machine. His head would not remain on his shoulders if Napoleon held sway.

'Norfolk is…Norfolk,' Gabe said with a brief smile, knowing they were not talking about Norfolk at all. Years ago in a moment of weakness, he had trusted Bane with his secrets. And hence his life. In return, Bane had allowed him to use his family estate in Cornwall as a secret base. 'Manners creeps around with snail-like efficiency. Boats come and go with cargo, both legal and illicit.' He always told the truth. Or as close to it as made no difference, whenever possible. You never knew who might be listening.

'It's good to see you back in town,' Bane said in his usual brusque manner. 'Come for dinner. Next week. We would be delighted to feed you.'

'I suppose you want to talk politics and the state of the British economy. Poor Mary.'

Bane's dark face lit up at the mention of his wife. 'She's used to it. And she has some pretty good ideas of her own. So, will you come?'

The elegant Lady Mary had a lovely and very delicate neck. Easy work for a sharp blade. With a conscious effort, Gabe shook off his black thoughts and inclined his head. 'It would be my very great pleasure, but I am not in town long enough, I'm afraid.' The news he'd just received made it imperative he leave as soon as he informed Sceptre of this latest development. Unlike agents of the Home Office, who reported to Parliament, the political arm of government, Sceptre owed its allegiance to no one but the House of Hanover. Fortunately, for the most part, the goals of these agents of security were in accord. Sceptre, however, tended to be more secretive and entirely ruthless in achieving its aims.

'Next time you are in town, then,' Bane said. 'Let me know your plans in advance and I will arrange a quiet evening at home. Meanwhile, stop racketing about. You are looking quite done up.'

He laughed. 'Surely not that bad?'

'Not so bad others will notice.' Bane strolled away.

The man saw too much.

Gabe sighed and glanced around the room for a suitable dance partner to help maintain his façade. One who would not immediately give him the cold shoulder. There were plenty of females who enjoyed flirting with a man of his reputed wickedness, provided he wasn't looking for more than a dalliance.

The babble on the far side of the room intensified. The stir of the *ton* at some new piece of gossip, some *on dit* or scandal, no doubt. The crowds at the edge of the dance floor shifted like water swirling in a strong current before parting around the object of their interest.

A woman he didn't know. She wasn't particularly tall, or even particularly short. Her hair wasn't brown, or chestnut or guinea gold. Strangely, it was all of them. Her features were neither classical nor pretty nor plain, because one only noticed her large cerulean-blue eyes framed by surprisingly dark lashes. Were they dyed or natural? And why would he care? She didn't glitter or sparkle as other females did, nor did she fade into the modest obscurity of a miss new on the town. She glowed with the incandescent warmth of the pearl choker around her throat.

And the *Beau Monde* hovered around her like bees over clover. Sumptuously dressed women hung on her every word, while the men mentally slavered over the flesh exposed by the low-scooping gown. The lure of shoulders and high, full breasts of palest white startlingly scattered with freckles. Instinct told him she was French. Few British women would dare such a diaphanous gown of silver and dampen their petticoats with such blatant unconcern. A recent *émigrée*, perhaps? One who had arrived during his absence these past few months.

A woman as sensual as sin. The words reverberated in his head. Surprising. Shocking. These days, he rarely had that kind of reaction to a woman, no matter how beautiful or fashionable.

Her gaze passed over him and flicked back. An almost imperceptible lift of brows as dark as her lashes. Interest. Followed immediately by an acknowledgement of desire. The look strummed every nerve in his body, a vibration followed swiftly by heat. Things inside him shifted, as if his spine had realigned. Stunned, he froze. His body stirred as he was caught in her clear-eyed gaze. A coolly calculating glance that spun out into timelessness before it fractured into naked vulnerability. Or not. A blink and the very idea seemed absurd for such a self-contained creature.

Realisation dawned. She was the one of whom he'd been warned.

The French, then. How typical of them to suppose he couldn't resist the wiles of a woman. Clearly, they'd let appearances deceive them into thinking he was an easy mark. Yes, he found the woman extraordinarily attractive, but so did every male in the room.

Damn it all. And if he was right, why test his

loyalty at such a critical juncture? That he now had to fight a battle on yet another front was irritating to say the least. Yet, if he'd been in their shoes, he likely would have been testing his loyalty too. His role had become pivotal to their plans. If he proved a weak link in the chain, it might set the invasion back by months. He certainly didn't want that. The more nervous they became, the harder it would be to put a stop to their ambitions once and for all.

If he told Sceptre of his suspicions about this woman, they would demand he eliminate the danger. Coldly. Brutally. Just as Marianne had been eliminated. His stomach clenched at the memory.

No. Not without proof. Suspicions were one thing, but it behove him to discover the truth of who had sent her and why. Only a fool would eliminate a danger without knowing from whence it came.

Tension tightened his muscles. A reaction to the knowledge of an upcoming skirmish. Retaining his outward easy calm, he sauntered through the ballroom, bowing and smiling, while his skin tingled and his body burned with an inner flame. He couldn't remember the last time he'd felt this much anticipation. Because of the way he had come alive during the space of a glance.

As he moved among his peers, he heard her name on their lips. Nicoletta, Countess Vilandry. Society's new novelty.

He drifted towards the refreshment table, glad to see Armande was nowhere in sight. He deliberately slowed his breathing, forced himself to think logically, sifting through the bloodlines of the French nobility. Vilandry. An old name. And one now extinguished, he thought. Lack of certainty made him uneasy. Ignorance was vulnerability in this high-stakes game. But no matter what he didn't know, his gut sensed she was the one of whom Armande had warned.

Heat leached away, followed by cold resolve. One way or another, he must delve the secret depths of the Countess Vilandry before returning to Cornwall. And quickly.

Without a doubt, Gabriel D'Arcy, Marquess of Mooreshead, would be Nicky's most difficult challenge to date. The gauntlet in his chilly blue eyes had been unmistakably thrown down before he coolly turned away. Not a man to be trifled with carelessly, she'd been warned, despite his reputation for charm.

Something had happened during the course of that brief visual encounter. Despite her every effort, the familiar mask of the Countess Vilandry, the seductive woman she'd become to survive her marriage, had almost slipped from her grasp. Leaving Nicky Rideau, the girl she had been a long time ago, open and exposed and unprotected. Perhaps it was Mooreshead's sheer physical beauty that had pierced her protective shield, his golden locks and masculine physique, with no sign of the corruption she'd expected to see in a man base enough to betray his country. The sweetly painful little flutter low in her belly when their eyes made contact had been a terrible shock, when she'd expected to feel nothing at all. Such a display of weakness would have earned her a slap if Vilandry had been alive to see such a beginner's mistake. There were no emotions involved in a seduction. The woman never admired the man. She only teased and tormented.

She'd realised her mistake in an instant and drawn the Countess around her like a domino made of steel. It was too late for Nicky Rideau. She'd been buried years ago. The Countess never let her own desires run amok. And no matter how handsome or charming he proved, he would pose no threat to a woman who had learned her arts from a master. She would expose all of his secrets and find the proof of his treachery.

Failure was not an option. Not if she wanted Paul to keep his promise to provide the false papers that would get her into France. The hint she'd received that her sister might yet be alive and alone was a bruise on her heart. And the sour taste of guilt in the back of her throat.

Exposing Mooreshead would give her the opportunity to know the truth once and for all.

It would take a delicate touch to reel in a man with his reputation. She'd made it her business to unearth the gossip about him. A man of fashion. A Corinthian. A man who drove to an inch and who displayed to advantage in the pugilist ring despite his whipcord leanness and rangy height. And an incorrigible rake. A man who took nothing seriously, unless it was the cut of his coat and the set of his cravat. A man who laughed easily, whether he won or lost a fortune. A man who needed a fortune to support his lifestyle, but who was rumoured to be penniless. That last alone made her suspicious.

But it would not be easy to pierce that carefully constructed armour of devil-may-care. At least, not easy for any other woman. The Countess had been well schooled in the art of seduction and male manipulation. Her husband had delighted in teaching his young bride how to please him as well as keep his friends and political enemies dancing to his tune. She shuddered at the recollection.

Still, Vilandry's lessons would stand her in good stead in this new venture of hers. And if in the end, Paul did not send her to France to help with Britain's war effort, she would have earned enough to pay her own way.

A quick scan of the room found Mooreshead near the refreshment table idly watching the dancing. Or appearing to do so. She smiled at her companion, the estimable, plump Mrs Featherstone. As a widow, Nicky did not need a chaperone, but the elderly matron, with her grey frizzled hair and placid expression, not only added a necessary aura of respectability, she was the link to her spymaster. *'Ma chère madame,'* she said idly, 'why is it the English must keep their rooms so warm? I swear I am parched.'

'Do you find it so, my dear?' the other woman said, looking vague. A habit she cultivated to great success. Her eyes sharpened as they fell on their target and she gave a small smile. 'Why is there never a waiter nearby when one needs one? Let me see what I can do.' She drifted in the direction the refreshment table.

A moment or two later Mooreshead arrived in Mrs Featherstone's wake, carrying two goblets of champagne. She smiled her thanks as he handed her a glass.

'Countess,' Mrs Featherstone said, 'may I introduce Lord Mooreshead, who so kindly came to my rescue. Mooreshead, the Countess Vilandry.'

Nicky gave him a warm smile, dipping her

knees and inclining her head, well aware that the advantage of his height gave him a clear view of the valley between her breasts. She felt his gaze linger there just a second too long. Any other woman might have blushed or simpered; she simply waited for his gaze to return to her face. She held out her hand. 'My lord.'

'Countess.' He held her hand in a firm yet gentle grip and made a bow of exactly the correct depth.

'Mrs Featherstone tells me you have been in town a month,' he continued. 'I regret my tardiness in making you welcome to London. Had I known the world was about to change, I assure you, I would not have left for anything so dull as a visit to the country.'

His voice was deep and well modulated and his eyes danced with laughter. At himself and at the world in general. Or so he would have it appear. She was once more conscious of shoulders that owed nothing to the skill of his tailor and a betraying pulse low in her belly. A woman's appreciation for a magnificent male. A warning that she must be wary of a man who so easily aroused her feminine desires. Such female weakness could only endanger her mission. But desire was not something she feared. It was a two-edged sword she knew well how to wield and she would have no hesitation in using its blade to put an end to his disloyalty.

She inclined her head. 'A charmingly expressed sentiment, my lord, but a gross exaggeration.'

He chuckled and placed a hand to his heart. ''Pon my honour, my lady, you wound me.'

'It was not my intention.'

Mrs Featherstone touched her arm. 'Would you excuse me for a moment, Countess? I particularly wished to have words with a friend of mine this evening and she arrived a few moments ago. I fear I may lose her in this crush.'

A planned excuse to leave her alone with her mark. 'Of course,' Nicky said. 'I shall be well entertained by his lordship in your absence.'

'I shall do my best,' Mooreshead responded and bowed as her companion departed. A moment later, his charming smile held sensual promise. 'In the interests of my duty to entertain, may I request your hand for this next dance, Countess?'

The urge to give in to the obvious strength of will in those piercing blue eyes, his absolute confidence she would not refuse, was an irresistible pull. A delicate touch, she reminded herself. Too eager and he would grow wary. Or bored. She gave a regretful sigh. 'Thank you, but, no, I am promised to another. Perhaps later?'

On cue, the young man who had sought the first dance the instant she entered the ballroom approached. He bowed and held out his arm with an expression of triumph. 'My dance, I believe, Countess.' His expression cooled as his eyes met those of Mooreshead. He gave a nod of his head. 'My lord.'

'She's all yours,' Mooreshead responded with the air of a man who had the right to relinquish possession. 'I will return later for our dance. The supper dance, I believe we agreed.'

She shook her head at the way he had finessed taking her to supper, but smiled. *'Bien sûr.* Until then.'

Mooreshead bowed and sauntered away

Well, that had been easier than she'd expected. Almost too easy.

She would have to be careful not to rush her fences and make him overly wary. A man who walked in the dangerous world of intelligence would not be easily fooled.

Fascination with a female. It happened occasionally. Even to a man as jaded as him. It was her boldness he liked. And the intelligence behind the seductive knowing in her cornflower-blue eyes with the starburst of grey in their centres. They were eyes that seemed older than her years.

Even so, under other circumstances, he would have sheared off at the obvious ploy by the Featherstone woman. It might be a coincidence that the countess had clearly decided to inveigle her way into his company at the same moment Gabe had been warned of treachery afoot. It might also be a coincidence that her appearance coincided with new orders from France. But when both occurred at one and the same time? Coincidence it was not.

The gauntlet had been tossed at his feet. He couldn't afford not to pick it up with matters at such a crucial stage. How annoying that despite himself, he was interested in her. As a woman. He huffed out a breath and forced himself to think logically. He needed to know why she'd been sent. What it was they suspected. He strolled around the ballroom, speaking casually to those acquaintances who would spare him a word, garnering the latest *on dit*. The life blood of the *ton*. Apparently little was known about the Countess Vilandry apart from the fact they all thought her divine.

She was the fashion. Her style admired by men and women alike. No doubt about it, the countess warranted a closer inspection.

His groin tightened at the thought of the pleasure such closeness might bring.

Inwardly, he froze. Not for years had he had such a visceral response to a woman. He certainly never let them get close. Marianne had cured him of any wish to open his heart. So why was this one different?

Something sharp and unwelcome twisted in his chest. The emptiness of his self-imposed isolation? The knowledge that there wasn't a woman alive who would want him? Was that why he was attracted to her? Because she was a creature of lies and darkness, like him?

He mentally cursed and shook off the shadows of the past. The task was simple. Find out if she was the one Armande had warned of and, if so, eliminate the problem.

With the supper dance still a good hour away, he wandered into the card room, passing the minutes until it was time to claim his dance by joining a game of faro. It certainly wouldn't do to be seen hanging around at the edge of the dance floor watching her like a slavering dog. Everyone knew he didn't run after females. They ran after him. And the only ones who caught him were those who were interested in nothing but good times and no ties. As far as the world was concerned, she must be no different from his usual fare.

The stakes at his chosen table were high enough to account for his inner tension. Yet the urge to return to the ballroom and see if he had imagined the whole attraction tugged at his mind. He raised the stakes to the groans of his companions. And again when he won. Their gazes turned questioning. He could read their minds. Had he cheated?

With studied slowness, he abandoned his place, picking up his winnings to disapproving stares, and headed out into the mêlée of swirling skirts and sparkling jewels. Despite the crowds, his eyes found her immediately. A mysterious woman who shimmered among lesser gems. Lust grabbed him low in his gut.

Devil take it, whether he was right and she was sent by an enemy or not, he was going to have regrets.

He bit back a curse.

The supper dance was a cotillion. To Nicky's delight, Mooreshead proved himself a skilled and graceful dancer. Graceful in a manly way. He was always just where one expected him to be, never turning the wrong way or forgetting a figure. And he conversed easily. No matter how difficult the step, his eyes said he was thinking of nothing but his partner. It was a skill few men managed with any great success. She was impressed.

'How are you enjoying London?' he asked as they came together, hands linked in a turn.

'I find it exceedingly respectable.'

A fair brow shot up. The ice in his eyes warmed with amusement. 'You would prefer it otherwise?'

The dance parted them and she smiled at her new partner, who turned red and stumbled.

Mooreshead rejoined her at the top of the set and they passed down the lines between the other couples.

'I do not have a preference for things not respectable,' she said, smiling up at him. 'But I do find it a little dull.'

'Then it seems the gentlemen in London are failing you badly.'

Ah, there it was, the offer for them to become closer. They separated at the end of the line. Three figures later, they joined hands for a fast turn. A shiver ran down her spine at their touch despite the layers of their gloves. Anticipation. Followed quickly by annoyance. Yes, the man was attractive. No woman could ignore the classically carved features of his face, or the sensual mobility of his mouth, or even the way the candlelight glinted gold in his hair, but she must never forget he was a traitor with the potential to cause the loss of hundreds of lives. Perhaps even thousands. And not just soldiers. Innocent lives. A cold calm filled her chest. Her work was too important to let her desire for a handsome man make her starry-eyed.

She arched a brow. 'I presume you think you would do better.'

A take-it-or-leave-it grin lit his face. So devil-may-care her stomach gave a pleasurable little hop. 'I know I would.' His deep voice was a velvet caress.

A tingle of warmth low in her abdomen cut short her breath. No. This was not about her desires. Duty came first. And Minette. Only by keeping her distance could she trap him successfully. He had to believe her indifferent. There was nothing more alluring to a man for whom women routinely swooned, than one who remained elusive.

She gave a non-committal shrug. 'So you say.'

Something flashed in his eyes. Frustration? Annoyance? Or something warmer? Only time would tell. He forbore to make any further comment, leaving her in the dark and awaiting his next move.

The dance concluded. It was time to adjourn for supper and she placed a hand on his forearm. It was a forearm with the strength of steel beneath an elegantly tailored coat of the finest cloth. Her fingers tingled with a longing to explore the detail of that strength. A surprising reaction, since in her experience, beneath their trappings, fashionable men either ran to fat or scrawniness. But not Mooreshead. The man looked to have the physique of a Greek god. It was a theory she would likely have an opportunity to test in the not-too-distant future.

To achieve her goal. Nothing more.

The cream-and-gold room set aside for supper was tastefully arranged with small, round tables that allowed guests to eat and talk in small groups after selecting their own food from the sideboard against one wall. He held both their plates in one large hand, while she selected the morsels she fancied: lobster patties, oysters and little, fancy cakes. He led her to a table in the corner. A perfect place from which they could watch the room as a whole and no one could approach without advanced warning.

It was the table she would have chosen if given the option.

As if by tacit agreement, no one else made an attempt to join them. It was not surprising, for they both lived on the fringes of good society. She knew that about him, even as he must know the same about her.

'No doubt all the gentlemen you have met tonight have told you how stunning you look,' Mooreshead said. 'May I therefore say how honoured I am that you chose to take supper with me?'

'Why, my lord, you have a silver tongue as well as good looks.'

'My lady is too kind.'

'*D'accord.* It seems we have reached a fine understanding of one another.'

His chuckle in response sounded so natural she was enchanted. Not something she wished to be at all. Not with him. She must keep a straight head on her shoulders.

'You must have been in England a long time,' he said. 'Your speech is impeccable.'

'*Merci.* I left France after the death of my husband.' She too could avoid the provision of useful facts.

He frowned as he attempted the calculation of age and circumstances. He would likely think her young to be a wife, let alone a widow. Appearances were deceiving. He would be horrified to know she'd been wed for nearly five years by the time she was twenty. 'It must have been a very difficult time,' he murmured in a tone that invited confidences.

'I survived when many did not.'

'You are to be congratulated on your escape.'

It was what she kept telling herself. As they so often did, the images of the fire flashed before her mind. The face of the soldier, Captain Chiroux, a demon's mask of satisfaction in the glare of the flames. If she had realised… But it was too late to change what she had done. She could only hope Minette had somehow survived, then she would indeed feel fortunate to have escaped from France. If not, then there was only regret.

'Where have you been until now?' he asked.

'Waiting for you.'

His eyes widened. And then he laughed. Yet the shadows deep in those icy-blue eyes gave his laugh the lie. The danger he exuded was not merely that of a male in pursuit of pleasure, though that was certainly there in good measure, the shadows hinted at darker pursuits that chilled her very soul.

She widened her eyes in feigned innocence. 'I see you do not believe me.' She gave a theatrical sigh. 'And to add insult to injury, here comes my companion, Madame Featherstone. I am afraid our delightful tête-à-tête is to be disturbed.' The poor dear looked quite harassed beneath her puce turban and its nodding peacock feather. Well, she would. She was supposed to keep a close eye on her and Mooreshead. At least until they were sure he suspected nothing. A cornered man was more than risky.

'Do you ride?' she asked with one eye on the widow's imminent arrival. 'I usually go to Hyde Park at seven in the morning. Before it is busy.'

His eyes gleamed with wickedness. 'So, you

like to gallop.' The innuendo was not lost on her, but she chose to ignore it.

After a brief hesitation, he continued smoothly. 'I'll take you up in my carriage at six. Bring your horse and your groom. We will breakfast afterwards.'

She smiled her acceptance of the invitation as Mrs Featherstone arrived at their table. Mooreshead rose to his feet and offered the older lady a chair with a bow and a charming smile. If he felt the slightest irritation at their lack of privacy, it did not show. Exquisite manners were his forte. But a storm lurked beneath the unruffled surface. She could feel it battering against her skin.

As was usual among the English, the conversation turned to the weather. Certainly no one was ever ill-bred enough to mention the war.

Chapter Two

The discovery of the Countess Vilandry's dwelling required little effort on Gabe's part. Her location in Golden Square was known by all and sundry. While not exactly desirable, the location was respectable. Her companion, Mrs Featherstone, was an unknown and generally described as bit of a mushroom. Not that Gabe put much store by stuffy conventions. While the countess might be considered fast, and a little *risqué*, his enquiries into her background and her obvious acceptance into society had made him wonder if his suspicions might be wrong.

Sceptre had been unable to tell him anything, good or bad.

Émigrés were nothing unusual these days. London seethed with refugees from Bonaparte's vision of France. The more he had thought about it, the more certain he had become that neither side was so stupid as to send anyone so obvious against him. Or was his reluctance to believe it the result of the smouldering attraction low in his gut every time he brought her to mind. Wanting a woman that much was dangerous to any man's sanity, but in his case it was completely out of character. The few relationships he had allowed since returning from France had been fleeting, an integral part of establishing his persona. Nevertheless, after Armande's warning, he could not afford to ignore such an obvious play for his attention. Not now when one stumble, one error in judgement, would bring down his carefully erected house of cards.

He drew his carriage up at her front door, pleased to see a waiting groom mounted on a staid-looking hack holding the reins of a showy little black mare who showed the whites of her eyes at the sight of his curricle. His tiger, Jimmy, jumped down and went to his horses' heads at the same moment the front door opened and the countess stepped out in a riding habit of pale blue that showed off her curvaceous figure to perfection. A curly brimmed beaver adorned with a veil set on severely styled hair made her look naughty.

Gabe leapt down and strode up the steps to meet her. He bowed. 'Good morning, Countess. I am encouraged by your promptness.'

A corner of her mouth curled upwards. 'Don't be, *mon cher* Mooreshead. My Peridot does not like to be kept waiting.'

'Your mare is as beautiful as her mistress.'

'And far more impatient.'

He chuckled. She was clearly a woman skilled in the art of flirtation with a lively wit. She would keep his thoughts from growing too dark for an hour or two. She might even be willing to slake his lust. His body hardened. He quelled his surge of desire with ruthless determination. He had other more important matters on his mind. Like leaving London for Cornwall at the earliest opportunity, which he would do as soon as he was sure the countess was harmless.

Taking her hand, he escorted her down the steps onto the flagstones. 'Then I must not keep either of you waiting. I have ordered our breakfast for nine.'

Her blue eyes sparkled. 'You are very forward, *milor'.*'

He inclined his head. 'Faint heart does not win fair lady.' He gestured to the curricle. 'May I assist you?'

'*Certainement.*'

As he lifted her, his fingers spanned her slender waist and, despite her very feminine curves, he was aware of the lithe strength beneath his hands. A woman who rode frequently and hard.

Once more his body stirred at an image of the kind of riding she might enjoy that would involve them being alone together. Between the sheets. Once more the urgency of his visceral response surprised him. He was without doubt going to enjoy their association, no matter how brief.

He walked around to his side of the carriage and climbed up. 'Your man will follow behind?'

'He will.'

'Let 'em go, Jimmy,' Gabe said. The little tiger jumped clear and Gabe set his horses in motion.

Countess Vilandry frowned. 'Your tiger does not come with us?'

Yes, this lady was unusually quick witted. 'We have your groom.'

'Yes, but who will mind your horses while we ride? Oh!' She laughed. 'You, *Milor'* Mooreshead, are a very bad man.'

He grinned at her. 'I've been on the town a long time, Countess. I have not failed to learn how to make the most of the company of a lovely and enticing woman.'

She settled herself more comfortably on the seat. 'I do not respond well to flattery.'

'And if it is the truth, Countess?'

She shook her head. 'Incorrigible.' She said it the French way and the caress in her voice was unmistakable. Velvet and honey and fine old brandy wrapped up in one word.

'But you should know, *Milor'* Mooreshead,' she continued as he wove between the slow traffic of carters and tradesmen about their business, 'your reputation precedes you. I have been warned that there isn't a lady in London who does not fear for her virtue when you smile her way.'

'Call me Gabe,' he said, deliberately avoiding her teasing glance by pretending to concentrate on feathering between two slow-moving vehicles.

'Gabe?'

'Short for Gabriel.'

'A devil named for an angel? *Très amusant.*'

'Indeed. But do not tell me you did not already know.' She had to know his name. And he would not have her think him an idiot. Nor did he want to play word games. Or not much anyway. He wanted his suspicions put to rest. Though that didn't make a scrap of sense, when he needed to learn just who had been sent and by whom. It really would be so much easier if she was the one. He could deal with her today and leave for Cornwall first thing in the morning. He turned his head and gave her a quizzical smile so he could read her expression.

Her eyes danced with amusement as if she had nothing on her mind but easy flirtation. '*Tiens,* you will spoil the jest?'

'It grows stale with age.'

She laughed. A light bright sound that spread unaccustomed warmth in his chest. 'So it is good we have such staleness out of the way, then. And you will call me Nicky. Nicoletta is such a mouthful for the English tongue, don't you think?'

'Nicky,' he said, tasting it on his tongue, sharp and tart, yet, like her, exotic. 'It suits you.'

A little frown creased her forehead. 'A compliment?'

'A woman as lovely as you does not lack for compliments.'

'Lovely? *Mais non.* Not at all. I think they call it *je ne sais quoi, n'est-ce pas*?'

'It seems we are at *point non plus.* At a standstill in this war of words.'

'War?' She raised a brow. 'Surely not. Relax, *mon ami*, and enjoy a ride on what appears to be the coming of a very fine day.'

He laughed and helped her out of the carriage. He could barely remember the last time he had found a woman so enticingly amusing. It was like coming into the light after days below ground. And she was right. Whatever she was, lovely did not adequately describe it. The sum of her was more attractive than the individual parts. And therefore undefinable. She was not going to be as easy to figure out as he had assumed. Not easy, but not impossible. And perversely he was looking forward to learning her secrets. And if his initial suspicion proved correct and she did come as a spy from the French? His chest tightened. Then he would leave her convinced that her masters had nothing to fear in regard to his loyalty. That way this vibrant creature wouldn't have to die. At least, not this time.

'I will certainly be interested to see you put that mare of yours through her paces,' Gabe said, as they mounted.

She glanced back at his gelding, a big bay, strong enough to hold a man of his weight and height and still go like the wind. 'I'll wager my glove that Peridot and I will leave you in our dust.'

Again a challenge. It must be part of her nature and it was alluring as all hell. 'Now that I look forward to seeing.' He clapped his heels to Bacchus's flanks.

The early-morning breeze stung Nicky's cheeks. The dew on the grass glittered like diamonds. She felt carefree. Giddy. As if the Countess was nothing but a bad dream and she was young again. Thank goodness, her companion was out in front. The ineffably charming Mooreshead was far too intelligent to insult her by letting her win. But one look at her face and he'd see the cracks in her hard-won walls. She let go a breath and gathered her composure.

Clearly Paul had been right to repeat his warnings last night. The man had a dark and dangerous allure. Beneath the urbane veneer lay finely honed steel forged in a crucible of fire. What turned a man with every advantage of position, wealth, intelligence and education into a traitor? She would have to be clever indeed to expose his treachery and bring him to justice.

The thought of this physically beautiful man mounting the gallows robbed the day of its brightness.

She forced herself not to think of the end, only the means, and urged Peridot to greater efforts as the big, rangy bay drew a good length in front. No catching them now. At the end of the Row, Gabe circled his horse around and greeted her with a boyish smile that caused her heart to flutter.

Mortified by her instinctively feminine response, she halted in front of him with a smile that felt forced. At her command, Peridot curtsied low, in acknowledgement of his win.

The smile turned into a delighted grin. 'What a little beauty. And fast.'

'Not fast enough,' she said lightly. 'He's not very pretty, your animal, but he is strong.'

Gabe patted his mount's neck. 'I see you know horseflesh.'

She pouted, but not so much that he would think her serious. 'If I knew it well enough, I would not have wagered one of my new gloves.' Repressing the tingle of anticipation at the thought of his touch, she held out a hand for him to claim his prize. Boldness was the only way to handle a man like him. A man who assumed he held all the power.

With deliberate slowness, as if he sensed her impatience and intended to punish her, he pulled off his own gloves and tucked them beneath one heavily muscled thigh. When her hand disappeared inside his palm, it clearly emphasised the difference in their size and strength. Even through the kid she could feel his warmth. A small shiver slid down her back, but she kept her smile steady, coolly amused, unflustered, despite the unwanted flutter of her pulse. Carefully he undid the tiny button at the wrist, then raised her hand to press his lips to the blue-veined pulse point he had uncovered. Her insides tightened in response to the velvety sensation.

When he glanced up at her, his eyes danced with mischief.

Her heart tumbled over, her body loosened. She swallowed her urge to gasp at the odd sense of discovery. The kind of feeling a younger Nicky might have experienced. Before the world changed and she became a pawn. A puppet with gilded strings. The naive child she'd been was dead and buried beneath her childish hopes and dreams. Only the Countess lived to play this so very dangerous game. 'You won the glove, sirrah. Nothing more.'

He fastened the button and gave her hand a

gentle pat. 'And you must keep it until I return you home. You need it for now.'

Generous to a fault. A wickedly clever move. She inclined her head as if approving of his thoughtfulness. Oh, yes, the man had charm from his beautiful burnished locks to his highly polished boots, making it hard to think of him as evil. She shored up her defences with a teasing smile. 'Do you make a habit of collecting ladies' gloves?'

'Only yours.'

Gathering her reins, she tossed him an arch look. 'A very small collection, then.'

He laughed out loud. Again, that deep joyful sound. It stirred something deep in her heart. Recollections of happier times. She squashed the surge of sentimentality. Men never did anything without a purpose and they were at their kindest when their intentions were at their worst. Her own husband was a prime example. She'd thought him their saviour, her and Minette. Instead he'd been her ruination.

She fell in beside him and the horses walked side by side down the slope towards the Serpen-

tine. 'Do you ride here often?' she asked, seeking neutral ground.

'Rarely. Even at this time of year there are too
many people.' He gave her the same charming
smile that seemed so friendly and open, yet did
not allow her to assume intimacy.

'You prefer the countryside, then, to town?'
she asked.

'Each has their place. What about you? Town
or country?'

Country. 'Town.' The Countess must always
prefer the town.

They brought the horses to a halt where a copse
ran down to the water and a huge gnarled willow
trailed the tips of leafy branches in the water. The
horses drank their fill.

They turned to head back at the same moment.
She looked over to make a comment about like
minds when several rooks took flight. His horse
reared. A crack rent the air. A sharp sound, like
the snap of a branch. He cursed, coming around
behind her on the left and grabbing Peridot's
headstall. And they were off, racing away.

Normally, had any man touched her mount,

she would have taken her crop to his hand. But that cracking sound, so innocent at first, had registered. A shot. Someone was shooting nearby. He galloped clear of the trees and bushes and brought the horses to a stop. His eyes when they met hers were blazing. 'Who did you tell about our assignation?'

Paul. 'No one.'

The hesitation was slight. Infinitesimal. But the slightest widening of his eyes said he'd heard it. Blast. The shock had made her careless.

'Who?' he said in a tone of low menace.

'My groom, naturally,' she said calmly. 'If one can call a groom someone.'

He breathed deep through his nose and looked back over his shoulder at the copse from whence the shot had come. She followed his gaze. There was nothing to be seen except the black birds circling and cawing their protest. She inhaled, but the wind was in the wrong direction to smell any trace of gunpowder and the undergrowth too thick to reveal the smoke. 'Someone hunting, do you think?' she asked, wrinkling her nose.

'Hardly. Not in Hyde Park.' He spoke tersely,

still looking back at the copse as if he could see into the shadows. He returned his gaze to her face. 'Or…perhaps that was what it was.' His face calmed. His voice evened out. But fires of anger still burned deep in his gaze. Almost instantly, the heat died away as if it had never been. Perhaps it was all in her imagination.

He released her horse. 'Time to return to the carriage.' His hand went to his upper arm. He winced and when he brought it away his glove bore the dark gleam of moisture.

'You are hit.'

He looked at his hand. 'A scratch.'

That certainly accounted for their wild gallop. 'We must seek a doctor.'

'No need.' He pulled a handkerchief from his pocket and bound it around his arm, while he held his horse in perfect control with his knees. He went to use his teeth to make the knot.

'Let me,' she said. She pulled the handkerchief tight and knotted it off. 'You need to have it looked at.'

'The innkeeper will see to it. He's an old friend

of mine. I've had worse wounds falling out of his front door.'

She frowned at him.

'I'm not going to let some damned idiot poacher ruin my plans, Countess.'

She glanced back over her shoulder. 'You think it was a poacher?'

He shrugged, but his eyes were intent on her face. 'What else could it be?'

Surely he did not suspect her of having a hand in this shooting? 'If you think so, then who am I to argue? I know little of English ways. But I must say that, in Paris, people do not go shooting...'

'Rabbits,' he said helpfully.

'*Tiens.* Rabbits, in what I understand is a Royal park.'

They rode at a steady canter, past the spot where he'd teased her with her glove to the gate where they'd left the carriage. All the time they rode, his gaze scanned for hidden dangers. As did hers. Who could have fired a shot? And why?

Paul? Surely he was far too subtle for such an overt act in so public a place. And besides, why would he? She did not yet have the information he sought. Did Mooreshead have other enemies? Someone as mundane as an angry husband, perhaps. Or a jealous lover?

When they arrived at the carriage, her groom was walking the horses as instructed. All seemed as it should. It must have been an accident. A poacher. Or someone undertaking a bit of early-morning target practice. Nothing to do with them at all. Yet she could not stop dread from trickling icy fingers along her veins.

She had learned to never ignore those instincts. If she had listened to them years before, she would never have married Vilandry.

Mooreshead climbed down from his horse and helped her dismount.

Reggie came and took Peridot's halter.

'Take the countess's horse back to its stables,' Mooreshead ordered. 'I will escort your mistress home later.' He led his horse to the back of the curricle.

Reggie looked at her. She nodded her acquiescence. 'Take it easy, Reggie. She's had a good run.'

Peridot rolled her eyes, showing the whites.

'She seems a little nervous, my lady,' the groom said, his stolid square face showing puzzlement. He frowned at Gabe's gelding, whose legs were trembling, and then at the makeshift bandage around Mooreshead's arm. 'What's amiss?'

'A shot,' she said calmly, smoothing her glove. 'Some idiot shooting in a thicket.'

The groom's frown didn't lighten. 'Shooting what?'

'A target. Or rabbits,' Mooreshead said, returning in time to hear the question. 'The fool must not have seen us. I'll speak to someone in authority about it later.' There was steel in his voice. Displeasure. 'Well, man? Do you plan to stand there all day while the mare takes a chill?'

Reggie drew himself up to his full height, though his head didn't come much above Mooreshead's shoulder. His resentment at the accusation was no less impressive. He touched his forelock and bowed to Nicky. 'I'll be going now, my lady.'

'Yes, Reggie. Thank you.'

He marched off stiff-legged to mount his hack. When Nicky looked up at Mooreshead to chide him for his ordering of her servant, she saw that the good humour was back in his face and his eyes were alight with amusement. 'A good man, that,' he said.

'Yes,' she agreed. 'A very good man.' Reggie had been one of the few people who had remembered her mother with any kindness when she arrived at her relatives' house. He could have been no more than a small boy when her mother left for France, but for some reason, he had expressed the desire to leave their employ and serve her instead. She'd come to rely on him and half-wished she could go with him and confront Paul about this failed assassination attempt. But she must stick to the plan and accompany Mooreshead to breakfast. The wound in his arm could not be all that serious or he would be fussing about it. Men always fussed about their aches and their pains.

'I'll apologise for my harshness next time I see him,' Mooreshead said.

He helped her up into the curricle and with little more ado they were on their way. From time to time his gaze flicked to her face with a considering expression and the lines each side of his mouth seemed to become more pronounced. Was he really wondering if she had some involvement in what had occurred? She waited for him to speak. To give her some hint of his thoughts. But his expression remained uncommunicative and his conversation commonplace. Near Kew Bridge, he turned off the road and took the lane to the village of Strand on the Green. He brought the curricle to a halt in the courtyard of the Bull, an inn overlooking the River Thames.

'What a pretty spot,' she said.

'I'm glad you are pleased.' Gabe took her arm and led her inside, where they found a private parlour ready and waiting. She glanced around at the comfortable surroundings. The low beams and panelled walls. A table with a pristine white cloth and an attentive servant. The unobstructed view of the river. 'You think of everything, my lord,' she said calmly, though her heart was beating far too fast. Because of the shot? Or was it the idea of being alone with him? It could not possibly be the latter.

'I'm glad you approve,' he murmured, pulling out her chair and seating her.

'Coffee or wine, my lady? My lord?' asked the waiter.

'Coffee, please.' She had the feeling she needed her wits about her.

'For me too,' Gabe said. 'Thank you. If you will excuse me for a moment or two, Nicky, I'll have my host make a better job of this bandage and be right back.'

She nodded her assent.

The waiter poured their coffee and placed several dishes on the table. Coddled eggs, rashers of bacon, slices of ham, toast, preserves and fruit.

'I hope you are hungry,' Gabe said, returning and giving her a charming smile as he sat down, no longer sporting the handkerchief around his upper arm. The innkeeper must have bandaged it properly.

'Starving. Riding first thing in the morning always leaves me sharp set.'

'Me too.'

'How is your arm?'

'As I said, it's merely a scratch.' He looked down with a frown. 'Ruined one of my favourite coats, though. For that he ought to be horse-whipped.'

Bluster. Nicky laughed. 'No doubt he went home with a couple of good rabbits to fill his stewpot.'

He picked up his coffee cup. 'Here's good luck to him, then.'

They tucked into the food and it was a good few minutes until they sat back in their chairs and sipped at their coffee. He was watching her again. Over the rim of his cup. Intently. As if considering his next move. Prickles of warning raced across her shoulders. If she had thought him dangerous when he played the charming rogue, she now thought him terrifying. She stiffened her spine against a surge of anxiety.

If he was what she suspected, he would pounce on any sign of weakness. She needed a distraction. She remembered their wager. 'I suppose it is time to pay the piper?' Once more she held out her hand, palm up.

He leaned forward, his eyes glittering with a kind of wildness she hadn't seen in him before. 'Ah, yes,' he said with an undertone of menace she couldn't quite fathom. 'The wager.' But he made no attempt to take her hand. He just smiled, a baring of teeth that was almost a grimace. 'You do it.'

She fumbled with the button, the leather loop making it difficult. The gloves had been made to fit tight around her fingers and the leather was whisper-thin, like a second skin. The button slipped free. She drew the glove off and held it out to him. When he didn't take it, she set it beside his plate.

He glanced down at it. 'You have small hands, Countess.'

She trilled an easy laugh, thankfully back on the ground she knew. 'And tiny feet.' She lifted the edge of her skirt and looking down, circled one foot in its riding boot.

'Delicious,' he murmured silkily.

She glanced up at his face. The devil-may-care rogue was back. The blue eyes crinkling at the corners, his posture relaxed and easy. He picked up the glove and tucked it inside his coat. Next to his heart. A small ache in her chest made her draw in a breath of surprise she hoped he hadn't heard.

'I am sorry our ride was cut short in so ugly a way,' he said.

She smiled, reassuring, as careless as he. 'No harm done, my lord. And I enjoyed our race. It is a long time since I galloped *ventre à terre.*'

'Something you did in Paris?'

What would he think if he knew she had never been to Paris? 'Certainly not. Only in the countryside around my home.'

'Do you miss France?'

'One always misses home.' It was the people she missed the most. The tenants on the family estate. Her parents who'd died long before she wed. And most of all her sister. Poor little Minette, who might yet be alive and all alone in a brutal world. But she must not think of Minette now. She must not let him see the longing in her heart. 'What about you? Have you been to Paris?'

Wariness flashed in his eyes, but his smile didn't falter. 'I went after the Treaty of Amiens. It is a beautiful city.'

A part-truth. He had been to Paris during the

Terror. A disaffected Englishman accepted into the ranks of the Jacobins, according to Paul. The thought made her cold. And angry. Yet if she wanted him stopped, she could not let him see this emotion either.

She placed her napkin beside her plate. 'Thank you for a delicious breakfast.'

'It was a pleasure. Now, it is time we left.'

Now that was a surprise. She had expected him to suggest they dally for a few hours. Take a room. Perhaps his wound was worse than he was letting on? But if so, why not have it treated properly? Why bring her here at all instead of immediately returning her home? Paul was going to be disappointed at her failure to woo this man into her bed today. But Mooreshead would want to see her again, of that she had no doubt. While he settled the shot with the innkeeper, she went to the necessary, joining him in the yard outside when she was done.

A carriage stood waiting, a dusty and unfashionable-looking equipage that had seen better days. A groom stepped forward and opened the door.

The hairs on her nape rose. A warning. She looked at Gabe in question.

'My curricle suffered damage when they turned it around. The pole is fractured, ready to break at any moment. The innkeeper has kindly offered us the use of his rig and his coachman to get us back to town.'

'How odd? Two accidents in one day?'

'I know. Dashed nuisance.'

These sorts of things did happen, but her sense of worry refused to settle. Unable to see a way to voice her concern without seeming unduly suspicious, she took his hand and he helped her in. He climbed up behind her and took the seat opposite, his legs sprawling across the narrow space between the seats. He seemed larger in here than he had outside on his horse or within their private parlour. He was a powerful man who would have no difficulty overcoming her, should he wish. She should have thought to bring her pistol instead of the knife she had slipped into the pocket hidden in her shift. She hadn't thought it necessary, given that Reggie would remain nearby. More fool her. Yet to have insisted on her groom following them to breakfast would have made any thought of seduction impossible. So now they were alone together in a carriage and she was defenceless.

Not defenceless. She still had her wits. She kept her breathing even, despite her unease.

The carriage pulled away and for all its dilapidated appearance it moved with considerable speed.

She glanced out of the window and frowned. 'Your coachman has missed the road. We should have turned right at the bridge.'

He followed the direction of her gaze. 'Perhaps he is taking a short cut.' Irony coloured his voice.

'What madness are you about?' she asked. 'We are heading away from London.'

'Yes,' he drawled. 'We are.'

'Turn around, at once.'

He shook his head. 'Sadly, Countess, I cannot. Do not fear. We will reach our destination soon.'

Heaven help her, it seemed she'd played right into his hands. Had he decided that she had led him into an assassination and now he was planning a way to get rid of her? It seemed all too likely.

She leaned back against the squabs with a bright smile. '*Tiens*. How exciting. First we are shot at. And now it seems I have been abducted.'

To her infinite alarm, his smiled deepened.

'Abducted?' Gabe drawled, settling deeper into a corner. The pain from the wound in his arm throbbed dully, a grinding ache rather than the stabbing pain it had been at first. The innkeeper had been another one who had wanted to call for the doctor when he realised the bullet was still lodged in his arm. Gabe didn't have time. Whoever had shot him would want to finish the job. He was just glad he had not told the countess where he intended to partake of breakfast. How disappointed she must be that the plan to kill him had failed. Though he had to admit she had played her part well. The surprise. The sympathy.

At least he now knew for certain she was the one Armande had warned him about.

The floating sensation in his head worried him more than the pain. It was due to a loss of blood.

If she guessed at just how weak he was becoming, she'd take full advantage and have them on their way back to London in no time flat. And straight into the arms of those trying to kill him, no doubt.

Maintaining his outward calm was becoming more and more difficult as he stewed over the clever way she had lured him in. With great effort, he offered her a charming, easy smile. 'A harsh word, don't you think? I want to know you better, is all.'

Her eyes narrowed, a small crease forming between her dark brows making her look like an irritated kitten. This kitten had claws, as the throb in his arm testified. 'You could do that in London, surely? Reggie will be concerned if I do not return at a reasonable hour.' She gave an expressive shrug.

'And to whom will Reggie run with concern?'

Her blue gaze settled sharp on his face. 'To whom? Mrs Featherstone, naturally.'

The question played for time. Time to prepare the answer he would find acceptable. Perhaps she did not realise yet that she could not beat him at the subtle game of evasion, though of course he had not expected the truth. It amused him to put her on the spot. To see how she would handle things. Hell knew he had little else to take his mind off the pain in his arm. He kept his face pleasant and smiling and watched the mask over her expression become more pronounced. So small a change, so indefinable, if he had not expected it, he would not have seen it.

A surprising sense of disappointment hollowed his gut. What? Had he expected her to cast aside her role of seductress and trust him with her secrets? He certainly wouldn't have done so in her place. And just because she was a woman it didn't make her any less dangerous. It was a man's nature to protect a female. And therein lay a man's weakness and why she'd been sent in the first place.

He'd let down his guard and she had very nearly succeeded in getting him killed. If Bacchus had not reared at the same moment the shot was fired, she might even now be carrying his lifeless body back to London in his own curricle. He almost laughed out loud. Almost.

It was no laughing matter when England stood on the brink of disaster. Not since the Normans had a Frenchman tried to invade her soil. Even after years of war, she was a ripe and juicy plum Napoleon would love to harvest. And until as recently as last night, he'd hoped they thought of him as the key to their success. But if they were trying to do away with him—

'Where are we going?' Nicky asked in tones of supreme indifference. She gazed calmly out of the window as if she wasn't taking note of their direction, but her bright gaze missed nothing.

He had to admire her lethal calm.

'Meak.'

She blinked. Naturally, she knew about Meak. She would not be a worthy opponent if she had not looked into every corner of his life.

'Your house in the country?'

My, but she was clever. Instead of feigning puzzlement, she coolly announced her knowledge, because she knew her face had given it away. Never had he met a woman with such *savoir faire. Careful, Gabe.* Admiration was akin to liking. One slip and she'd have him at her mercy. The thought riled him, yet anger did not diminish his appreciation. Or the desire thrumming along to the beat of the pulse in his arm.

'You have heard of Meak?' he asked casually.

'An inheritance from a distant relative, wasn't it? Before you came into your title.'

Meak wasn't any great secret if one cared to ask the right questions of the right people. He stretched out his legs. 'A very small property.'

'And quite convenient to town.'

'I wonder what sort of convenience you imagine?' Indeed, his body tightened at the thought of the kind of convenience a house in the country might offer to a single gentleman. His thoughts must have shown on his face, because her smile became more sensual.

'Why bother to go such a distance?'

No doubt she'd been expecting him to take a room at the inn. But then she didn't know the whole story. Didn't know how badly he was wounded. The stakes had risen by leaps and bounds. Given a choice, the last place he would have taken her was Meak. He always stayed there on his way to Cornwall. There he took a breath, shed his man-about-town persona and became himself. A point of departure to the dangerous underhanded work that would ruin him completely if it became known. Meak served as his bastion. The line of defence between the reality of the life they were about to enter and his fictional existence as an idle rake. Hopefully, whoever had sent her had not breached that particular wall. If so, he was in trouble. Which was why he could not let her go. He needed to plumb the depths of her masters' knowledge. 'We can be entirely private there. Alone.' He flashed her a wicked smile.

She laughed. The warm, sultry sound of it made his groin harden. He imagined her naked on his bed. 'How intriguing,' she said. 'I was told you were a shameless devil, Gabe, but I did not realise the lengths to which you would go for an afternoon seduction.' She gave a small chuckle. 'You underestimate your charms if you think such draconian measures are required.'

A brave player indeed. He tried to remember what that felt like. The belief. The commitment. The sureness of purpose. Risking all for the sake of an ideal. He stared into the past and with a faint sense of surprise realised he couldn't do it. Could not recall even an ounce of the youthful zeal that had once burned so bright in his veins. First his father, then Marianne, had doused the flame, he supposed. But he had held on to his sense of duty. His knowledge of what was right kept him from falling entirely into darkness.

His eyelids drooped as if weighted. Sleep wanted to claim him. But he could not sleep yet. Not until they reached Meak and he could be sure he held her fast. Then and only then could he see to his arm properly and seek some rest.

He inclined his head. 'You honour me,' he said. 'But with half the *ton* hanging about you, I fear I would be lost in the crowd.'

At that she laughed outright. 'You, *mon cher* Lord Mooreshead, could never be lost in a crowd.'

Something inside him warmed at her words. It was as if she had touched him with a gentle caress. Nonsense. He was light-headed and she was playing her role as he played his. And so they would circle the truth, for a while at least.

He reached down. He was unable to prevent an

exhalation at the unexpected sharp dart of pain from his arm.

'Your wound bothers you?' she asked.

Inwardly he cursed at having revealed so much. 'Hardly at all. I had forgotten all about it until now.' He drew forth a rectangular box from beneath the seat. 'Since we have a good few miles to go, we might as well entertain ourselves. I assume you play chess?' A woman of her supposed ilk would learn all the arts to entertain a man. It was their stock in trade.

'I do,' she said. 'I choose white.'

'Of course you do.' He set the travelling set on its legs between them and set out the pieces. Chess would stop him from falling asleep and eliminate the need for conversation.

Conversation required too much careful attention to avoid falling into one of her traps.

To Nicky's increasing concern the journey went on and on. They had changed horses twice now, at small inns along the road. Not posting inns or coaching houses, tiny village inns along narrow lanes off the main road. And at each inn it became quite obvious that the horses were his own. Kept ready should he need them. They were changed without comment or fuss. Food arrived on a tray within moments of their arrival. At one, when she stepped down to use the necessary and take stock of her whereabouts, she quickly discovered there was no possible route for escape. The places were too small, the gaze of her captor too sharp, too aware of her every movement, to give her the slightest opportunity to disappear.

Where was Meak exactly? West of London. Berkshire, if she recalled correctly. The property had been included in the document on his background as a place he rarely visited.

And regardless of where it was, during the course of their games of chess, in the silent moments while he weighed his next move, she had decided not to attempt an escape. Fate or his lust or something else had presented an unexpected opportunity to become more closely acquainted and she would follow wherever it led. *Carpe diem.* Seize the day. And there was no need to worry. Once Reggie reported to Mrs Featherstone, she would go to Paul and he would move heaven and earth to discover her whereabouts.

If Mooreshead had not been so good at hiding, she would know their ultimate destination. It could not be Meak. Or the family estate in Norfolk, where he had claimed to be these past few months. He had…disappeared over the summer. Perhaps to France on his yacht that came and went from port to port around the coast, doing what, no one knew. But their Parisian contacts had not seen him, according to Paul. Now the chance had presented itself to discover where he went and what he did, and, more importantly, to know for certain where his loyalties lay. A chance she would not pass up.

And if Paul was right and Mooreshead was a turncoat—for some reason she could not fathom, she felt slightly sick at the thought—then he would pay for his crimes. And she would have the satisfaction of knowing she had prevented him from doing further harm, as well as being one step closer to finding her sister.

'Checkmate,' he said, winning their third game.

She leaned back and began unbuttoning her

remaining glove. 'Two out of three to you. Your collection of gloves grows larger by the hour. I see I shall have to go shopping very soon.'

His eyes twinkled as he caught her gloved hand in his right hand and raised it to his lips. Tingles ran up her arm. Unruly heat warmed her blood. She cast him a sultry glance as he nipped the end of the glove's forefinger between his teeth and tugged. A pleasurable shiver ran down her spine. With each nip of his teeth at her fingertips of leather, something darker and more dangerous tugged deep in her core. Desire.

It had been a long time since she had felt such a deep sensual pull of male allure. In the years of her marriage, she had learned how to turn male lust to her advantage, but her encounters were never about her desires. Vilandry had never appealed to her that way, though she'd done her wifely duty, and the other affairs had been reciprocal arrangements encouraged, if not arranged, by her husband. To keep Minette safe. She pushed the memories away. Now was not the time to remember the betrayal or the fear. The threats had come close to breaking her then and she could not let the recollection of them near the surface now.

She needed to seduce a man into trusting her. A man who wouldn't simply fall beneath her spell, like some green youth, or an old man who needed firm young flesh to get him interested. Beneath Gabe's charm lay a cold, hard man. A man full of suspicion and steely resolve. She would need to find out what drove him. Money? Ideals? Power? All things she could understand, though rarely in her previous life had ideals played much of a part. It would make her task easier if she understood his motives. For that she would need to get into his bed and under his skin.

Certainly a man of his calibre and experience would be a worthy adversary in the arena of amour. And any other arena, she admitted to herself. But seduction was her best weapon. She let her visceral pleasure at Gabe's touch show on her face as she lifted her chin to meet his gaze.

The glove was loose now and an inexorable pull by strong long fingers drew it free in a slow slide. The fine hairs across the back of her hand stood to attention in the cooler air. She shivered and his smile widened. The teasing smile on his lips turned distinctly sensual.

Looking into her eyes, he turned her hand palm up, his thumb massaging the tender flesh. 'Such a pretty hand,' he murmured. 'So white. As delicate as a bird's wing.'

And as easily crushed by his superior strength. The comparison was not lost on her.

'You mistake, my lord,' she said her voice full of amusement. 'The whiteness is clearly marred for such flights of fancy.'

He glanced down, his long gold-tipped lashes shielding the ice-blue of his gaze. He pressed his lips to the flesh brought to life by his thumb. Hot, dry lips. Softened by desire. And she ached to feel those lips on her own. Shocked by the strength of her carnal response, she curled her fingers, but if he noticed her protective reflex he did not react, but rather turned her hand knuckles up. 'Freckles,' he said as if making an extraordinary discovery.

'Yes,' she murmured.

'Charming.' He brought his gaze up to rest on her face. 'You have been kissed by the sun.'

'Everywhere, except my face.'

'Everywhere,' he repeated, his voice deepening with desire. It strummed a chord low in her belly. A flutter of inner muscles turned her limbs liquid with longing. 'I looking forward to learning them all. One by one by one.'

'And so we go to Meak,' she whispered. And something inside her wished there was no other purpose.

The carriage turned and swayed, rocking on its springs, scattering the chess pieced to the floor.

With a cry of surprise, she knelt to gather them up.

A soft sound made her look up.

Naked desire carved itself on his face.

Heat flared in her cheeks as if she was an innocent schoolgirl when she realised the image she presented kneeling between the thighs of this virile male. But the light in the carriage was dim and hopefully hid her blushes. 'Later,' she said and tossed the small wooden pieces into the box. A promise made was a promise kept. And in truth, she was looking forward to keeping her promises for her own sake. Anger welled up at her traitorous thought. The man was her enemy. Passion was her blade, not her pleasure.

With a smile she returned to her seat on the opposite side of the carriage at the same moment it drew up. The coachman, as he had at all their stops, opened the door and let down the steps.

Gabe stepped down and helped her to alight.

While he turned to give instructions to his driver, she glanced up at the house. A square stone house. A house of good proportions, but modest without ornament or grandeur. She had heard much of Bagmorton in Norfolk. The seat of the marquessate. This was a poor secondary dwelling for a nobleman such as Mooreshead. Not a single window glimmered with light. Not even the lantern at the front door glowed a welcome, though dusk had the day well in retreat.

'I see we are unexpected,' she said.

'You mistake the matter.'

The coachman returned to his box and the carriage pulled away, turning into a smaller drive at the side of the house.

He held out his arm and she placed a hand on his sleeve. Rock-solid strength. All virile male.

Now the game would begin in earnest. A game she must win.

The front door opened as they reached the top step. A young man with tousled mouse-brown hair peered out. The candle in his hand flickered in the wind, casting shadows over his moon-round, pimply face. His eyes lit up when he saw Mooreshead and yet there was a slackness about his expression. Nicky instantly recognised the vagueness of an innocent soul.

'Good evening, Walter,' Gabe said. 'Let us in, dear old chap.'

The boy, for she really couldn't think of him as a man though she judged his age to be about thirty, grinned and stepped aside, his eyes growing wide and round as his gaze fell on her. He gave his master a puzzled look.

'She's a friend,' Gabe said. He leaned closer and muttered a few words in the boy's ear. He shot off, leaving them to enter the gloom of the hall. Gabe chuckled. 'He'll bring us something to eat. Nothing much, I'm afraid, since the house is mostly shut up.'

'I thought you said we were expected?'

'I was expected.' His voice was as dry as dust. 'I am always expected.'

It didn't look much like it. She kept the thought behind her teeth. An Englishman's house was, after all, his pride and joy. His castle.

Mooreshead's movements were sure in the semi-dark and the sound of steel striking flint preceded the flare of light. Instinctively she closed her eyes and turned away, so as not to ruin her vision. And when she turned back, he was lighting a branch of candles set by the door.

The marbled entrance hall boasted a grand set of carved stairs leading up to the first-floor landing and…nothing else. No tables or chairs or pictures on the walls. Just a floor of marble in squares of pink and grey and walls of white.

'This way,' he said, holding the candelabra high. They passed an open door. A drawing room, she thought. It too was bare. Completely empty.

Her stomach sank. She knew what this place was. Not a home. Not a sink of iniquity where he brought his latest paramour as the gossips would have it. It was a halfway house. A halt on their journey, not their final destination.

He ushered her onwards with a press of his hand in the small of her back. Their footsteps echoed on the tile and on the bare wooden stairs as they made their way upwards. There was not a stick of furniture or floor covering anywhere. He flung open a door. This room contained a large bed sumptuously accoutred with bedding and pillows and hangings from a canopy of embroidered green silk. In the centre was a table with two chairs, and a cold hearth, laid ready for a fire.

'Welcome to my abode,' he said, his voice full of amusement and, if she wasn't mistaken, a smidgeon of regret.

Chapter Three

Gabe closed the door and turned the key.

The countess swung around, her eyes wide and suspicious. With a grin, he tucked the key into his fob pocket. 'We wouldn't want to be interrupted, now would we?'

Her gaze went back to the bed. 'No,' she said, her voice low and husky. 'We wouldn't.'

Incredibly, despite the ache in his arm, his body tightened at the velvety caress in her voice, causing his head to spin. No, it wasn't her, it was lack of blood, even if she was the most enticing female he had encountered in a very long time. He had to keep his head here. She was a woman around whom he dare not lay down his guard. Which didn't mean he wouldn't enjoy what she offered; he just wouldn't let lust overcome reason. But

right now there were other more practical matters requiring his attention.

He knelt at the hearth and touched a candle to
the spills left ready. Poor Walter never let him
down, no matter how long between visits. There
was always a fire ready to be lit, and food to
be had from his mother's kitchen at the not-so-
distant cottage he'd provided for them. A guest,
though, was a novelty.

The back of his neck prickled. Awareness of
her moving closer. He turned sideways to keep
her in view at the edge of his vision. Her expression was calm, but resolute. She had come to
some sort of decision. To flee? To murder him
while he slept? She wouldn't have the chance
for either. He touched the flame to the spills laid
neatly between the kindling. They caught at once.
'Sit by the fire,' he said. 'Warm yourself.'

She sank onto the *chaise* and held her hands
out to the blaze. She was taking it all much too
calmly to be innocent. He'd made the right decision to bring her along. He certainly wasn't going
to leave her to Sceptre's tender mercies.

A scratch came at the door. He unlocked it, then opened it to Walter carrying a tray. 'Come in.'

Gabe carefully pocketed the length of rope curled around the beer mug while his back was to the countess, then took the tray and set it on a nearby chest.

'You will bring the rest as I instructed?' Gabe asked the lad. It was always best to deal with one thing at a time.

'I will, my lord,' Walter said, doing his best to look properly serious.

Gabe closed and once again locked the door behind him. The countess got up and went to the table, seating herself in one of the chairs. 'I'm famished.'

He wasn't surprised. She had eaten little on the road. Likely she feared he might drug or poison her. Or it might have been a case of nerves held under tight control. Whatever it was, she needed food. One-handed, he carried the tray to the table. In addition to beer, his usual tipple, Walter had thoughtfully provided a pot of tea. It was what the lad's mother drank and therefore he thought all females would be the same.

'I can ask for wine, if you prefer,' Gabe said. 'Or cognac.'

'So your cellars are furnished better than your house,' she said with a smile. 'Tea suits me very well. I am practically English, *n'est ce pas*?' She buttered a slice of bread the size of a doorstep, placed a hunk of cheese on top and bit delicately into it with small white even teeth. She had a lovely, generous mouth with lips of just the right lushness. Not too full or too red. Just right for kissing.

He dragged his gaze away and buttered his own slice, careful not to show the pain the movements caused.

'*Tiens*, where do we go next?' she asked.

Startled, he stared at her.

'You do not intend that I stay here.'

Not a question. He swallowed the urge to laugh at the sharpness of her attack. Nor would he pretend she had not scored a hit. 'You will see when we get there.'

They finished eating in silence and she took her cup of tea back to the hearth. Any other woman would be trembling with fear at this point. But she wasn't any other woman. She was his enemy and likely carefully chosen. He might admire her. Even lust after her. But he would not underestimate her.

Another scratch on the door.

Her expression turned wary. As well it might. She would not like what he would do next.

He gestured to the bed. 'Please, lie down.'

A flare of anger sparked amid the blue. 'Why? Are you planning a *ménage à trois*? I assure you it is not to my taste.'

'Good grief,' he said, before he could stop himself. 'What would make you think such a thing?' He pulled his pistol from his pocket. 'The bed, if you please, Nicky.'

She responded to the note of command in his voice with an upward tilt of her chin. Her gaze dropped to the pistol as if considering her options. He bit back a smile at her courage. Finally, clearly unwilling, she climbed gracefully onto the bed.

'Hands together, if you please.'

She rolled her eyes, but complied. 'Really?'

He caught both hands in one of his, set down

his pistol and pulled the rope from his pocket. He made quick work of the knot then tied it to the bedrail above her head.

She gave a small tug, shook her head and smiled. 'You pervert.'

'Sorry. I just don't need to be worrying about you for a while.'

He let Walter in. 'Well timed.'

'You said to wait fifteen minutes.'

Gabe could imagine him down in the kitchen watching the minutes tick by. 'You did very well indeed.'

Walter flicked a sideways glance at the countess. His jaw slackened.

'I need your help,' Gabe said.

'Yes, my lord.' The lad's eyes were clear and guileless.

Gabe sighed. This was about to get very difficult. And very painful. 'Put the things I asked for on the hearth and help me out of this coat, if you please.'

Walter knelt and produced several items from his capacious pockets. A knife. A box of basilica powders. A bandage. His lips moved as he laid the items out on the grey-veined marble. He looked up at Gabe for confirmation that he had all that was requested.

'Well done, old fellow,' Gabe said. Damnation, he did not want to ask Walter to do this.

The lad stood and Gabe turned to let him peel the coat over his shoulders and down his arms.

Walter gulped. A gasp came from the bed.

He glanced down. He wasn't surprised to see the bandage the innkeeper's wife had applied soaked through with blood.

'You idiot,' Nicky said. 'It looks a great deal worse than a scratch. Do you have a death wish?'

He looked at her and was surprised by the anger in her face. 'It is not as bad as all that.'

She made a scornful sound in the back of her throat.

She was right. Beneath the bandage, his arm was a mess. By rights, he should be calling for a surgeon. Not something he had time for. He glanced at the greenish tinge to Walter's face.

'Dear fellow, fetch me a bowl of hot water, will you, please?'

Walter swallowed and nodded, his gaze still fixed on the bloody bandage.

'Off you go, then.' Gabe watched him gallop out of the room. Carefully, he untied his cravat and laid it over the chair, then worked at the knot in the bandage.

'Can I help?' Nicky asked.

He glanced over at her, stretched out on the bed, her arms over her head, her face framed by her elbows, her lush breasts pushed up against the confining fabric of her riding habit. Again a surge of unwanted lust. He grinned. 'The sight of you lying there is keeping my spirits up.'

'More than your spirits,' she said, pointedly glancing at his hips.

'Hussy,' he said, with a laugh. 'Your kind of help I can do without.'

'I don't think your Walter is going to be of much assistance,' she retorted. 'He's likely to cast up his accounts and have you playing nursemaid.'

'Too true.' He got the knot undone and pulled the bandage away from the wound, sucking in a breath of pain when it caught in the dried blood crusted around the edges.

'*Mon Dieu,*' she muttered. '*Les hommes.*'

No doubt she was rolling her eyes again. With the bandage off, he pulled his shirt over his head and inspected the wound he'd only glimpsed when the woman had bound it up for him. An inch or two to the right and it would have hit his heart. He probed it gently with a fingertip. And cursed.

'The ball is still in there.' she said.

He wiped his bloody fingers on his shirt. 'Apparently so.'

Nicky glared at him as he got up and draped his shoulder with a towel from the washstand in the corner. The man was an idiot if he thought he could take a ball out of his arm himself.

The boy returned with a kettle of steaming water and a bowl. 'Set it down on the hearth, lad.' Walter did as requested and then beamed at his master.

Mooreshead frowned. 'I should have asked you to bring up some brandy.'

The boy looked worried. 'What does it look like? Me mam went back to the cottage.'

Mooreshead shook his head. 'It's all right. I'll get it. You wait here with the countess.' He strode out of the room.

'Walter,' Nicky said with a beguiling smile. 'Untie me. Please.'

He giggled, but didn't move.

'Walter,' she said again, more firmly but gently. 'He can't possibly remove that ball from his arm. He needs my help. Untie me.'

'I don't take no orders from anyone but him.' He stuck out a lip.

She sighed and let her head fall back. 'What makes you so loyal to a man like him?'

He stared at her in puzzlement. Innocent loyalty. What would he say if he knew the truth about the man he served? Would he care? Probably not. She certainly thought better of Mooreshead for his kindness to this poor benighted man-child.

'Tying people up is wrong, you know.'

Shadows filled his eyes. 'I know,' he mumbled. 'Mam wouldn't like it. But she said I must always do as he asks.'

'Why?'

He frowned and stared off into the distance as if he was trying to recapture a memory, then smiled in triumph. 'Old marquess tossed us out with not a penny in our pockets—' he inhaled a quick breath '—so we must do all we can to help my lord. It's only right.'

The words came out so fast it took a moment to make sense of them. 'His father tossed you out?'

'When Pa died. He…he needed the cottage for the new man.' He frowned. 'I don't know the new man. My lord was very angry. I thought I was bad. *He* was bad. Old marquess.'

He started to look upset.

'And so Lord Mooreshead brought you here, to his home.'

'Lord Templeton.'

She closed her eyes. Right. He would have been Templeton while his father was alive. 'Walter, I want to help Lord Mooreshead, but I can do nothing with my hands tied.'

He shook his head, his bottom lip protruding. 'No one tells me what to do 'cepting milord.'

She huffed out a breath. 'I am not telling, *mon ange*. I am asking. Please.'

He took a hesitant step towards the bed.

'Leave Walter alone,' Mooreshead said harshly from the doorway, his face as dark as a thundercloud. He had a dusty bottle tucked under his arm.

Walter shrank back.

'It's all right, Walter,' Mooreshead said, gentling his tone. 'It is her I am angry at.'

Walter glared at her. 'Bad.'

'Not bad,' he said. 'Stubborn.'

He looked at her. 'You are right, I cannot do this by myself. Yet, to be honest. I am loath to let you free and put a knife in your hand.'

She smiled at him sweetly. 'Quite the conundrum.' Bah, she should not be rising to his bait. 'Why did you bring me here, Mooreshead? What is it you want from me? If it is ransom, you are at outs. I have no one who cares enough to pay for my release.'

'Don't play games, Countess,' he said setting his bottle down on the hearth. 'Whoever you told about our assignation this morning had me shot.'

The only possibility was Paul. She shook her head. 'It makes no sense.'

He gave her a hard look. 'So you do not deny you told someone in addition to the members of your household. Who?'

Her heart jolted at her mistake. 'I told no one apart from Reggie and my companion, Mrs Featherstone, about our plan.' She gave a shrug of indifference. 'I thought nothing of it. I ride every day in Hyde Park.' She glanced at the window that clearly showed it was full dark outside. 'By now she and Reggie will be worried out of their wits. They will no doubt contact the authorities. Eventually someone will think to look here.'

He regarded her for a long moment, then inhaled, his wide chest expanding, the frown between his brows deepening. Pain. She pretended not to notice.

He removed the key from his pocket and handed it to it to Walter. 'Walter, no matter what she says, no matter what you hear on my side of the door, you are not to let her out of this room unless I say so. Now be a good lad and lock the door from the outside. I'll call for you when I need you.'

Aghast, she stared at him. 'And if you die? You could, you know.'

'You'll be stuck here until your friends come looking.'

She laughed bitterly. 'Leaving me locked in a room with a corpse for days, if not weeks.' No, it wouldn't be days or weeks. Ultimately, Walter would fetch his mother. What little she could see of Mooreshead's wound did not make her think he would die. She'd seen men survive worse after an injury on the hunting field. Much worse. And women too. But sometimes the smallest of things could result in death. A shiver passed down her back.

His eyes narrowed as he looked at her, then he nodded. 'Very well. I'll make provision for the worst. Wait a moment, Walter.' He sat down at the desk and dashed off a note. He folded it, addressed it and sealed it. 'Walter, this goes to my friend. You know who I mean?'

Walter nodded.

'Take it to him if I do not call you to open the door in the morning.'

So she had one night to make her escape. If

that was what she was going to do. She glanced at the windows.

The man seemed to read her mind, blast him, because he shook his head. 'They are nailed shut.'

And each pane too small for her to squeeze through if she broke the glass.

'This friend of yours, what will he do if he comes?' she asked.

'He'll have you arrested for murder.'

'Then I had better ensure that you survive.'

He gave her a charming grin. 'Countess, you are a constant source of delight.' He handed the note to Walter. 'Turn the key in the lock on the outside, lad. And no matter what she says, you are not to open that door without my permission.'

The boy left. The key grated in the lock.

Mooreshead picked up the knife. 'Let us go too, then.'

Gabe looked down at the knife in his hand. The ball had to come out. He could send Walter for a surgeon. But the fewer people who knew of his comings and goings at Meak, the better he liked it. Still, putting a knife in his enemy's hands... It was either tempting fate or…or what? Madness? Aye, it was madness.

But he had to die some time. And it wasn't as if a great many people would mourn his passing. One or two good friends, that was all.

And besides, it likely wouldn't suit her purposes to have him die. Not if she wanted information. And that was where his greatest value lay. He knew too much about both sides in this war. So why shoot him? His head spun as a wave of dizziness hit him hard. The dizzy spells had been coming with increasing frequency. He had no choice in this. He had to get on the road in the morning.

He strode to the bed and smiled down at his prisoner. 'I hope you know what you are doing, Countess.' He cut the rope.

She sat up, rubbing at her wrists. He saw with gut-wrenching anger that the rope had chafed the pale delicate skin. Blast it all, he should have thought to protect her flesh before tying her up. He shook his head at himself. He didn't hurt women. They were too fragile. Too easily broken. It was likely the last bit of decency he had left. And it appeared someone had figured it out or they would not have sent her. 'I'll send Walter for some salve.'

She gave an impatient shake of her head. 'It is nothing. Believe me. Your wound is far worse.'

He hesitated.

'Gabe. We will look at it afterwards.'

Bossy. He was glad to see her spirit still very much alive. Wounds of the flesh were one thing, but a man could destroy a woman without ever touching her. He'd seen it with his parents. 'Very well. Where do you want me?'

A spark of amusement lit her blue eyes. 'Now what sort of question is that, my lord?'

Surprised, he chuckled. 'So you can operate,' he amended.

She looked at the bed and then pointed at the floor. 'It is better if you lie completely flat.'

He raised a brow. 'Have you done this before?'

'I have helped. When leaving France there were shots fired.'

He wanted to ask for more details. But then there were all sorts of questions he wanted answered about this woman. This was neither the

again, shaking her head. 'I might be able to find it without doing any more damage,' she muttered. She poured brandy over her fingers and then inserted her forefinger into the wound.

Pain. Burning. Sharp. The edges of his vision darkened. 'Aaagh!' The groan forced its way behind his clenched jaw. Black laced through with red veins claimed his mind.

And then he was crawling out of the darkness. Fighting for breath.

'You are fine,' a light, gentle female voice tinged with a French accent said from a great distance away. 'I have it.'

Have what? What had he lost?

Marianne. He'd lost Marianne. He should have…

Recollection flooded back. Marianne was dead. And she'd been lost to him before she died. The old bitterness rose up in his throat at the recollection of her treachery. *Never trust a beautiful woman in this work,* a voice whispered in his mind.

'Mooreshead,' the same female voice said, demanding, commanding. 'Wake up.'

He opened his eyes, spat the rope from his mouth and looked up into her worried face. 'You have a freckle on your nose.'

She drew back with a frown. 'How ungallant of you to notice.'

'I like it.'

His head was in her lap, he realised, and her lush lips curved in a smile as she saw the realisation dawn. Her blue eyes twinkled. Her hair hung around her shoulders in long, feathery strands. She was lovely. How could he have thought her not stunningly beautiful the first time he saw her? He frowned. She looked different. Younger. More vulnerable. As if a mask had fallen away, for all that he had been sure he knew who she was. What she was. He suddenly felt as if he didn't know her at all.

He glanced down at his arm. It was bleeding again. And aching like the very devil.

She held up her hand in front of his face. Gripped between her finger and thumb was a round metal ball. 'You are a lucky man. It is all in one piece. I think it was almost spent when it hit you. I also found this.' She put the ball down and held up what looked like a lump of bloody flesh.

He grimaced. 'What is it?'

'The missing part of your coat and shirt.'

He made to sit up. She pushed him down and he discovered he didn't have the strength to resist her. 'Weak as a cat,' he mumbled.

'Yes, well, you better tell Walter you are fine. Every time you moaned, he screamed as if he was being tortured.'

He squeezed his eyes shut. He should have guessed poor old Walter would remain close by. 'Walter,' he called.

'Yes, my lord,' a weak voice said from the door followed by the sound of sobbing.

'I'm fine, Walter. The countess is going to bandage me up and then you can come in and see for yourself. All right, Walter?'

Walter hiccupped, which Gabe took for a yes. He looked up at the countess. 'If you would be so good.'

'If you could lift a little higher,' she murmured, 'I can get the bandage under your shoulder.'

Her voice sounded different. Gentler. Younger.

Her face said she cared. He wanted to bask in that caring, shut out the world and enjoy it. Seduction. It was her stock in trade. Yet it was different.

He gritted his teeth and forced himself up on his right elbow. She sprinkled basilica powders on the wound and then began the painful process of tying it up.

'You likely should have it sewn by a surgeon,' she murmured, tying off the knot.

He grimaced, holding back the urge to groan as the throbbing intensified with each pass of the bandage. 'Let's see how it does.'

'Typical,' she said.

He got slowly to his feet, tossed the bloody shirt onto the fire and went to the chest where he kept a spare set of clothes. He pulled a fresh shirt over his head and, tucking it in, went to the door. 'Walter, you can come in now.'

The lad opened the door, looking as pale as milk. Gabe tossed a cloth over the bloody water and handed him the bowl. 'It's all right, Walter, take this away. I won't be needing you any more this evening.'

He took the key from the lad and ushered him

out, closing and locking the door behind him, finally looking at the countess. She watched him put on his waistcoat and tuck the key in his fob pocket. He frowned. 'It seems I am in your debt. Thank you.'

'I didn't have much choice, now did I?' She tilted her head, her expression changing, becoming harder even as it teased. The mask had returned. A subtle shift, yet he felt an odd sense of disappointment. He shook it off as a trick of his imagination as she smiled and said, 'I presume repayment does not involve returning me to London?'

He bowed. 'You presume correctly.'

'What happens now?'

An excellent question. What he really needed was rest. A day or so for his arm to heal. Yet, her friends would lose no time in looking for her. As he saw it, he had two advantages. First, assuming the groom had informed them he'd been winged, his enemies would suppose it was superficial. And second, they didn't know where to find him. If they had, they would not have shot him in such a public place. What he didn't have was time.

'Gabe,' she said sharply. 'You didn't answer my question.'

He couldn't prevent a smile as he strode towards her and placed his hands on her shoulders, gazing down into a face that retained its calm by dint of incredible courage.

'What do we do now?' he murmured softly, feeling those fragile bones beneath his hands and the rise and fall of her gentle breathing. 'Now we go to bed.'

The hitch in her breathing heated his blood.

Nicky lay with her eyes closed, listening to his deep, even breathing. Dratted man. First he teased her, then he ignored her. Never before had a man lain in her bed like a log of wood. Certainly not the men she'd seduced at her husband's request. Fortunately for her, very few of them had demanded she fall into their beds unless the attraction was mutual. Those she had bedded had been excellent and skilled lovers, unlike Vilandry, whose jaded appetites preferred untouched girls. Once he'd had her, she'd been of no further interest. To her relief. And if he had not eyed her sister, she might well have been content to live a celibate life.

So why did she care that Gabe seemed indifferent to her charms? Frustration made her want to flop over onto her side. Caution held her still. She breathed as if she had fallen asleep. Dare she sleep? Ought she to steal the key he had tucked into his waistcoat pocket? She had no doubt she could do it without him feeling a thing.

Slowly, carefully, she eased up on to one elbow and looked into the face on the pillow beside hers. The glow from the fire behind her cast his features in sharp relief. In repose, unsmiling, he looked harder, grimmer, as if only now he could let the burdens he carried show on his face. What sort of burdens? The guilt of a traitor? Her fingers tingled with the urge to trace the line of a blade-like jaw softened by a day's growth of beard. To test the texture of his firm, carefully sculpted lips. Now that would be more than foolish. It would be tempting the devil.

But wasn't that why she was here?

'You are awake,' she said. 'Afraid I will murder you in your sleep?'

He cracked open one eye, then the other, and heaved on to his right side, resting his chin in his palm. 'Do you like what you see, Countess?'

Vain creature. He'd known she was watching him, if that slightly self-satisfied smile was anything to go by. If his face was lit by the glow of the fire, then her face must be in shadow. Yet she felt as if he could see her as plain as day the way his gaze searched her face. The man must have the vision of a cat, or some other nocturnal creature. Or her imagination was playing tricks. 'Your wound troubles you?' Realisation dawned. 'Or is it some other part of your anatomy that keeps you awake?'

'I am a man, am I not?'

Cheeky beast. She grinned at him and let her unruly fingers have their way by tapping him lightly on his large, manly nose. 'So why lie there pretending to be asleep with a face as grim as death?'

'You object to my gentlemanly conduct?'

'Gentlemanly? Is that what you call an abduction?'

He chuckled softly. One large, warm hand came up to do to her what she had been longing to do to him: he stroked his knuckle across her cheek, then touched her lips with his thumb. Her insides clenched. Oh, yes, she wanted this man. And not because it was part of the job. She just wished she understood why. She'd met many attractive men during her marriage, but never had any of them elicited such a feeling of uncontrollable desire in the Countess. Was she losing control? She could not. She must not.

No matter that she found his cleverness as alluring as his physical beauty. She still had trouble grasping how quickly he'd reacted to that shot and the change in circumstances. As well as his gentlemanly conduct.

Admiration would imply she cared about him as a person. It was dangerous to care about people. They rarely turned out to be what you expected. Or hoped. And quite often the ones worth caring about were the ones you lost. No, it was physical attraction. Pure and simple. Physical she understood. The pleasures of the body impacted parts of the mind. The parts one couldn't always control. But they did not rule unrestrained. Never.

His fingers left her skin, his hand dropping to rest on his hip, and she felt suddenly cold, bereft. He was, of course, leaving it up to her to decide where this would go. How it would go. He was a man of experience. Interested, yes, but he had no need to press his case. If not she, there would always be another waiting in the wings.

The thought gave her a little stab of anger in the region of her breastbone.

It would serve him right if she turned away from him. Cut off her nose to spite her face, in other words. She almost laughed at her own foolish thoughts. Instead, she leaned forward the inch or two that separated their faces, feeling the warmth of his breath on her cheek, her lips, and kissed him.

With lightning speed, he pulled her close, lifting her so she lay on top of him, and swept her mouth with his tongue, tasting her as if she was the most delicious of sweetmeats.

The kiss was deep, searching, ravaging and

expert as he cupped her face in his hands, angling her to give him his tongue greater access. The wall of his chest pressed against her breasts, her thigh slipped between his, bringing the hard ridge of his arousal against her belly. Not one to give a man all the control, she kissed him in return, cradling the back of his head, raking her fingers through his short cropped hair, swirling her tongue around his, forcing him into retreat, then darting away, so he followed. She sucked on his tongue, thrilled to her core with his rumbled groan of pleasure.

She ached with the pleasure of that sound. Almost of their own accord her hips rolled against his groin, seeking to deepen the deliciously wicked sensations scorching through her body.

He flipped her on to her back, gazing down into her face, his features now in shadow, the lovely, heavy weight of his lower body pressing her deep into the mattress. Even though he tried to hide it, she felt him wince.

'Be careful of your arm,' she murmured. 'I won't have you bleeding all over this gown. It is the only one I have.'

'Then I suppose we had better remove it from danger.'

'Excellent suggestion.'

He kissed the tip of her nose, the rise of her cheekbone, the lobe of her ear. Shivers ran rampant through her body to settle with excited little pulses deep in her core.

'You,' he said, punctuating the word with a lick of the pulse point below her ear, 'are—' he licked the hollow at the base of her throat '—wicked.'

She sighed contentedly. 'I know.'

He cupped her breast and blew heat through the fabric to torment her flesh. Her nipples tightened in response. Her breasts felt full and heavy. Aching for his touch, which she instinctively knew would be as delicious as his kisses. He was, after all, a renowned hedonist and much-sought-after lover among ladies with less-than-stellar reputations. He was not the kind of man who sought out the untried or the virtuous. A point in his favour, she supposed.

And yet… The thought slipped away as he began releasing the frogging of her riding habit. Impatient, she lifted her arms above her head to give him better access. She wished she had disrobed before lying down; it would have shortened this delay. Fortunately he was only wearing his shirt, waistcoat and breeches. They had helped each other remove their riding boots before they lay down.

Fastenings undone, she helped him slide the sleeves off her arms. He soon had the tapes at her waist untied and the skirts stripped away, leaving her in stockings, chemise and stays. She stretched beneath his hot gaze, wanting to purr like a cat as she basked in the heat of those sapphire eyes and the smooth strokes of his large, warm hand down her length.

'Lovely,' he murmured. 'I wish I could see you better.'

'Ditto,' she said, unfastening the buttons of his waistcoat. 'Light the candles.'

'So you are brazen as well as wicked,' he said, slipping out of the coat and swiftly pulling his shirt over his head. The bandage around his arm and chest stood out white in the gloom.

'You like your women shy, then?'

He shook his head. 'Not at all. I like a woman

who knows what she wants and how she wants it.' Three long strides took him to the table, where he picked up the branch of candles, kindling them at the fire in an instant. Pretty much as he had kindled her desires only moments ago. As he prowled back to the bed the candles provided light enough for her to see the beautifully de-fined musculature of his torso, the crisp blond hair scattering his chest, the power of his arms and the clear evidence of his arousal confined by the soft leather of his breeches.

She licked her lips and raised her gaze to meet his.

The sensual expression on his face made her want to moan. She managed a shallow breath and once more let her gaze drift down his magnifi-cent body, stopping at his waist. 'Take them off.'

He muttered something that sounded a bit like a prayer as his hand went to the buttons on his falls.

Words held no meaning for her right now; it was all about sensation and vision. She wanted to see and touch and explore this splendid male as much as she sensed he wanted to do the same to her. It was a mutual ungovernable desire. For a moment, the fear she might not be able to accomplish her task if she let the yearning inside her have its way almost made her retreat. A strange wayward feeling that this man pulled at some far deeper emotion than lust.

A feeling of regret filled her. A feeling there was more to life than she'd experienced with her husband. Could this man free her from the walls the Countess had built around her heart? It was too late for her, she answered herself with desperate haste. She wasn't an innocent schoolgirl with dreams of romance and love. She understood the carnal creature that was man far too well to have such fanciful notions.

Besides, there was far too much at stake. Not just her mission relied on her keeping her head. There was her vow to track down Minette. Her hope that her sister still lived. No man, not even one as attractive as Gabe, would make her forget her sister. And to find her, she would do whatever was required. And making love to Gabe was certainly no hardship.

Heart pounding against the walls of her chest, not in terror, but in impatience, she watched as he peeled the leather trousers over his hips. His erection, freed of the confines of fabric, sprang free, jutting towards her from its nest of dark-gold curls. Knowing the size of his hands, she should have known he would be big there too.

Her insides melted to the texture of warm honey at the thought of the pleasure he would bring.

'Now you,' he instructed, his voice a harsh rasp.

A faint quiver of worry took her by surprise. She was not a voluptuous woman, but the sensuality she had learned under the tutelage of her husband usually more than made up for her lack of curves. Yet, for some strange reason, she feared to see disappointment in his eyes.

Such missish foolishness. With a quick tug, she released the ribbon of stays designed to fasten in front so they could be easily managed by a woman who had no maid or sister or friend to give her aid in dressing. Two more pulls at the laces and she was free to sit up and slip them off her shoulders.

His eyes widened a fraction as the sheer muslin fabric of her shift revealed her breasts, the nipples already taut and thrusting at the filmy fabric.

He inhaled a breath through his nose. A slow smile curled his sensuous mouth. 'More delicious than I imagined,' he murmured softly.

She gazed at him from beneath heavy lids. 'I can't wait to discover if the reputation I hear of you is true.'

'It nowhere near does me justice,' he said, his eyes hot as he gazed down at her. 'The reality is so much better than the myth.'

She opened her arms, offering welcome. If he was half as good as she had heard, he would be tremendous. And she would be more than his match.

Not only did this woman engage in the art of verbal swordplay, she was lovely. Not beautiful, or pretty in the shallow, accepted sense. Simply lovely. Slender, yet delicately curved. Bold without being blatantly wanton. A woman sure of her feminine allure. The freckles he had noticed on her shoulders and breasts in the ballroom covered every inch of her skin in a dizzying array. Colours from palest fawn to dark brown scattered willy-nilly across skin the colour of milk.

He had never seen anything so fascinating. He had the urge to count each one. To kiss each one as he did so. And only one single one on her face. The one on her nose. He wanted to kiss that too.

Extraordinary.

No woman had ever mesmerised him the way Nicky did. Not even Marianne, who had dazzled him with her bluestocking mind and philosophical ideas. He'd set her on a pedestal. Treated her like his goddess to be worshipped from afar.

The way Nicky eyed him with such obvious and earthy approval aroused him beyond understanding. And now, the sight of her body, her small, high breasts and narrow waist, the delicate flair of her hips, displayed without pretence of modesty, and yet without any loss of her dignity or pride, left him in awe.

All that was not what had him unsettled. It was the sense that, if he wasn't very careful, things between them could become much more complicated than two enemies seeking the advantage in seduction. He found her too intriguing. And there was this other deeper emotion, the urge to protect her from Sceptre, that he didn't much like. The organisation was ruthless when it came to guarding its secrets, as they had proved when Marianne had tried to betray him. Caring about Nicky would make him vulnerable and at this stage of the game it was a weakness he could not afford.

'Like what you see?' she asked, her blue eyes dancing in the candlelight, her mouth sultry from his kisses.

She threw his own words back at him. He could not help but smile. 'Very much.' He joined her on the bed, kneeling beside her, cradling her lovely face in his hands as he plundered her deliciously soft mouth.

His body ached painfully, protesting the delay, but a gourmand of the flesh did not rush such a delicacy. He savoured the sweet, honeyed taste of her and eased down onto the bed beside her, absorbing the sensation of her satiny-soft, heated skin along his length. He explored her finely wrought curves, the dips and swells of her sweetly feminine body and touched his tongue to every freckle within easy reach. Her soft moans of pleasure served like spurs, intensifying his anticipation. Never had he felt so impatient to be inside a woman as he was with this one. He wanted to be sink into her heat, to rise over her and claim her, like some uncivilised beast.

He swallowed a groan at the pain and the pleasure as he broke free to look into her eyes. To gauge her need, to learn what gave her the greatest pleasure as he caressed and stroked her small, perfect breasts.

Heavy lidded, she gazed back at him, one hand exploring his back, the other's fingers circling first one, then the other of his nipples. She pinched one lightly, then grazed the tightly furled nub with a nail. His body tightened unbearably and he gasped.

A small, wicked smile curled her lips. It was the smile of a woman who knew what she wanted and knew how to get it. And yet there were shadows in her eyes that spoke of a yearning that had nothing to do with the pleasures of the flesh. But even as the thought occurred to him, it slipped from his grasp as she lifted her head and latched on to his nipple.

Blood roared through his veins, heading south.

His head emptied of thought. Such overwhelming lust. Such extraordinary pleasure.

Teasing at his nipple with her teeth, she pressed hard against his shoulder, forcing him back against the mattress until he lay half beneath her. She pressed one smooth knee between his thighs and he shifted his legs, widening them to the steady pressure, mindless as he felt her thigh brush urgently between his legs, gripping the sheets in his hands to stop from begging for the same attention at his other nipple.

She released his nipple with a soft sucking sound and gave it a lick, then raised her head to look into his face with a saucy smile.

His heart pounded in his chest. His breath was ragged. And his body shook with the force of his need to take her like a rutting animal. Never had he come so close to losing control. He met her gaze as her hair tumbled in waves on to his shoulders and chest. 'Would you ride me, then, Nicky?' he asked in as teasing a tone as he could manage, when he really wanted to growl. 'Is that what gives you pleasure?'

The thought of her slim form rising over him jolted heat through his body.

'Many things give me pleasure, *mon ange*,' she breathed, her mouth full and rosy as her eyes spoke of secrets. 'But I told you, I would not let you ruin my work, *n'est-ce pas*?'

His wound. 'As if I can feel a thing,' he said, shifting his hips beneath the pressure of her silken flesh against his shaft, wanting to lift her and have her slide down his length. 'There is only one part of me that hurts at this moment and it is a very pleasurable ache, my sweet.'

She settled her other leg between his thighs and stretched up to plant a brief kiss on the point of his chin. 'Oh,' she said innocently. 'Would you like me to kiss it better?'

Hot images of her mouth on him, her hair spread over his hips, ran through his mind. His throat dried. He could barely speak for wanting. 'If it would please you,' he rasped, shocked at his eagerness.

All right, so it had been a while since he had taken a woman to his bed, despite the rumours. And while what she offered was nothing new to him, here she was making him pant and sweat and want to beg like a lad. He pulled the threads of himself together. 'But only if it gives you pleasure.'

She dropped a kiss on his lips. 'You must promise to lie very still,' she whispered against his mouth. 'Can you?'

Again she challenged his manhood. And heaven help him, he wasn't exactly sure he could. He swept her hair back from her face, looking deep into those mischievous eyes. It was quite deliberate, this challenge. But there was something else in her gaze, a kind of desperation. As if somehow his seduction was important. Did she think then to bend him to her will?

'I can,' he said firmly. Convincing himself. But he had no choice. He needed to learn her secrets and to do so, he must earn her respect.

And so he must endure or be damned.

She rose on her knees, leaving his body wanting her touch, the wicked hussy. It was quite deliberate. But he hadn't gained his own reputation among the wicked ladies of the *ton* without foundation. He cocked an arrogant brow. She laughed and shook her head in admonition. 'Patience is a virtue.'

To hell and back with patience. He swallowed a growl. And she slowly lowered her lips to his shoulder, still careful to avoid any contact with his lower torso, the wicked tease.

And he endured a trail of teasing kisses across his chest, the licks, the sly little nips when least expected, all designed to drive him mad with anticipation while he waited for the promised kiss where it counted most.

Were it any other woman, when she reached his navel and teased it with her tongue, he might have flipped her over and taken what he wanted, and found his partner well pleased. But that would not do for this one. He stared at the pattern on the canopy above his head, a swirl of vines and leaves, and concentrated on breathing deep and trying not to measure the distance from her lips to her ultimate destination, nor count the seconds until she arrived.

She sat back on her heels, her lips full, ripe and luscious.

Forcing himself not to demand she continue, he

rose up on his elbow, eyeing her dainty breasts briefly before flashing her a grin. 'Is there something I can do for you, my lady?'

'Oh, I am sure there is,' she said huskily.

He reached for her and she leaned back with a teasing smile. 'Later.'

His control slipped a notch. He hauled it back on a huff of breath. 'So it is your intention to torture me until I beg for mercy, is it?' he growled.

Her nipples tightened. Her eyes turned smoky with the onslaught of her own passion.

So she liked a little roughness from a man. But he was equally good at sensual torture. 'Then perhaps it is time you make good on your promise, Nicky?'

'Promise?'

He flicked a glance down at his groin and the full-blooded erection straining upwards.

She looked down and blinked. *'Mon Dieu,'* she said softly.

The awe in her voice was reason enough to smile, though he had the feeling it was more like a grimace of pain. She nodded slowly and scooted backwards down the bed. For a moment, he thought she was going to abandon her task, but then she planted her hands either side of his hips, leaned forward so all he could see was the amazing colours of her hair burnished by candle-light. She took him into her mouth. Deep.

It was bliss. It was searing flame.

It was heaven and it was hell. Because he could not drive into her heat, he could only lie there and take what she dished out. With her tongue. With her teeth. With a mouth meant for sin.

He sank back on to the pillows and shuddered as her tongue circled the most sensitive spot at the head of his shaft. The pleasure of it was un-bearable. Yet when she moved on to lick her way down to its base, he wanted her to return, with him buried deep in her moist heat. She cupped him in her hand and tasted with such relish, he had the feeling she might devour him whole.

And he'd had enough.

Silently, he rose up, grasped her beneath her arms and flipped her over on to her back, ignor-ing the stab of pain from his arm as he would ignore the bite of a gnat.

'Now it is my turn,' he growled from a throat that felt as if it had been scored by gravel.

The agony of denial was etched into his face as he bore down upon Nicky. His reputation hadn't done him justice. The man had impossible control. She'd thought he would never break. And he still hadn't, she realised, looking up into his eyes. Despite the lethal speed of his reaction, he was still in control.

And he intended to make her suffer for bringing him so close to his climax and not letting him finish.

She was both fascinated and terrified.

Terrified he would be more than a match for her. If she did not rule here, in bed, his greater strength would give him all the advantage. It was not to be borne. She lifted her chin with a smile of triumph. 'Am I too much for you, *mon cher* Gabe?'

There was no resentment in his grin. 'Not too much, sweetling. Just enough.'

He took her lips in a kiss that was at first gentle, almost chaste, and then deepened to wildly erotic as he plundered her mouth and the taste of him mingled in their mouths. Her body clenched with excitement, little thrills tightening her unbearably, until her insides turned liquid with heat and longing. She cast her arms around his neck, pressing her breasts against the hot, hard expanse of his chest, and joined the dance with her tongue tangling with his.

Dizzy with desire and panting, she lifted one leg and wrapped it around his hip, bringing him close to where she wanted this young, virile man who heated her blood in a way the Countess had never known. With Gabe, it was different. Enticing. Exciting. He fed a yearning for closeness she hadn't known she wanted. Until now.

A large hand reached down, slipping between the swollen folds of her cleft, finding the core of her pleasure, then teasing and circling. 'Yes,' she breathed in his ear and felt his shiver of pleasure dance across his skin beneath her fingers. 'Now.' For it would not do for him to think she was overwhelmed.

Even if her limbs felt as if they had melted to his heat.

time nor the place. He had to get back to Cornwall and Freddy so they could begin their preparations. He lowered himself to the floor and stretched out. 'Do your worst.'

'You had better hope I do not,' she muttered. She soaked one of the strips of bandage in the bowl of water, which she set close to hand, along with the basilica powders, then picked up the brandy bottle. 'You'd better have a good swig of this since we do not appear to have any laudanum.'

He shook his head. 'I prefer to keep my wits about me.' He held up the rope he'd used to tie her. 'This will do.' He put it in his mouth and bit down hard. He nodded.

Her face grim, she knelt beside him and uncorked the brandy. He didn't blame her at all for needing some fortification. To his surprise, she poured it over the wound.

It stung like the blazes. He breathed in, hard, through his nose.

She swabbed at his arm. Glancing down, he could see the hole in his flesh now, ragged and raw. She picked up the knife. And put it down

He positioned himself in the cradle of her hips, nudging at the entrance to her body. He raised his head and looked down into her face. Lust darkened his expression, his eyes, his very soul, yet he held himself apart, gazing at her, waiting.

It wasn't supposed to be like this. 'Gabe?' His name was wrenched from somewhere deep inside.

An expression crossed his face, one she couldn't read. Surprise. Anger. Why didn't she know?

'Together,' he said roughly.

Instinctively she knew. As she pushed upwards, he thrust into her and in that moment it was all over, heat and light and languid bliss. As startling as it was powerful.

'Gabe,' she breathed as they shivered and shuddered through a climax that seemed to rip open the very fabric of the dark.

'Nicky,' he groaned. The deep pleasure in his voice resonated through her body, as if some chord had been plucked.

Slowly his weight pressed her down into the mattress as they clung together, two people shattered and reformed as one.

What had happened?

Gradually, the warm mist receded from her mind. Slowly he withdrew from her body and moved to her side, pulling her against his chest. Two. They were two. Not one.

What had happened? The question spun out of control as she realised that she had not, as intended, brought him to his knees, but nor had he taken full advantage of her weakness.

Together.

The word clenched like a fist around her heart, squeezing. He'd given something she wanted.

By chance. Purely by chance. And she must not let him see how deeply he'd struck. No one must know that about her. She wasn't even sure it was true any longer. There was only one thing she wanted. To bring Minette home safely. And if she could spoil Napoleon's plans to do so, it was no bad thing.

She eased back from his body and he relaxed his grip, albeit a little reluctantly. His eyes were open and he was watching her with the wariness of a predator whose prey had just turned around to fight back. 'I suppose my hard work is ruined.'

She inspected the bandage around his arm as if she had no other concern and frowned. There was indeed a dark stain on the pristine white of the bandage.

She huffed out a breath of annoyance.

'Leave it be. It is fine.'

Likely. And if not, why should she care?

'Please yourself,' she said, with all the indifference she could muster.

He drew her head against his uninjured shoulder, and pulled the sheet over them both. 'Sleep. We have a long way to go in the morning.'

'A long way to where?'

'You'll find out when we get there.'

She glanced over at the waistcoat thrown so carelessly over the chair. The waistcoat with a key in the pocket.

'Don't give it a thought,' he murmured, stroking her hair where it spread over her shoulder. 'I sleep with one eye open. You don't stand a chance, *ma belle.*'

Beautiful. Did he think she was a complete fool? 'Pray, then, that you don't develop a fever,' she said, stung by the lie for no good reason she could think of.

'There is no doubt you and I hope for different outcomes.'

She smiled at his swift response and the heat it contained. Now the world was back in balance. They both knew where they stood. On opposite sides. She had no intention of trying to escape, but he did not need to know that. Her biggest worry was that he might decide to leave without her. Which meant she dare not sleep.

But sleep she did. Against her will, she drifted off. Too sated to remain alert through the night.

As she had feared, she awoke alone.

Oblivious to the chilly air, she leaped out of bed and ran to the closed door. A tug on the handle answered her immediate question. Locked. And no doubt Walter guarded the key. Blast Gabe.

She strode to the window. There was no sign of her host galloping into the distance. He'd probably left hours ago. What on earth could have got into her, sleeping so soundly, when she had known the danger? What now? She ran her fingers over the window frame. Nailed shut, as he had said. It would take her hours to get it open. Morose, she gazed at the far distant ground. And once she did get out, she'd likely break her neck climbing down.

A small sound behind her, a cross between a cough and a laugh, had her whirling around, ready to leap on the intruder.

Chapter Four

When Gabe had unlocked the door and left the room, a half hour before, the countess had been so dead asleep she hadn't stirred. He'd returned expecting to find her still asleep. Instead, a wonderful surprise awaited him. The countess, naked, at the window. The sight of that high, round bottom tapering to delicately muscled thighs had sent blood racing from Gabe's head to his groin. He was harder than granite and the urge to leap onto her and carry her to the floor had him gripping the edge of the door. Restraining himself around her wasn't getting any easier, despite how sated he'd been when he fell asleep. Utterly oblivious to her nakedness, with her long, wavy hair falling in disarray over her small, high breasts and halfway down her elegant back, she prowled towards him. By thunder, he'd thought her lovely by candlelight, but in the grey light of early morning, she was a goddess come to earth. Apparently, a very angry goddess.

She halted. 'I thought you had gone.'

Ah.

He eyed the distance between them. One stride and she would be in his arms. But her claws were still out.

'Still here, Countess.'

Her eyes flashed. 'You could have said something.'

'I didn't want to disturb you. You were sleeping so peacefully.'

If anything, his words seemed to make the anger in her eyes glow brighter. He thought about the passion that anger might spark, then forced his mind into action. He could not afford to delay his departure. He had no idea how quickly her people would come looking for her. Despite the fact that his arm felt a great deal better this morning, he was in no shape to fight off an enemy. Not when he had one inside his lines. 'Do you need help dressing?' he made himself ask, glancing down her length pointedly. 'There is warm water in the jug on the washstand.'

'I can manage for myself.'

Too bad. Or not. If he so much as touched her, he was going to go up in flames. 'We'll be leaving shortly. In the meantime, Walter has gone to fetch us a picnic from his mother. We'll break our fast on the way.'

She frowned at him. Looked him up and down, then her gaze fixed on the collar at his throat. 'What on earth…?'

He put his hand to his heart and bowed. 'Doctor James, humble curate, at your service, Countess.'

Her eyes widened, and then finally—thank goodness, finally, she realised she was naked. She snatched up her gown and held it in front of her. Far too late to do him any good. 'You pretend to be a man of the cloth?'

'It allows me to travel without remark.'

Her expression said she didn't like it. No doubt she had realised it would put anyone trying to find them off the scent.

'Have you no shame?'

'None at all.' As a man without honour, shame wasn't an option.

'What if you are called upon for some official duty?'

'Unlikely. I merely pass through places. I do not stay.' He gave her a humourless smile. 'We leave in ten minutes, whether you are dressed or not.'

'I will be ready.' She gave him a stiff nod, clearly not comfortable with him in this new guise and, taking it for his dismissal, he went out and locked the door behind him. He leaned against the wall and took a few deep breaths, adjusting his grey trousers, getting himself under control, if not exactly comfortable. Ten minutes would be enough time for Walter to get back from his mother's cottage and for him to be fully in command of himself.

The coach he'd taken from the inn was already on its way back to London. They would proceed from here in the small light vehicle he always used for his trips to Cornwall. Small and mean-looking, but lightened to be swift and sprung to be comfortable. Even so, two days on the road shut up in a carriage with Nicoletta was going to drive him mad. It served him right. He deserved to be punished for falling for her allure.

Perhaps his disguise would keep her at a distance. The thought gave him little pleasure.

Nicky closed the book she'd been reading, one of many Gabe had thoughtfully provided for their journey, and held it in her lap. It was fortunate she did not become travel-sick when she read. Or not. If she got sick he might be forced to tell his coachman to pull over. In a carriage this small, with only one seat facing forward, it was impossible not to be aware of the width of Gabe's shoulders or the spread muscled thighs that pressed against her leg. Aware in the worst possible way, given her longing to lean against him, to touch and stroke and enjoy.

While he behaved like the perfect gentleman. Keeping his distance. Doing his best not to crowd her by sitting tight into the corner, giving her as much room as possible. Something which could not have been very comfortable for his injured arm. Despite its rundown appearance, the carriage was well sprung and moved swiftly through the countryside. Gabe had pulled down the blinds at the start of the journey and refused to allow her a peak outside. Still, she was sure they had continued travelling west.

As on the journey the previous day, they stopped at regular intervals to change horses. She was free to leave the carriage at each of these stops, to stretch her legs, to sip at coffee while he downed a tankard of ale, but there was nothing to tell her where they were. The inns were small and off the main road, deep in the English countryside. Sometimes there were rolling hills, at others the countryside was flat, then rugged. Beautiful green vistas so different from the countryside around her father's estate. And yet so much better than the dirt and the noise of Bristol or London. Here, she felt as if she could breathe. Her mother had told her about England. About its beauty. And its greenness. The truth of it was far lovelier than anything she could have imagined. Minette would be happy here. If she lived. Her grip tightened on the book. She must.

'Where are we?' she asked. 'I believe we are travelling west?'

He shrugged and smiled.

Better than an outright lie, she supposed.

She picked up her book and read until it was too dark to see the words.

'Will we spend the night at an inn?' she asked, noticing that Gabe, who had been dozing, right now seemed alert and ready for something.

'Sadly, no.' His deep voice sounded so velvety smooth in the dark she had to repress a little shiver. 'We will keep going until we reach our destination.'

'Soon?'

'Tomorrow evening or perhaps the following morning.'

Given their speed, by tomorrow evening they would have travelled a very long way. Could she be wrong about the direction? Could they be moving north? Over the border to Scotland? 'Your business must be urgent,' she said lightly as if making conversation. She tucked her book into the pocket in the squabs at her elbow.

She sensed, rather than saw, his smile. 'Not in so much of a hurry that we can't stop for dinner.'

The basket of bread and cheese Walter had

brought from his mother had been consumed within the first few minutes of their departure. And lunch had been hours ago. Her stomach gave a pleased little gurgle at the thought it might soon be fed. She laughed and pressed a hand to the offending spot.

'I must express my gratitude, Nicky,' Gabe drawled, his voice sounding amused.

For last night? When he hadn't mentioned it once in all the hours they had been shut up in this coach. Not made one gesture that said he wanted to do it again. She could not prevent herself from stiffening. Was he perhaps going to offer her money? 'Gratitude for what?'

'For not having a fit of the vapours when you realised I would not return you home.'

'Peu importe.' Was it really of no importance? Perhaps a fit of the vapours might have made him think twice before carrying her off. Or might have made him less suspicious of her. Had she made a mistake by not protesting more? But she was where she wanted to be. At his side, learning his secrets, she hoped. The big problem would

be communicating what she learned to Paul. She doubted Gabe would let her write a letter.

She couldn't help smiling at the thought.

'What?' he asked.

'I beg your pardon?'

'You are smiling.'

'A passing thought.'

'But not one you wish to share.'

'Not at this moment, no.'

The motion of the carriage changed. It was slowing. It turned, rocked along a rutted lane for several minutes. She grabbed the hand-strap to stop herself from crashing into him. A strong arm came around her waist to steady her. Finally the carriage halted.

'Dinner,' he said.

She couldn't wait. Not because of the food, but because it meant she could stretch her legs and look around. Perhaps this time there would be a clue as to their direction.

When he handed her down, she inhaled a deep breath. The scent of summer. Ripening grain. Clover. Warmth. She'd grown up in the country and the smells were so similar that a rush of homesickness filled her. A longing she had never experienced in her weeks in town. Growing up, she'd always imagined her life being similar to that of her parents, having children of her own and a loving husband by her side.

Everything had changed when Maman and Papa had been killed by rioters in Paris. Her uncle had taken charge of her and Minette. He had arranged the marriage with Vilandry as a way to protect them. Only later had she learned that Vilandry had paid him well for the arrangement. Her marriage had been a shock. Her elderly husband revelled in political machinations and he'd blatantly offered her favours in exchange for power. She'd been horrified. But when he'd threatened to be rid of her and take her sister instead, what could she do?

In the end, it had done none of them any good. The soldiers had gone on a rampage authorised by Paris, throughout the Vendée. Only by chance had she survived.

She glanced around, hoping for some sort of landmark. It was far too dark to make out anything except the creaking sign above the inn door.

'The Bell, Book and Candle,' she interpreted from the crudely drawn painted figures. No village or town name. She nodded at the sign. 'How appropriate, given your current calling.'

'Indeed.' He opened the door in the stone wall and bowed her in to what was clearly the taproom. A pot boy glanced up from polishing a pewter mug. His eyes widened. 'Reverend James,' he said in a piping voice. 'Back so soon?'

'Good evening, Tom,' Gabe said. 'I have indeed returned. How are you, my boy? Behaving yourself, I hope.'

The transformation was shocking. Gabe suddenly sounded stern and the look from beneath his lowered brow was that of a man who would let no sin escape his notice.

Astonished, Nicky covered her mouth with her hand to prevent the escape of a giggle.

The boy, on the other hand, paled. 'Aar, Reverend,' he said in the accents of the West Country. 'I done just as you said the last time you was here.'

'Glad to hear it, young man,' Gabe said in

a deep rumble, but there was a twinkle in the depths of his blue eyes.

The boy turned to Nicky. She'd done her best with her hair after Gabe had given her a few minutes to dress, but she knew strands of it had escaped their pins and now straggled around her face, and certainly her habit was creased after so many hours in the carriage, but there was no reason for the boy to look quite so shocked. Or to dash off like a startled fawn.

She looked to Gabe for an explanation.

He grinned. 'He thinks you are my wife.'

She gasped. Her heart tumbled over at the word. A deep well of yearning rose up to block her throat. 'Your wife?'

'Well, you see, the innkeeper's daughter has been looking for a gentleman to take her away from this world of hard work and poverty. A curate, even one as poor as me, seemed like the very best of opportunities.'

'Not to mention that the curate is devilishly handsome,' she mumbled. 'And so you invented a wife.'

'Yes. Will you mind?'

Mind? Why would it matter at all? But some-how it did. Because it was something that could never happen. Something she never wanted to happen again. One marriage was quite enough. Now she had freedom. And she certainly would not want to be married to him. A man who had sold his soul to the devil. A man she would do everything in her power to bring to justice. She gave him an enquiring look. 'Will it make a dif-ference, if I mind?'

'It would be rather awkward if you denied it,' he said. He gave her a look of grave severity. 'Given my supposed line of work. We could skip dinner, I suppose.'

He had an answer for everything. 'Wretch. You know I am starving. Very well, I will play your wife and you will play the besotted husband.'

He must have seen something in her face, be-cause he gave a mock groan. 'Besotted, is it?'

'If I am to compete with an innkeeper's daugh-ter? Yes, indeed. Besotted.'

She removed her bonnet and handed it to him. The amusement in his eyes caused her heart to give a little hop. Foolish heart. This man was dangerous, to her, to her work, perhaps to every female in England if the truth was known.

A middle-aged woman in a mob cap and apron bustled in through the door, wringing her work-reddened hands and looking quite harassed. She bobbed a quick curtsy. 'I am so sorry to keep you waiting, sir. I've been calling and calling for our Sue to attend you, but there's nary a sign of the girl. What can I get for you and the good lady?'

Likely her brother had delivered the bad news that the *doctor* had brought his wife and the girl was off sulking.

'Please forgive us for descending on you at so late an hour, Mrs Barge. Are you able to provide us with a meal? No need to go to a great deal of trouble, for our business is pressing and we must depart within the hour. A little bread and cheese, perhaps?'

He smiled gently at the woman and she fluttered her hands. 'No, by George, sir. Mr Barge'll have a strong word should I treat you so mean. There's a stew over the fire in the kitchen and I dare say I can find a slice of pie.'

'You are too kind.'

'Ah, well, I would feel a lot kinder if I could lay a hand on that girl o' mine.'

'Please,' Nicky said. 'Do not treat her too harshly. We were all young at one time, *n'est-ce pas*?'

The woman frowned. 'A Frenchie? Well, Lord love a duck, I never did.' Her harassed countenance turned distinctly unfriendly.

Gabe's mild manner turned deadly. 'Perhaps I will have a word with Barge since I gather my business is no longer welcome.'

The woman looked horrified. 'Nay, sir. You take me wrong. You are always welcome here at the *Candle*. Go you into the parlour and I'll have that meal put together in a trice, never you fear.' She fled.

Gabe ushered Nicky through a door into an adjoining dark-panelled room with low blackened beams and furnished with a sofa and a dining table set for four. A small fire burned in the hearth.

Once inside, Nicky faced Gabe. 'I beg your pardon. I should not have spoken.'

''Tis no matter,' he said. 'I think the problem

can all be set at Sue's door. I will have a word with Barge, though. I want to check on my horses. You will remain here, will you not? As you can see, the locals are far from friendly to strangers.'

A warning. Not that it troubled her. If she wished to leave she would. The locals were the least of her worries. But it did not suit her purpose to leave him now. Not when she was about to learn one of the things Paul had asked her to discover. The location from which Moores-head operated. 'I will be here when you return. I promise.'

He nodded and left.

That he accepted her word made her feel— warm, when she should be feeling relief and nothing more. Well, she had wanted him to trust her, so it seemed she had accomplished one goal.

The lad, Tom, shambled in with a scuttle full of coal. 'Ma says I'm to build up the fire.'

Nicky inclined her head in permission. She spied the writing desk in the corner, strolled over and found it well supplied with writing materials. Dare she? She glanced at the boy kneeling at the hearth. 'Thomas?'

The boy turned to look over his shoulder at her. 'Yes, ma'am.'

If I gave you a letter, would you deliver it to the post office in the morning?' she asked. She dug around in her reticule. 'For a shilling.'

The boy's eyes lit up. 'I s'd be glad of a shilling.'

Nicky sat at the table and dashed off a few words, folded the single sheet and addressed it.

Finished with his task, the lad came to stand at her side. 'Where be it going?'

Naturally the child couldn't read. 'London.' She smiled at him and handed him the shilling. 'Shall we keep it as a secret between us? After all, if you tell anyone, they might want their share of the money.'

A smile split his ruddy face. 'Aar. And I've been wishing for a shilling, I have. The blacksmith has a fine pocket watch for sale. Left there on account and never claimed.'

'Then it is yours. But only if you say nothing to anyone.' She got up from the desk and wandered to the fire and held her hands out to the warmth. The boy took the hint and took himself off.

No one but Paul would understand her coded note. While she'd addressed it to Mrs Featherstone, she would pass it along. There was no doubt that Mrs Featherstone would have immediately contacted Paul about her disappearance.

When Gabe returned he glanced around. 'No food yet?'

'Not yet. But the fire is warm. I am sorry my presence caused difficulty with the mother as well as the daughter,' she said. 'Did you find the innkeeper more accommodating?'

'Barge will follow his orders.'

Something had changed. She couldn't quite put her finger on it, but he seemed tense. Preoccupied. Had she made a fatal mistake in trusting the boy with her note? If he had given it to Gabe... 'Is something wrong?'

'One of my horses is lame.'

She almost sighed with relief. 'And your arm? Does it bother you?'

He flexed his hand, opening and closing it. 'Not unless I move it.'

'I should look at it.'

'When we get to—' He pressed his lips together. 'When we arrive at our destination.'

She laughed and shook her head at him. 'I don't know why you are so intent on keeping it a secret. There isn't anyone I can tell.'

'Isn't there?' He looked grimmer than ever. 'Well, then, what is the purpose of you needing to know?'

The logic of the man was infuriating. 'It is a woman's lot to be curious.'

The tight expression on his face eased into a reluctant smile. 'You have heard the old adage, I suppose?'

'Curiosity killed the cat.'

'Precisely.'

A shiver ran down her spine and she hoped it wasn't an omen.

The carriage had rocked and bucked through their second night on the road. Gabe shifted in the confines of the interior, easing his arm while settling Nicky's head more comfortably on his shoulder. Damn the woman. She had snuggled up to him beneath the carriage blanket with a warm brick at her feet and fallen asleep. Really fallen asleep, like one dead. And now his good arm was numb where she lay on it while his wounded one was aching like it was being jabbed with a pitchfork, as was his head. The closer he got to Cornwall the more he realised what a mistake it was to bring her along.

If she had been a man, he might well have killed her out of hand. Or turned her over to Sceptre. More likely the latter. But the thought of this woman in Sceptre's hands was not to be borne. She might be strong and courageous, but she was no match for that sort of ruthlessness. Guilt twisted in his gut. She was a spy. An enemy. The fact that he found her so damnably alluring should not enter into his decisions. They were on opposite sides of a war.

But *she* didn't yet know that, not for certain. If he continued to keep her guessing, he might be able to brush through this without the need for violence. And he might even convince her to reveal all she knew. If so, he might stand a chance of convincing Sceptre to let her be.

Damn it all, he was in the very devil of a quandary. And over a woman, to boot. After what happened with Marianne, he'd thought he was immune.

The journey he usually slept through felt interminably long. Thank goodness the torture of having her hand on his hip and her head nestled against his shoulder would soon end. He inhaled the scent of her hair. Lavender and sage. Some sort of exotic soap. Everything about her was exotic. Clearly he found her far too attractive. Yet if he did not get close to her, how else was he to learn her secrets? Secrets were gold in his business. And betrayal was death. As Marianne had learned. A sour taste filled his mouth at the recollection. She should have trusted him. If she had, if she'd truly loved him, as she'd said she did, she would not have died.

But he was not going to let this one die if he could help it. And not because he loved her. He didn't. She was doing what she thought was right. And he respected that. But women had no place in a war between men and soldiers. It wasn't right.

His only course was to keep her close by, incommunicado, so she couldn't do any damage.

Any more damage, he amended, flexing his arm. And if he could convince her to give up some of her knowledge, then so much the better.

The carriage slowed and made the turn into the drive.

Nicky stirred. Opened her eyes and stretched. The woman had the reflexes of a cat.

'We are here,' he said as the carriage halted.

She sat up patting her hair. 'What is the time?'

He opened the door and let cold air and daylight enter their small space. 'Mid-morning.'

'So late? I must have slept.'

'Really?'

She chuckled softly. 'Wound troubling you?'

He rubbed at his numb arm. 'Not at all.' The coachman let down the steps and Gabe leaped out and turned to help Nicky alight.

Daintily she took his hand and stepped down as if she was a queen. Only when her feet were firmly on the ground did she look around. The sound of the sea was a low growl in the distance and the ruined part of the abbey made an imposingly bleak view despite the summer sun trying to break through the clouds. Her eyes widened as she slowly took it all in, then flew to his face. 'You bring me all this way to a ruin.'

'Look again, Countess.'

With a hand low on her spine he guided her around the boot of the carriage. She gazed at the ancient house with its ramshackle wings, towers and chimneys stark against the sky.

She grimaced. 'I am not much comforted, but at least it appears to have a roof.'

Without doubt the place had an air of neglect. Deliberately so. Not to mention it was rumoured to be haunted, a tale he gladly encouraged to keep the locals away. It was perfect for Gabe's purposes. 'Welcome to Beresford Abbey.'

'Beresford. The earl who is your friend. It is his house.'

'It is.'

'Cornwall. He has mining interests here. Tin. Copper.'

'I see you have made it your business to study my friends.'

'It is a woman's prerogative to ask about any man who asks her to go riding.'

'If you wish to maintain the pretence, Nicky, who am I to say you nay?'

A blank stare met his gaze.

The woman was certainly a worthy opponent. Once more, he fought his admiration. 'This way. It's chilly out here in the wind. Let us hope Manners has a fire lit somewhere in this old pile.'

She shivered. 'Is it possible he has not?'

'Very possible. It is, after all, midsummer.'

The coach pulled away, heading back down the drive.'

She turned to watch. 'Where is he going?'

'I stable my horses elsewhere when I visit. The earl keeps very few staff here in his absence.'

'How delightful.'

By the time they reached the door, Manners already had it open.

'Another place where you are expected.'

'No matter what time of day or night I arrive, Manners always seems to hear the carriage turn into the drive.'

'So you come here frequently.'

There was no point in dissembling. 'As often

as needed. The house has some unusual and useful attributes.'

She glanced towards the cliffs. 'It is close to the sea, for one thing.'

'Closer than you might think.'

He saw the question in her face and grinned. In the confines of the coach, unable to sleep, he'd been irritated by her presence, but now they had finally arrived, he found himself charmed all over again. Here at Beresford, he would have no difficulty keeping her from escaping, so where was the harm in enjoying the company of a beautiful woman provided he never let down his guard? 'I will take you on a tour later. First we need food.'

'Good day, my lord,' Manners, the ancient butler, said as he bowed them in.

'Good day, Manners. This is the Countess Vilandry. She will be spending a few days with us. I hope you will do all you can to make her stay comfortable. She is not to leave the house without an escort with the cliffs being so unstable.'

'Yes, my lord.'

Nicky's back had stiffened, but her smile was

pleasant as she addressed the butler. 'I am pleased to meet you, Mr Manners.'

'Welcome to Beresford, my lady,' the old man said in his creaky voice. 'There's a fire lit in the breakfast room, my lord. I can have the cook prepare you luncheon, if you wish?'

'Excellent,' Gabe said. 'Would you prepare a chamber for the countess, if you please? The one at the base of the North Tower.' The one he usually occupied.

Manners didn't betray by so much as a flicker of an eyebrow any surprise. The old earl, the one before Bane, had been a holy terror by all accounts and the butler had no doubt received far more unusual requests.

'I don't suppose you have any gowns tucked away in your closets?' Nicky said. 'I left London in a hurry and did not bring any luggage. I would really like a change of clothing. Or perhaps we can arrange a visit to a seamstress?'

Manners's lips twitched. Amusement or disapproval? It was hard to tell.

'I shall ask one of the maids to see what might be available.'

'You are kind,' Nicky said calmly.

'If you would follow me, my lady. My lord. I will show you the way to the breakfast room.'

'No need to worry, old chap,' Gabe said. 'I will make sure the countess doesn't get lost. You see, we are both rather famished after our long journey, so would appreciate it if you would head straight for the kitchen.' Manners bowed and shuffled off.

Gabe tucked her hand under his and headed off down a narrow corridor. 'It is a very confusing old house,' he warned. 'I suggest you don't attempt to explore alone.'

Naturally, that was like waving a red flag at a bull, but he was going to enjoy saying *I told you so* when she became hopelessly lost.

Chapter Five

As Gabe guided her along the musty-smelling corridors, cold damp seemed to ooze from the old stone walls and into Nicky's bones. Strange prickles ran up and down her spine in quick succession. It was an odd sensation of dread, as if there was something unusual at work in this house. The sensations had begun the moment she stepped down from the carriage when her gaze had been drawn to a flicker of movement beneath an arch in the crumbling wall of the ancient ruin. A dark, shifting shadow of what she thought was a woman.

Who on earth would be prowling around in the grounds? The glimpse from the corner of her eye had been fragmentary. Could Paul have found her already? Her heart lifted in hope and then sank again. It wasn't possible. Her note would not have reached London as yet. Then what woman would be wandering around the grounds in such a strange manner? Perhaps she was a visitor to the ruins. They were certainly the sort of thing some people found fascinating.

The steady pressure of Gabe's arm hooked through hers propelled her along as if he half-expected her to flee. Or was he truly worried that she might get lost in the rambling passages? They came to a junction, Gabe turned right and they were faced with another long stretch of window-less corridor. They'd turned east, she thought.

'I'm glad you know the way,' she said, more to hear her own voice than anything else.

'It took me a while to find my way about,' he said. 'The Beresfords have been adding bits on to the house for untold centuries. I'm surprised none of them ever decided to pull it down and start again.'

'Sacrilege.'

He laughed. 'Some might think so, but not the current earl, let me assure you. He has little time for his noble ancestors and no love for this place.'

She had heard something similar about the man. That he was a bit of a commoner. More industrialist than peer. Perhaps even tainted by revolutionary ideals. 'What about you? Do you feel the same about your forefathers?'

'I grew up with mine. Hanging all over the walls at Bagmorton. They gave me the shivers as a child. Now I never give them a thought, one way or the other. What about you?'

'A heritage such as this is beyond price.' It was the way she had felt about her own home, given to her family for years of honourable service to the King of France. A home that was now nothing but ashes. The image of flames dancing in the windows while soldiers with demon faces watched seared her vision. The screams of those inside echoed in her mind. The English knew nothing about such terrible losses. But they would learn if Bonaparte wasn't stopped. 'If it was mine, I would do everything possible to restore it.'

'This draughty old place?'

'A place where you spend a considerable amount of time. Why would that be?'

He stopped outside a door. 'The breakfast room.' He flung it open and gestured for her to enter.

She stepped in and was pleasantly surprised. 'But this is *charmant*.' The room was painted pale blue with the cornice and mouldings picked out in white. Delicate furniture in the style of Chippendale gave it a light and airy feel. Whatever she had been expecting, it wasn't something that would have looked perfectly appropriate in a London town house.

'The place is full of surprises. I'm afraid the bedrooms are more on the medieval side and rather dingy. The current Countess Beresford has had little time to make her mark on the place. This is one where her presence can be discerned.'

'She has very good taste.' Idly, Nicky strolled to the window to look out, to get a sense of her surroundings. In horror she stared at the empty landscape. Nothing but rolling craggy moors as far as she could see. 'I don't believe I have made her acquaintance.'

'Likely not. She's considered a bit of a blue-stocking by the old tabbies who rule the roost.'

She turned to ask him what he meant, but before the words formed on her lips Manners entered, staggering beneath the weight a silver salver, followed by a footman similarly encumbered. Manners set the tray on the table and arranged the cutlery and dishes before pulling out a chair. 'Would her ladyship care to be seated?'

She sat at one end and Gabe at the other. It was not a very large table. Indeed, the whole effect was rather cosy and domesticated. So opposite to the truth.

A stab of longing pierced her heart, instantly squashed. Her marriage of convenience had taught her that a husband had all the power and wouldn't hesitate to control a wife, not only her body but her very thoughts, should it suit his purpose. Fortunately for her, there had been no children from her union, though for a time she had longed for one with all her heart. Now all she needed to make her happy was to find her sister alive and find a place of refuge far from the horror that was France.

'This is cosy,' Gabe said, shocking her by how close he had come to reading her thoughts.

'Indeed,' she said calmly.

Gabe cocked a brow at her as if he sensed something amiss. 'I think we can serve ourselves, thank you, Manners.'

'Yes, my lord.' The butler headed for the door.

'A moment, Manners,' Nicky said. 'Were you able to assist with my request as regard to clothing?'

'Yes, my lady. There are some items left in Lady Beresford's wardrobe. However, since her ladyship is taller than yourself, there may need to be some adjustments. I have asked one of the maids to see what she can do.'

'*Bien*. Then may I request a bath in my room, once we have finished here? I would be rid of the dust and dirt of our journey.' She looked at Gabe. 'If that is all right with you, *mon ange*?'

Gabe gave her a wicked grin that did not suit his sombre clothing at all. 'I think I'll join you.'

Manners didn't blink. 'The bath will be ready in one hour, my lady.' He ushered the footman out ahead of him and closed the door.

'I hope it will be a large bath,' she said and

smiled provocatively at the hitch in Gabe's breathing.

She hoped her satisfaction did not show on her face. Gabe D'Arcy might be a cunning spy and a worthy opponent, but he was still a man. Warmth skittered through her veins. And she was definitely a woman.

The chamber Gabe took her to after breakfast was in one of the old, crenellated towers. 'Most of the rooms apart from the library and the breakfast room are under holland covers. No sense in opening everything up just for me.'

In the distance, Nicky heard the sound of the sea. A low grumble, as if from beneath her feet. She went to the window. Beyond the ruins, she could see cliffs and distant waves. 'What a beautiful view.'

'I'm glad you approve. My chamber is one floor above.'

'Can you see France from there?'

'Not even on a clear day. The distance is too great.'

Of course it was. This far west, the Channel

opened into the Atlantic Ocean. Normandy was a long way away. The room she'd been given was an odd shape, not the round of the tower, or square, but a vague kind of half-circle, the only straight wall of any length the one with the hearth and the chimney. Candles in iron wall sconces flickered on each side the chimney breast and at various points around the room. A hip bath occupied the rug in front of the fire and the wall opposite sported a bed canopied in blue damask.

'I hope you will find it comfortable,' Gabe said.

'Will you find something else for me, if I do not?'

'No. This is it, I'm afraid. These are the only rooms I use. Poor old Manners does enough.'

She frowned. Something sounded off about what he had said, but she could not quite figure out what. She glanced at the bath. 'Not big enough for two, sadly.'

'I hoped you wouldn't notice. Clearly Manners is not my friend.'

He was teasing her, his easy charming smile displayed to full effect. Effectively keeping her at a distance. Was he afraid that she might tempt him into doing something he would regret? Did he not realise his withdrawal would simply make her all the more determined to get close? Likely he was underestimating her resolve. Or her abilities. As he was supposed to, she admitted. Well and good. But right now she really needed that bath.

A maid appeared in the doorway, bearing several gowns laid over her arms. She bobbed a curtsy. 'I'm Tess, my lady. Right good with a needle, I am.' She glanced at Gabe and blushed. 'If you are ready for me, that is?'

'Indeed, I am, Tess,' Nicky said.

Gabe bowed, amusement at her rejection in his eyes. 'If my aid is not needed, I will see if Manners thought to provide my bath upstairs.'

'Oh, he did, my lord,' Tess said. 'George and Freddy took it up after they brought in my lady's bath.'

Gabe cast Nicky a look of mock disappointment. 'Foiled.'

'What about your arm?' Nicky asked.

'Freddy, my valet, will see to it.' At her doubtful expression, he continued. 'Anyone can change a bandage, Countess. You did all the hard work.'

And there was nothing more she could say. Oh, yes, he was really intending to keep her at a distance now he had carried her off to his lair. The man lived at the edge of danger and he clearly trusted no one. She would have her work cut out to change his mind. He would have to believe he had won her over. And that would take time. Nicky gave him a calm smile. 'I will see you later, then, when we are both refreshed.'

'At dinner. I have business matters requiring my attention this afternoon. I suggest you rest. You did not get much sleep these past two days.' He gave her a knowing smile. The wretch. He was making it sound as if— She looked at Tess, who was blushing again.

Irritation welled up in her chest. How many other women had he brought here? He probably brought one every time he came, judging from the way the servants took it in their stride. And why on earth did that make her feel unreasonably angry? 'Dinner, then,' she said with as sultry a smile as she could manage given her anger.

He nodded and left. Nicky heard his steps as he climbed the winding stone steps to the room above.

'Will you bathe first, or try on the gowns first, my lady?' Tess asked.

'Bathe,' Nicky said. It would help calm her down. Though what had sparked her anger she didn't know. It wasn't as if she cared whom the man slept with. Or where.

Gabe couldn't believe how hard it had been to drag himself out of that chamber. He'd wanted to send the maid away and bathe her himself. Like some besotted schoolboy tending his first lover. Nicky wasn't anywhere near the most beautiful woman he had ever taken to his bed, but when he recalled her delicious body covered from neck to toe with freckles and remembered the way she had responded to his touch, he almost groaned aloud.

'Finally,' Freddy said, as he limped into the upper chamber. He was a fragile-looking young man, with dark hair and eyes who some might say was cruelly disadvantaged by his deformity.

His slenderness, his poetic air, belied his inner strength.

'Good morning, Freddy.'

The lad crossed the room to help him out of his coat.

'Be careful how you go with my left arm, I took a bullet.'

Freddy tutted. 'How very careless. Who shot you?'

He snorted. 'A sniper. And not a very good one.' Gabe pictured the event in his mind. The crows flying up. The horse twisting awkwardly beneath him. 'I was lucky. Bacchus must have sensed something. He reared at the same moment the shot was fired.'

Freddy frowned, but said nothing as he eased the coat first off his right arm and then gradually off the left. He tutted some more after he helped pull the shirt over his head, but Gabe was pleased to see that there was no sign of fresh bleeding.

'Whose house is lacking sheets?' Freddy said, unwinding the strips of linen.

'Meak,' Gabe bit out through clenched teeth at the pain disrobing had cause.

'Manners said there was a woman. Not like you to bring your fancy bits down here. They won't like it.'

'They won't know. And I didn't have a choice. She was with me when it happened. And she's not exactly a fancy bit.' Now he really hadn't needed to add that last. There was absolutely no need for him to defend Nicky to anyone.

Gabe hissed in a breath as Freddy pulled the bandage free of the dried blood around the wound. The exposed injury showed that his arm was swollen and sore looking, but without pus or other signs of infection. The basilica powders had done their work. Along with the brandy?

'What is she, then?'

'I think she's a French spy. Sent to discover our location, I'm guessing.'

Freddy stopped what he was doing to look at his face. 'And so you obliged her by showing her,' he said drily. 'Are you mad?'

Out of his mind. With lust. 'I need to know what she's up to. What they know.'

Freddy grunted and went back to poking at his arm. 'You could have used a stitch or two. You'll have quite the scar. But whoever patched you up did a fair job. Not that lad of yours at Meak, I'll warrant.'

'She did. The Countess Vilandry.'

He lowered himself on to a chair while Freddy set about cleaning the wound with a damp cloth. 'She could have killed you.'

'Hardly likely, if she wanted to know our location.'

'You can't tell me that's the only reason you brought her. Manners says she was hanging on your arm like a limpet.' He shook his head. 'Women. Nothing but a blasted liability.' He wrapped a fresh bandage around his arm with a sure but careful touch. Freddy was clever. A brilliant spy. He could have been anything he wanted: a brilliant political orator, clever philosopher, mathematician, even a doctor. But Freddy was the one thing he had ever failed at. Freddy was a ducal heir.

The bath in front of the roaring fire steamed temptingly. 'I suppose it was your idea to send such a small bath to the countess's room?' Gabe said to keep his mind off the pain.

'I have news you need to know right away.'

Gabe grunted. 'Then tell me.'

Freddy was another of those handful of people Gabe trusted. Another man despised by his father. They had been through a great deal together these past few years. He might not be much good as valet, but it made a good cover story when they were at Beresford. And he was an excellent comrade-at-arms. Like his friend Bane, Gabe had met Freddy at school. They'd stuck together against the other boys. Boys could be cruel, especially if they sensed weakness. In that place, even the scrawny son of a duke had needed friends.

'The delivery you ordered comes tonight,' Freddy said.

A cold stillness gripped his body the way it always did at the start of a mission. 'None too soon. We are to be ready to move the day after tomorrow.'

A grim expression hardened Freddy's jaw. 'So soon? I had no idea they were ready. Does Sceptre know?'

'There was no time to report.' He'd been distracted by the countess first, and then the damned sniper. 'We'll send word today.'

'So, until we hear back, we are on our own with a spy in our midst.'

'Apparently.'

'Did you not speak to Sceptre at all?'

'Earlier in the week. They worry about who on this side of the Channel is helping the French. This woman might be the key to uncovering their network.'

Freddy grunted noncommittally. A few moments later he tied off the knot. 'Just don't get it wet.' He picked up the discarded bits of bandage and gave Gabe a hard look. 'It's unlike you to take such a devil of a risk to bed a woman.'

Gabe glared at him.

He put up his hands. 'All right. I'll leave you to your bath. And then we must get a note off to Sceptre.'

Tess had been correct in her claims of being good with a needle. It hadn't taken her long to shorten the three gowns and alter them to look as if they had been made for Nicky. Fortunately, their original owner wasn't much more generously endowed than Nicky was herself. Hopefully Lady Beresford would not mind the loss of part of her wardrobe too much.

The morning gown was a pretty shade of rose, not a colour Nicky would have normally chosen, either as herself or in her role of seductress. But beggars could not be choosers and she could not continue to wear her riding gown for days on end. Or however long it took to accomplish her task.

'Your mistress must be a generous person, if you think she will not mind donating half of her wardrobe to a stranger,' she said to Tess as she eyed herself in the looking glass.

Tess took a pin from between her lips and shook her head. 'She's a lovely lady, she is. Give anyone the clothes of her back was they in need.'

'Not while she was wearing them,' Nicky joked, somewhat intimidated by the description of this paragon.

Tess of the good needle was also quick witted. She chuckled. 'Now if you could just turn a bit, my lady, I can untie you and we can try on the dinner frock.'

Nicky complied. 'Do we dress for dinner, Tess?'

Tess stopped pulling. 'As to that, my lady, I

don't know. Lord Mooreshead ain't usually one to bring a guest with him.' She resumed pulling the tapes free.

Oh, well, there went that image of a hedonistic hideaway. She wasn't sure if she was glad or sorry. The latter, because if this wasn't a place he bought his women then its purpose was definitely suspect. An unexpected sense of disappointment made her heart sink. She didn't want him to be guilty. Her heart twisted painfully, knowing that what she wanted was not relevant. No matter how he touched her emotions, she must not shirk her duty. But in all fairness, she would not come to a conclusion about him until she had proof of his guilt. 'Does he come to this house often?'

'I think so,' the girl said. 'Manners and Freddy usually look after him. I was at the house this afternoon because it is cleaning day.'

This must be where he hid from the authorities. Paul had described him as a will-o'-the-wisp. Showing up where he was least expected. 'He spent the summer here?'

'As to that, my lady, I don't know exactly when he was here. Busy helping my ma with the fish my da caught, I was. Manners don't talk much about the doings of the grand folk. It isn't seemly.' She hesitated. 'He'll have my guts for garters if'n he thinks I've been gossiping.'

'Oh, I am sorry, Tess. I don't want you to be in any trouble because of me. Be assured I will say nothing. It was idle curiosity. Things I can easily ask his lordship.' Not that he would answer. 'Shall we try on the other gown?'

It was a beautiful green silk. A perfect colour for her. But the neckline? If she was to keep Mooreshead's interest she would surely need to be a little more daring. 'I think we should remove this edging,' she said, tugging at the wide band of lace.

Tessa's eyes widened, then she smiled. 'Oh, yes, my lady. I can do that. There's a pretty length of strung pearl beads taken off another gown in the sewing basket. Look right nice with that silk.'

'And the sleeves. Can you alter them so they are off the shoulder?'

Tess frowned. 'I can give it a try.' She looked at the construction of the sleeve from the back.

'I think I can. I might have to lower the back of the bodice a bit.'

'That would be fine.' More than fine. The more skin the better, Vilandry had said when he wanted her to blur the mind of a business rival or an unfriendly representative of the local government.

'If you just want to slip on this robe then, my lady, I'll get this morning gown ready for you in a trice.'

'Thank you. And, Tess, don't worry about the undershirt with that gown. I won't need it.'

Tessa's eyes rounded as she envisaged the effect of not wearing anything beneath the tiny bodice. 'Very well, my lady. I'll see if her ladyship has left a nice shawl that would go with it, shall I? The house can be a bit draughty.'

'So I imagine,' Nicky said as Tess helped her into the robe. 'It is very old, is it not?'

'Built in the time of Henry the Eighth, so they say. This here is the oldest part of the house. Then there's the ruins.' She gave a little shiver. 'Stay away from them, my lady. They say they's haunted.'

The maid's eyes were wide with fear. Nicky remembered the shadow she'd seen when she first arrived. 'Ghosts? What do they look like?'

Another shudder shook the girl's sturdy frame. 'Never seen one. And don't want to. But there's others that have. The White Lady, they calls her. Murdered by her husband, she was. Walks around them ruins at night, wringing her hands.'

Surely not the shadowy figure she had seen? 'I'll be sure to stay away,' she said gravely. 'Thank you for the warning.'

'You are welcome, my lady.' She gestured to Nicky's riding habit. 'I'll give this a cleaning, shall I? You won't be needing it right away?'

'I think not. Thank you.'

The maid gathered up all of the gowns. 'Will there be anything else, my lady?'

She wanted to find out what Gabe was hiding down here in the wilds of Cornwall. But until she had clothes, she wasn't going anywhere. 'No, nothing else, thank you, Tess.'

The girl left, closing the door behind her.

Nicky paced the room. She felt like a prisoner. And effectively she was, without anything but a robe to wear. She winced. Perhaps she should have told the girl to leave the cleaning of her riding habit until later. But what excuse would she have for making such a request? The thing was grimy from the journey. No self-respecting lady would don such a filthy garment if she did not have to. Nicky had lived in her clothes for weeks on end when she escaped from France. It had been none too pleasant. A couple of hours of delay wasn't going to make much difference in her quest to discover just what it was that Mooreshead was up to.

Heaven help her, he'd been right about her needing rest, she'd been living on her wits for the past two days and she was exhausted, even though she had managed to nap during parts of the journey. She glanced at the bed, which looked very comfortable. So tempting. A glance at the clock on the mantel revealed it was mid-afternoon. She strolled over to the bed and picked up the book on the night table. It was a small book bound in brown leather with gold lettering. *A History of Beresford Abbey.* Now that might keep her mind occupied for a while. Perhaps it would have more about the ghost. She plumped up the pillows and stretched out on the bed.

Within moments, her eyelids drooped. Whoever had written this history, they had decided to make it as dull as possible in addition to writing it in an almost indecipherable handwritten script. No doubt that was why it had been set on the night table. It would send even the most avid scholar to sleep. Nicky yawned. Sleep it was, then. And besides, she would be better able to deal with the wiles of Gabe D'Arcy if she was well rested.

She snuggled beneath the covers. Sleeping during daylight hours. Whatever next? She would just close her eyes for a few moments.

Something startled her out of her doze. Sounds from above her head. Men talking. Then the sound of two sets of footsteps coming down the stairs from the room above, passing her chamber and moving on. Oddly they seemed to echo in such a way as to sound as if they were coming not through her door, but from the wall on the other side of the room. Confused, she peered at the clock across the room. Five o'clock? Surely she could not have slept so long? But she had. Fortunately, if that sound was anything to go by, Mooreshead hadn't abandoned her and gone off on his own. What on earth had they been doing up there? Whatever it was, they had gone.

And with them gone, it might be an opportune time to visit Gabe's room and see what she could discover. She could always say she was looking for him, if he returned. She stood up and glanced down at herself. The silky-sheer robe hid little. Yes, it would serve as a fine distraction if he returned. A pleasurable little shiver of anticipation ran through her body.

She glared at her reflection in the mirror on the dressing table. How could she be so attracted to him, knowing he was a traitor? She frowned. She didn't know. Not for sure. And Paul could be wrong, couldn't he? Oh, dear, was that lift in her heart a feeling of hope?

No matter how hard she tried, clearly she wasn't invulnerable to Mooreshead's charms. Which meant she had to be doubly on her guard when in his presence or find herself at a disadvantage. She opened her bedroom door and looked around.

No one about. She stepped out and closed her door behind her. Hearing nothing, she made her way quietly up the winding steps to the sound of the wind whistling through the ancient arrow loops piercing the old stone walls. She halted on the upper landing. Two doors. One went out to the battlements. The other led to the chamber above hers. Expecting the chamber door to be locked, she pulled a pin from her hair, ready to put her training to use.

On a deep breath, she lifted the latch.

Chapter Six

The door creaked and opened a fraction. Startled, she froze. She had not expected Gabe to be so careless. But like so many others, perhaps he underestimated the abilities of his houseguest. He wouldn't know that she had been taught things no lady should know in preparation for this task. Men did not expect a woman to be brave or clever.

Composing a sultry smile on her lips, her excuses rapidly forming on her tongue, she pushed the door wide and stepped inside.

Empty.

She closed the door quietly and glanced around a room that was identical to the one below. The fireplace on the same wall, the window looking in the same direction, even the same-style iron wall sconces either side of the chimney. But the furniture was nowhere near as fine. A small battered wooden desk with a chair in front of the window containing writing implements and a ship's lantern. A chest beside the door. A bench in front of the hearth. And in place of the comfortable four-poster bed on which she had rested was a cot. The kind one might make available for a servant.

She frowned. Surely he did not use this room when he stayed here? Oh. Of course. He had put her in his room and this must be where his valet slept. Servants didn't normally sleep in the same wing as their masters, but in this sprawling place and with most of the house closed up it made sense he would want his man nearby.

She crossed the room to the window and looked out. From this vantage point she had no doubt the view on a clear day would be far out to sea. Today was grey and gloomy, though not raining. Waves the colour of slate and flecked with white horses raced towards land. Every now and then spray appeared above the cliff edge a few yards away from the tower.

Off to the right, she also had a good view of the abbey ruins. And beyond that, nothing but sea or moorland stretching out vast and empty. The perfect place for secret arrivals and departures by sea or by land. It was a wonder that Paul had not found this place on his own, it was just so perfect. But then who would suspect Beresford of being complicit with an enemy of England?

A movement at the corner of her eye had her searching the ruins. Nothing. But she had seen something down there. The woman she'd seen before? Someone obsessed with the history of the abbey? It couldn't be a servant. They'd have no reason to behave in such a secretive manner. She held still for several seconds, opening her vision to take in as much of the scene as possible in case the figure reappeared. Nothing. Perhaps she'd imagined it. It could have been a trick of the light. No. She'd definitely seen someone prowling around. The strange sensation she'd felt earlier slid over her skin. Imagination. Tess's tales colouring her thoughts. She shook it off and went back to her task. She might be interrupted at any second.

A peek under the blotter on the desk. Nothing. Inside the drawer? Blank paper. She lifted the top one and held it to the light. It held no impression of any previous writing. The drawer on the left? Empty. She heaved a sigh. He'd be a fool to leave any evidence of what he was doing about for anyone to find. Still, he likely had some place he could hide things. Either here or in the room downstairs. She gently pushed the drawer closed.

A small sound made her whirl around.

Gabe was standing in the middle of the room, eyebrows raised in question.

Her gaze flew to the door. It was closed. How had he got so far into the room without her hearing him?

Gabe enjoyed the expression of shock racing across Nicky's face, almost as much as his body was enjoying the sight of her in the filmiest of dressing gowns. She'd been asleep when he'd looked in on her an hour or so ago. But where the hell was Freddy? He'd left him on guard. He glanced around, half-wondering if she might have done away with the poor chap, then let his gaze roam down her length. Clearly there was nothing beneath the ivory silk but naked skin. He hardened even more. Annoying as well as frustrating. Since when did merely the sight of an almost naked woman have him lusting like a schoolboy? Albeit a very attractive woman. Who had been delightful in bed. Blast it. He was master of his desires. Yet, against his better judgement, he let his lascivious thoughts show on his face. 'Can I be of assistance, Countess?'

To his annoyance, she remained supremely calm. 'I heard a noise. I thought perhaps you had fainted. Because of your wound.'

The breathlessness in her voice revealed more than her face. She was nervous. And so she should be. He gave her his most charming smile. 'An angel of mercy, then.' He touched a hand to his heart and took a step closer. 'You will find me full of gratitude.'

Her slender body was only a foot from his. He was sorely tempted to reach out and encircle that tiny waist with his hands and pull her close. Ever since he'd enjoyed her company in his bed at Meak, he had wanted her again. It was why he had been unable to rest and had gone off to check on his boat in the underground caves, to make sure it was ready for tonight's enterprise. Thank heaven he kept nothing in this room for her to discover. 'Did you find anything of interest?'

'I beg your pardon?'

'You were searching the desk.'

A faint hint of pink coloured the edges of her delicious cheekbones. A memory of the flush of her skin during their lovemaking tormented him. Only by dint of will did he stop from kissing her while he waited for her answer.

'It is a woman's prerogative—'

'To be curious.' He couldn't hold back his laugh.

She pouted. 'I am glad I amuse you.'

'You do more than that.' He prowled closer, drew her hard up against the full length of his body and inhaled the scent of lavender and sage wafting from her hair, and the scent of warm woman fresh from her bath rising up from her body. Irresistible. Not that he had to resist what her body had to offer. But he did have to resist the desire to keep her safe when the safety of his country was at stake.

She inhaled too and her nose wrinkled. 'You smell like…seaweed.'

He grinned. 'Thank you.'

She frowned. 'It was not a compliment.'

He caught her chin between thumb and forefinger and looked down into her face. 'This is a very old house,' he warned. 'And some of it is not in good repair. You need to have a care where you trespass.'

Her blue eyes twinkled. 'And where were you, *mon ange*?' She glanced at the door. 'I did not hear you come in.'

Damn Freddy for leaving his post. He was now left with no alternative but to redirect her line of thought. He kissed her.

She melted so sweetly against him he could not stop the groan of pleasure that rumbled up from his chest. And then, to his deep and primal male satisfaction, her small hands attacked his buttons, tugging and pulling his coat over his shoulders while her lips clung to his. Pain flashed outward from his arm. He winced.

Her hands stilled. 'Oh, your wound. Forgive me.'

'It is nothing.' Nothing compared to the ache between his legs.

She pulled back. 'Perhaps this is not such a good idea...'

In counterpoint to her words, he captured her mouth with his lips, delving deep with his tongue while he divested himself of his coat and waist-coat. The sound of their ragged hurried breathing filled the room, along with her little moans and her gasp as he plunged a hand inside that ridiculously flimsy robe and cupped her breast, feeling her gasping breath in his mouth and her shiver of pleasure as the peak hardened against his palm. He pressed one thigh between her legs and she widened her stance, rocking her hips to take pleasure from the pressure.

He broke the kiss, stepped back and pulled his shirt off over his head. She licked her lips as she stared at him and, plague take it, he was harder than granite and breathing so fast he couldn't think. Not that she was in any better shape—she was panting, her small breasts, revealed by the gaping robe, rising and falling in quick succession.

Her hands went to the tie at her waist at the same moment his went to the buttons of his falls. Unable to look away, he stripped off his pantaloons, glad he had gone barefoot down to the caves. Her gaze fixed on what he was doing, she pulled the end of the tie free and dropped it at her feet.

More. Had he said that out loud?

Whether he had or not, she seemed to know just was he wanted, because with a little wriggle of her shoulders the robe slid down her arms to fall in a puddle of gleaming iridescence at her small delicate feet. She was also barefoot. He swallowed and slowly skimmed his gaze up her lovely slender legs to the light brown nest of curls at the apex of her parted thighs, to skim over the curve of her belly and the indentation of her waist. The high small breasts jutted towards him as if they longed for his touch.

Her gaze remained fixed on his naked body for long seconds and again she licked her lips. Oh, yes, he wanted that. But not now, not when he was so out of control. He had to be inside her heat. Now. He winced when he recalled the cot, but it was either that or the floor. They stepped towards each other at one and the same moment, her arms went around his neck and one leg lifted around his hip and her mouth melded with his. His right hand went beneath her buttocks and he raised her without effort. Such a small woman, whose courage made her seem larger than life, but who in truth was dreadfully vulnerable. The idea gave him pause. She nibbled at his ear and then he couldn't think about anything but being inside her. 'Hold tight,' he gritted out.

Her legs gripped his waist, her tongue explored his mouth and, ignoring a twinge of pain from his arm, he guided himself into her with his other hand, felt the heat and the slick dampness surround his flesh and almost exploded. He fought for control. Found a shred, but it wouldn't last long. Hands pressing down on his shoulders, she lifted herself and slid down with a deep sigh that scorched heat through his veins. Urgent, unthinking, he took the two steps to the nearest wall and with his hand between her back and the rough stone, he drove hard up into her body. With each thrust of his hips she opened wider and took him deeper. And then his vision went red and he was... He thrust again, reaching desperately between them, finding her little bud of pleasure, pressing and stimulating... She tensed. Cried out at the rush of her climax. Helpless to stop, he followed her with his own thundering release.

It was hours. Or it was seconds, when thought finally returned. He was standing, thighs trembling with the strain of holding them both upright, his forehead pressed to her shoulder while she rested her cheek against his temple. Bliss raced through his veins in wave after wave, like the incoming tide.

By thunder, what the devil had occurred? He'd taken her like some rutting beast up against a stone wall. Where was his famed art of seduction? His clever hands and tongue and teeth that kept a woman at the brink for hours before he let them fall into bliss?

She had fallen.... Hadn't she? She had. He was sure of it. At the same moment he had. Hard and fast. 'Are you all right?' he croaked. And swallowed against the dryness.

She nodded weakly.

Oh, yes, she had.

Carefully he lifted her free of his body and carried her to the cot, setting her down carefully on the rough blankets. And still he couldn't resist drinking in the sight of her and marvelling at the perfection of her form and the magically swirling patterns of her little sun kisses. She wriggled closer to the wall and patted the cot in a peremptory summons. Normally he would have laughed and walked away. It didn't do to let a woman know you sought anything beyond completion, but he wanted to join her and hold her. And, weak or not, wrong or not, he stretched out beside her and encircled her in his arms. He pulled the counterpane over them, and let himself go lax. She couldn't go anywhere, not without waking him, and the unusual tender pleasure of the feel of her so delicate and so sweetly yielding against him was something he didn't want to miss out on.

Lying beside her, he marvelled at what had occurred. At his loss of all sense of self along with his loss of control. At some point he'd had the strangest feeling that they were one person. They were not. It was not possible. His life did not allow for permanent connections. It was why he had chosen it.

She stirred in his arms and he lifted his head and glanced down to find her face tipped up to look at his. He smiled.

Rosy lips answered with a tender curve. He did not think he had ever seen anything quite so beautiful. Her beauty shone from within.

'Gabe, whose side are you on?' she asked softly.

Shocked from his daydream, he could only stare.

Nicky inwardly winced. She had not intended to question him so bluntly. Deep-seated contentment had made her speak without thinking. The Countess had dropped her guard and the innocent girl she protected from the harshness of the world had taken advantage of the moment of freedom. Something about this man made it harder and harder to maintain her role. To stem the unfurling hope that Paul was wrong and somehow Gabe was not a traitor. Foolish, foolish woman.

Hoist by her own petard. Seduced into speaking when she should have remained silent.

He let his head fall back with a sigh. 'So, you want to end this game and play truth or consequences. Are you prepared for the outcome?'

Was she? A band tightened so tightly around her chest, she could scarcely draw breath. 'I am prepared for anything,' she ventured.

'This is a dangerous game for a woman, Nicky.'

'I can look after myself.'

He made a scoffing noise in his throat. 'And will you believe what I tell you?'

She hesitated a moment too long and he laughed softly, bitterly. 'Who sent you, Nicky? It was the French, wasn't it? They've never trusted me.'

Her heart sank. 'You want their trust?'

'It would be…nice.'

Nice was not the word he had been about to use. Though he had sounded regretful. Lack of trust was an obvious impediment for a man like him. Certainly she did not dare trust him. And clearly he did not trust her wholly either. Yet. It was a barrier she had to find a way to break through.

Her heart hammered in her chest. She'd opened

this conversation and now she had no choice but to try to force the issue. 'What would you do, if I admitted the French sent me?'

She held her breath, hoping he would denounce her, send for soldiers to make an arrest. It was the only possible outcome that would be good.

He rolled on to his back, staring up at the canopy, his mouth set in a grim line. 'Then I would say, welcome aboard.'

Deep inside, she rode out the sickening sensation in her stomach. Was this the truth? He assumed she was in his power. He had no reason to lie. 'I will be sure to let your superiors know.' His English superiors. Who would be arriving at any moment, provided her message had reached London.

The man was a traitor. A man who would let the French ravage his country, force their revolution down his countrymen's throats. The very idea made her feel ill. That and the fact she had to find a way to destroy him. Her foolish heart ached at the thought of what she must do. And yet it was right and just. Men of his ilk, men who cared nothing for whom they hurt in their hunt for dominance, had killed her family. Whatever these revolutionaries spouted about equality and liberty, in the end they were no less corrupt than the *ancien régime* who had at least been open about their views, even if she did not agree with them either. She preferred the English way of doing things. At least, so far.

The ideals of the revolution were grand. Much of its philosophy appealed to her sense of what was right and fair. It was the way that they went about it that she hated. Wreaking havoc on innocents like her sister.

She sat up and leaned over him, running a finger down his lightly stubbled cheek. 'I am glad we are working on the same side.'

'Are you?'

She cast him a sultry smile. 'Of course. There are many advantages, from my perspective.'

He caught her fingers in his large, warm hand and brought the tips to his lips. The warm, dry pressure sent a shimmer of sensual awareness across every inch of her skin. The hairs on her arm stood up. He smiled briefly at her response to his touch. 'The question is, Countess, do I believe you?' The teasing humour was back in his voice. The man wore his sensuality like a masquerade domino, to be put on and off at will. In that, they were very much alike. The thought was a deep well of sadness.

She stroked his palm. 'Why would I lie?'

Another sigh. 'Everyone lies when they have reason.'

'Cynic.'

He rolled on his side to look at her. 'Without question. What if I told you I work for the highest bidder?'

Her stomach clenched in a kind of sick horror. 'You mean like a mercenary? A soldier for hire?' Was there anything more dishonourable? 'A man with no ethics. No principles. No loyalty to anyone.' Even misguided loyalty was better than what he was suggesting.

He rose up on one elbow and looked down into her face with a smile so seductive her breath caught in her throat. His thumb traced a path across her lower lip. 'Passion suits you, *ma belle*.' His eyelids drooped as he focused on her mouth. 'I can think of better ways to put it to use.'

She stroked his hair back from his face, looking into those keen blue eyes with their deeper shadows and sank into their promise of forgetfulness in bliss. A flush of warmth rippled through her body.

Sensual distraction. The man was a master. A good thing she wasn't fooled.

The door opened. Freddy stuck his head inside, saw them both on the cot and whipped his head out again. He knocked on the door.

'Go away,' Gabe said.

'My lord, there's an urgent message.'

Gabe groaned. 'Wait for me in the library. I'll be down in a moment.' He climbed out of the cot and picked up his pantaloons, pulling them on as fast as he had stripped them off. Nicky enjoyed the view of those lovely, tight male buttocks and firm flanks until they were covered, then glanced up to find him watching her, his face set in grim lines. 'We will finish this discussion later. By the way, please do not forget you are still my prisoner. Return to your room and stay there.'

Her jaw dropped. But what could she say? Feeling rather foolish, she got up and wrapped herself in her robe. 'I will see you at dinner.'

He bowed. 'I look forward to it.' He opened the door and she trotted down the stairs under his watchful eye.

She was no further ahead now than when she had arrived. He had not denied he worked for the French. Nor had he really confirmed it. Indeed, he had thrown another option into the mix. One she had never considered. Nor had it been suggested by Paul. Was it possible he was a mercenary? Selling secrets to both sides of the war. The very idea drove bile up into her throat. It was far easier to accept that he was a spy for the French, a man misguided, than that he was a man with no conscience. The idea that she could be attracted to a man with such a lack of moral fibre was more than shocking. It left her feeling disgusted. With her own lack of good judgement.

A pain in her chest made her want to cry out. Dash it all. She liked him more than she dared admit. Look at his kindness to the boy at Meak. And the obvious loyalty of his less-than-able valet. The more she got to know him, the more she did not want him to be a traitor. And if she wasn't very careful that would be her downfall.

But a mercenary? It was simply unacceptable. And why would he do such a thing? For money, as he had implied? He was a marquess. It made no sense.

Or was it simply a clever ruse? An attempt to pull the wool over her eyes? But why?

Because he didn't believe she had been sent by the French? It was the only possible explanation. She had not convinced him she was not his enemy.

Then she needed to try harder. She surely hadn't expected him to drop into her palm like ripe fruit after so brief an acquaintance? After all, he had caught her snooping in his room. The man was no fool and unlikely to spill his secrets to every woman he bedded. The thought of him bedding other women made her grit her teeth as she went down the stairs to her room.

Tess wasn't in her chamber when she stepped in, but the rose-coloured morning gown was laid neatly over a chair along with her stays and a delicate chemise of the finest lawn. More of Lady

Beresford's generosity. She would need something warmer than that when she finally made her escape.

She glanced inside the wardrobe for her riding habit. It had not yet been returned.

As she turned away, she stilled. How odd. The sea sounded much louder on this side of the room. She glanced at the window across the other side of the chamber and shook her head. Not possible. To prove herself wrong, she went to the window. The noise seemed more muffled.

How very strange. She went back to the wardrobe and, yes, the sea did sound louder in this corner. She peeked inside the cupboard, but saw nothing but pine boards. It must be something to do with the stone walls. Some sort of echo coming up from the foundations. Perhaps she would ask Tess if she had noticed the odd phenomena. Or Gabe.

His last words came back at her like a slap.

Prisoner indeed. Did he think he could keep her locked up if she wanted to leave? But she didn't. Not yet. Not until she knew exactly what he was up to. So his prisoner she would be. For now.

* * *

Freddy was pacing the library when Gabe arrived. He held out a sealed note. 'It was waiting at the post office.'

Gabe took the folded paper. The small mark in the corner, an eight-pointed star, the personal sign of the Sceptre, indicated its importance. He broke the seal.

The note was in cypher. His blood turned cold when he recalled where he had left his book. On the night table beside his bed. It wasn't the text he'd been interested in the night he'd left it there, it was the maps. Maps to the tunnels beneath the house. He almost groaned. If Nicky saw those maps, it would be like giving her the keys to the gaol.

And if he went there now, seeking it, she would realise the book had significance. Obviously the woman had brains. She was certainly more trouble than he needed right now. How could he have been so careless?

Actually, it didn't take a genius to figure out his problem. Lust. When they'd first arrived, he had been so anxious to be rid of her before he lost control again, his brain had ceased working. Not that being rid of her had done him a bit of good. At the first opportunity, at her first appearance upstairs, he'd let the beast loose. He could only be grateful she hadn't seen him enter by way of the secret door or the fat really would be in the fire.

And now she was in possession of his cypher as well as the maps. He cursed.

'Bad news?' Freddy asked.

Gabe grimaced. 'I don't know. I'll need to transcribe it.'

Freddy frowned.

'The book is in the countess's bedroom.'

A grin lit Freddy's usually serious face. 'Lucky you.'

Gabe shook his head. 'No, lad. You are the one who is going to have to retrieve it while I keep her busy elsewhere. The chances are she hasn't looked at it, but…' He went to the shelves and pulled out a book of roughly the same size and colour. A book of poetry. 'Replace it with this one.'

'What if she has already looked inside?'

Gabe stilled. What had she said? It is a woman's role to be curious. Yes, likely she would have looked at it. 'All right, forget exchanging it.' He replaced the book on the shelf. 'Have Manners send her maid up to clean the room. Make it very obvious that it has been cleaned.' He frowned. 'Go with the girl. Collect some of my things. There have to be other items of mine in that room. If you bring all of them, then it won't look so singular that the book is gone.'

Freddy nodded. 'Shall I let the countess know you want to speak with her?'

'No. I'll collect her myself. I promised her a tour of the house. That should keep her busy for a while. Give me fifteen minutes to get her to the other end of the abbey.'

Gabe strode back to the tower along the maze of dark and dreary hallways and with some difficulty forced himself into his usual state of calm. Only a clear, cool head would serve him with an enemy inside his walls. Dash it all, he couldn't remember the last time he'd done anything as careless as leaving something so important out in plain sight.

Clearly he needed to be rid of her. And soon.

If he could just think of some way of putting her out of commission that did not result in her death. His blood ran cold. Life was a balancing act on a knife blade. One foot wrong and someone died. He cursed. He did not want the blood of this young woman on his hands, no matter that she, like Marianne, would betray him without a second's thought. The old sick sensation invaded his gut. Marianne's betrayal had been a painful revelation and her death lay on his soul like a dead weight. If nothing else, he had learned never to trust words of love.

He rapped on the chamber door.

Nicky opened it. She had changed and she gave him a practised smile he didn't much like. He preferred her real smiles, though they were rare and fleeting. 'Ah,' she said. 'The gaoler comes to check on his prisoner. Is your messenger gone already?'

Well, the woman was bold. How could he not admire her courage? If time wasn't quite so desperately short, he might have been content to continue to enjoy their battle. 'Gone, but not forgotten.'

She gave a little pout of disappointment. 'I barely had time to dress. I had hoped to catch a glimpse of him.'

'Or her.'

She bridled. 'So you wish to insult me with another woman?'

He laughed out loud. 'Not at all. I promised you a tour of the house.'

She frowned. 'Then your message was not so urgent after all.'

'Did you want to view of the house or not?' Any agent worth his or her salt would want a good look at the lie of the land.

'*Bien sûr.* Let me get my wrap.'

She turned away from him and he admired the way the rose-coloured fabric moulded to her legs and swayed at her ankles. He frowned. She was wearing her riding boots. 'Couldn't they find any slippers to fit you?'

'*Mais non.* The lady has larger feet.'

'I'll send Freddy to purchase something that fits.'

'Do not bother, *mon ange.* I will not be here that long.' She caressed his cheek and he very nearly turned his head to kiss her palm. And that would never do. Because if he started that again he might very well not leave this room for a considerable time and he needed to read that note. He resisted the temptation to peer into the room and check where the book lay and instead gave her a brief smile. 'If you are ready?'

She swept past him and out of the door. He took her arm. 'This is the North Tower. There used to be one at each corner, but there are only two now. South and North.'

'The two closest to the sea. I hear it loud in my room even with the window closed.'

The noise came through the tunnels behind the walls. 'The sound echoes off the rocks beneath the house. There are sea caves all along the cliffs. Some of them go pretty deep.'

She gasped and looked up at him. 'The sea is under the house.'

'Not under. Not yet at least.'

She pressed a hand to her lovely bosom. 'You relieve my mind. I would not like to think of the house falling into the sea.'

He stopped and flung open a door. 'The library.'

'*Magnifique.*'

'Feel free to make use of it during your stay here.'

'So I am not now to be locked in my room?'

'Only when necessary.'

Her blue eyes sharpened, but she simply smiled.

'Oh, and by the way, there is a hound here who is an excellent tracker, should you by chance become lost.'

A flash of fire in her gaze, gone in an instant, indicated her thoughts on his threat. He was sorry he had to make it, but he had no doubt that if she decided to leave she wouldn't let a little thing like bad weather or a long walk hold her back. The thought of being tracked by a dog might keep her in check.

'I should like to meet this so amazing dog,' she said blithely.

'Then I will introduce you when we go for a walk in the grounds tomorrow.' If there was a tomorrow for them. The thought that he might not have the opportunity was…disappointing. Something he should not be feeling. He smiled at her. 'He is already aware of your scent, from your riding habit, you understand. He needs to know you belong here,' he said kindly.

He was sure she was gritting her teeth behind her sweetly delivered word of thanks.

The rest of the tour proceeded without event. He took her only to the public rooms, the drawing room and the breakfast room. He was surprised at her excellent sense of direction. He began to wonder if she had already studied the maps in the back of the book he had left in her room.

'I understand a ghost walks in the grounds,' she said as they made their way back to the library.

He gave her a sharp glance, but saw nothing but innocent inquiry in her expression. 'Where did you hear that story?'

'From Tess. The maid assigned to me.'

'The Cornish are a superstitious lot,' he said, wondering if she was telling the truth or whether she had read about the ghost in his book. As far as he was concerned it was nonsense. He had wandered the house, its grounds and its underground passages at all times of the day and night and never seen so much as a glimmer of a spirit.

'Tess seems terrified at its very mention.'

Might as well force the issue as not. 'There is a history of the house somewhere. It has a whole section devoted to the mysterious apparition. Each owner of the house has added their own experience of sightings to the original story.'

'Oh,' she said. 'That must be the book I found on the night table beside the bed. I only read a couple of pages and it sent me to sleep. If I had realised it had a ghost story, I might not have given up.'

Hell, she had looked inside the book. Fortunately, she seemed to think nothing of it. He would have to be careful not to arouse her suspicions once she discovered it missing.

'They call her the White Lady,' he said. 'Killed by a husband or a brother. All rather dull and predictable.'

'How disappointing. If one has a ghost, one would like it to be novel, at least. So you do not believe it exists?' They arrived back at the library and he ushered her in. 'Shall I ring for tea?'

How very domestic that sounded. And pleasant. He could not quite believe how much he had enjoyed her company on this walk around the house, not just the challenge of outwitting an enemy, or the seduction of a female, but the enjoyment of her womanly presence. For all her sharp wit, there was something indefinably comfortable about having her on his arm as they strolled along corridors and peeked into this room and that. What the devil was wrong with him? If anyone had described an hour spent it such a manner he would have thought it tedious in the extreme. It was all to do with her. And he was beginning to think he had made the greatest mistake in his life bringing her here.

'Yes, please. Tea.' And then he really must find Freddy and read that note.

They sat down side by side on the sofa, so close they were almost touching. She glanced at him with raised brows, as if she was waiting for something. 'My question?' she prompted.

'Your question? Oh. Do I believe in the White Lady? I thought it was obvious. No. I don't believe in ghosts at all. And surely no woman as intelligent as you could possibly believe in the occult.'

'*Bien sûr*. While I thank you for your compliment, I think there are many things about the world we have never seen, but that we believe in. If there is a hereafter, why should there not be ghosts?'

He shook his head and grimaced. 'Two very different things in my opinion.'

Manners entered. 'You rang, my lord.'

'Tea,' Gabe said. 'If you can manage it, please, Manners.'

'Of course, my lord.'

Gabe settled back against the cushions and tried not to look as if he was in a hurry to leave. Any kind of urgency would arouse her curiosity. At least that was the excuse he gave himself for remaining in her company instead of returning her to her room and locking her in.

Chapter Seven

'Well?' Gabe said the moment he returned to the upstairs chamber.

'Job done.' Freddy handed him the book with a flourish.

'Well done, my friend. I'll buy you a brandy at White's when this is over.'

'If it ever is.'

'It will be.' Sooner or later. One way or the other. He ran a hand over his jaw. 'I really must shave. It wouldn't do to sit down to dinner looking like a gypsy. Would you mind?'

'Only because you have a bad arm.'

On a short laugh, Gabe went to the desk and sat down with the letter and the book and worked his way through the cypher. It wasn't complicated when one had the key.

He sat back and stared at the transcription, hoping he didn't look as shocked as he felt.

'What does Sceptre want?' Freddy asked from the other side of the room where he was stropping Gabe's razor.

'Apparently Bonaparte handed out medals to the troops at Boulogne on August the fourth accompanied by a stir of activity that makes invasion look imminent. Sceptre wants the date of embarkation.'

Freddy scowled. 'How are we to get it? Go to France and ask Boney point blank?'

'If that would work, then yes.' Sceptre didn't care about what was possible, just about information. 'I'll report that things are coming to a head. That we should have something in the next day or so.'

Gabe drafted the letter swiftly and handed it to Freddy, who tucked in a hidden pocket in his jacket with a frown. 'Is it possible Sceptre sent the Countess?'

'Too clumsy. If she was working for the British, it would be for the Home Office. You know what a set of suspicious idiots they are.' Gabe sat down on the chair beside the hearth.

Freddy draped a towel around his neck. 'Chin up, old fellow.' He picked up the razor.

The sight of a blade so close to his neck was a little unnerving. Or it would be in anyone else's hand. He did as he was bade. Freddy lathered his chin and scraped the razor up his throat.

'She's admitted she works for the French,' Gabe murmured.

Freddy's hand stilled. His mouth was smiling, but his eyes were hard. 'So what do you plan to do with her?'

'I haven't decided.'

'I have a feeling we are both going to regret this. Where is she now?'

'I left her in the library. And, Freddy, do not doubt that I have this under control. No one knows where she is, so there is no need for draconian measures.' What was going to happen was a very pleasurable evening and with luck some of his more pressing questions would be answered by Nicky.

'I'll trust your judgement.' The words were grudging.

A knock at the door sent Freddy to answer it. 'Manners?'

The old man sounded breathless. 'The boy brought a letter for the Reverend James up from the village. I thought I should pass it on to his lordship at once.'

Gabe sat up, wiping his chin on the towel.

Freddy handed the note to Gabe. When he opened it another note fell out. Freddy picked it up and stared at the address. 'Mrs Featherstone, Golden Square,' he read.

Gabe snatched it from his hand and ripped it open. He looked at Freddy. 'Bloody hell.'

The clock on the mantel in the library struck seven. Nicky looked up from the book she'd been reading and wondered why Gabe hadn't returned. Not that she expected to discuss whatever business had drawn him away after tea. Indeed, she wasn't quite sure why she had hoped he would reappear. He made her feel things she should not be feeling at all for a man who by his own admission betrayed his country for money. She hated him for that. Or at least she did when she forced herself to remember.

When he was close she seemed to lose sight of her purpose. And now, not only was she a prisoner in this house, but having gone through all the drawers in the desks and tables in the library and found nothing, she had discovered she was a prisoner in this room. When she had thought to return to her chamber, the footman outside the door had gently suggested that she wait in the library for his lordship's return.

Clearly he'd had strict instructions to keep her *in situ*. While Gabe did what? Dash it all, she should have realised he had something planned when he left her to her own devices. Still she had decided it would not do her any good to embarrass the poor footman, so she had been charming and friendly and compliant. Much to the man's obvious relief.

Nicky tapped an impatient toe. Gabe must be up to something in that upstairs chamber that he did not want her to know about. Likely, had she been in her room, there would be more mysterious noises above her head. And having had her check up on him once, he was not about to risk it again.

Which brought her back to the conundrum of where he had sprung from when she was searching his room. He had not been there when she'd first entered. She frowned. Nor could he have gained egress through the door by which she had entered. She would have heard the lift of the latch. And yet there he had been, standing in the middle of the room, looking as handsome as sin and smelling of salty air and seaweed, as if he'd been down on the shore or...or in some sort of cave.

And if he hadn't gone by way of the outer door there must be another entrance into that room.

Mon Dieu! Was she blind? Or just too infatuated with the man to think straight? All these old houses, especially abbeys, had had priest holes and secret entrances installed in times of religious upheaval. From the Tudors through to the Stuarts, one group or another down the ages had been hiding their beliefs. Not to mention the smugglers who infested the coast with their secret ways. Too bad she hadn't read more of the little history book she'd found by the bed. Never mind ghosts, it probably revealed the house's real secrets.

And that was why it was on the bedside table. Gabe probably used it as a handy reference when undertaking his nefarious activities. She shot to her feet. Then remembered the footman.

She paced from the sofa to the hearth, staring down into the flames. She needed to go back to her room.

A small sound made her spin around with a gasp.

Manners. 'His lordship asked me to remind you that dinner will be served in half an hour, my lady. Would you like me to ask Tess to attend you in your chamber?'

He was hinting that it was time for her to dress. She almost laughed out loud at the nerve of Mooreshead sending such a message, knowing he had kept her pinned in here for the past hour. 'Is dinner to be formal, Manners?'

'It will be served in the breakfast room, my

lady. Where you ate earlier. *En famille*, so to speak.'

And she was certainly not company, even if she was an unwilling guest. She was his lover. All the servants would know that and their dinner would be intimate. She smiled. 'Thank you, Manners. I would indeed like you to send Tess to me.'

At least it would give her a chance to look at that little book.

'Do you need me to direct you back to your room?' Manners asked.

'*Mais non*. I can find my way, thank you.'

'Very well, my lady.' He bowed and held open the door for her to leave. The footman from earlier was nowhere to be seen.

She arrived back in her room seconds before Tess and it was easy to see that someone had tidied the room in her absence. The dresses were put away, the bed made and the fire stoked. And there was no sign of the book. Might one of the servants have removed it?

'There was a small book on the nightstand,

Tess,' Nicky said idly as the girl unbuttoned her dress. 'Have you seen it?'

'Oh, yes, my lady. I meant to return it to the library when Mr Manners asked me to ready the room for you earlier, then I forgot. I saw it when I came to build up the fire and tidy up a bit when his lordship was showing you around the house. Freddy asked me to check to make sure he hadn't left any of his lordship's things behind.' She eased the gown over Nicky's shoulders and down over her hips. Nicky stepped out of it.

'So you gave it to Freddy?'

'I gave it to Mr Manners. He said he would put it back in the library.'

Nicky tried not to show her fury. She'd wasted time locked in the library—well, not locked in, but unable to leave—with the very book she wanted to look at close by and hadn't known it.

It was enough to make a girl curse.

'Did I do wrong, my lady?' Tess asked anxiously.

Her anger must be showing and that wasn't right. 'Not at all. I glanced at it and found it interesting. I thought I might read it later.'

'I am sure Mr Manners will be able to put his hand on it for you.' She went to the cupboard.

'I'll wear the green gown, please, Tess.'

Her way of punishing Gabe D'Arcy for holding her prisoner.

Gabe sat back in his chair and looked at the woman across the dinner table. Where in the devil's name had she found such an extraordinarily sensual gown? He could not imagine Bane's wife wearing such a thing. Not in public anyway, though knowing his friend he didn't doubt the woman was far less severe in nature than she appeared to the world. To be honest, it wasn't really the gown that made Nicky so damnably alluring, it was the way she wore its plunging neckline and shimmering sea-green fabric. The way she teased and tormented with each glance or each movement of her delectable body. The elegant turn of her wrist. The way her voice strummed against his senses.

Clearly feeling the intensity of his gaze, she looked across the table with a smile hovering on her delicious lips. 'Sated already, my lord?'

Only Nicky would ask such a blatantly salacious question without blushing and make it sound ladylike. Was that the secret of her allure? Her ability to be thoroughly wicked, yet seem almost innocent? 'Not yet.'

Her low, enticing laugh held not a morsel of discomfort, though her eyes said she knew exactly what he meant and what he was expecting. His body hardened in anticipation. Against his will. Shocked, he drew in a quick breath and demanded obedience from that unruly male appendage.

'Then let me help you to some apple pie.' She offered it as if she was offering him her body.

Again, he fought his arousal and shook his head. 'Thank you, no. That is not the sweetmeat I am interested in tonight.'

'Sweetmeat.' She rested her chin on the back of her hand and leaned close enough that he could smell her perfume and the undertone of spice that was all her. It was a scent he would never forget, he suspected. He could only hope the memory wouldn't be laced with guilt. 'You have a way with words, I must say.'

He laughed lightly. 'I've had lots of practice.'

'You are not the only one.'

There was something slightly off about her low voice. As if the memories were not particularly pleasant. He stored the observation away for later use. Women needed a careful touch at the best of times. Particularly when they wanted something. He hadn't forgotten the way Marianne had manipulated him into believing she agreed with his opinions. It had almost got him killed.

Nicky tilted her head and looked at him, as if considering him and not his words. As if she could see into his mind and his thoughts. 'Is it so very wearisome, all the female attention?'

It seemed she could. Was it wearisome? Or was it that he had trained himself not to care? Not to delve too deep into the hopes and dreams of his partners, so it was easy to walk away. He grinned, trying to make light of her words though they had struck far too close to home to be comfortable. 'It very much depends on the woman.'

'Ah. I see I will have to be very careful, then.'

'Careful?'

She lightly brushed his hand where it rested

on the table and the base of his wine glass. 'Not to bore you.'

He caught her fingers in his, held her gaze with his and brought her knuckles to his lips. At the last moment he turned her hand over and placed a brief kiss in the centre of her palm. 'You could never be boring, Nicky.' He moved his mouth to the base of her thumb and gave a little nip.

He felt her shiver of arousal.

It was good to get a little of his own back after spending the past hour resisting the urge to see what lay beneath the gown she was barely wearing.

He progressed to the pulse point on the inside of her wrist, touching it with the tip of his tongue, feeling the beat of her heart like the flutter of a wild bird anxious to escape. He kissed her there too.

Her eyelids drooped in pleasure. He liked how sensitive she was to his touch and how easily she showed it.

Was it all an act? It was hard to be certain.

'Shall I leave you to your port and retire to the

library to await your pleasure?' she asked in sultry tones.

'Port. Alone? Lord, no.'

'Then you will take tea with me?'

'If that is what takes your fancy.'

'I would like tea,' she said. 'In England it is *de rigueur* after dinner, I have learned. One becomes accustomed to such little rituals, no? And then I shall no doubt have other fancies you will satisfy.'

He grew iron-hard inside his pantaloons. He shifted, leaning back casually to ease the pressure of the fabric. 'I will do all in my power to please you, Nicky, as you know. And what about in France?' he asked lazily pushing to his feet. 'What is *de rigueur* there, after dinner?'

'Bed.'

Heat shot straight to his groin. He stifled the urge to groan. 'Then I am sorry we are not in France.'

'Perhaps we soon shall be.'

Her daring stole his breath. He could ask her to explain, but he had no wish to rush his fences. She would not like it if he spoiled the sensual game she had embarked upon this evening. She wanted him to fall beneath her spell so she could continue her probing. Likely that would reveal her purpose. But he'd already revealed far more than he'd intended. He wondered if she realised that even if he wanted to let her go, she knew far too much for him to do so. Still, he was looking forward to doing a little probing of his own and not all of it verbally. He took her hand and brought her to her feet.

'Should we not ring and let Manners know our intention?' she asked, her voice a husky purr.

'I have discovered that Manners has a sixth sense about these things. I don't doubt that we will find tea awaiting us in the library.'

The tea tray did indeed await them in the library as Gabe had predicted.

She sat behind the tea tray, going through the motions of a ritual she had been taught as a girl.

'What a delightfully domestic picture you make, Nicky,' Gabe said, sitting down beside her, leaning back against the cushion, relaxed and calm, yet underneath something seethed. She'd sensed it at the dinner table, but now he seemed to be giving it free rein. Lust? Desire? Something else? She wasn't sure.

'Domestic? *Moi?* Something no one has ever accused me of. Do you take sugar, *Milor'* Moores-head?'

'Are we so formal?'

She pouted at him. 'Tea is a matter of the most serious manners, *mon ange*. My English companion is very strict on the subject.'

'Mrs Featherstone.'

'Yes. And the poor woman must be out of her mind with worry by now.'

'Oh, does she have one? A mind?'

She tried not to laugh, she really did, but it bubbled up against her will. 'You are very wicked.'

'I know. And, yes, I do take sugar. And cream.'

'It will make you fat in your old age.' She handed him his cup and dropped a slice of lemon in hers.

'Not a chance.'

'Forgive me?'

'There's not a chance of me being fat in my old age. I won't live that long.'

The teasing words had a strange effect on her heart. It twisted painfully inside her chest. Because he spoke with such calm conviction. He expected to die young. And accepted his fate almost as if it would be welcome. How could this be? Cup and saucer in hand, she shifted to lean back against his broad chest and tucked her feet up, careful to show just a flash of ankle. She turned her head to look up at him. 'No one can tell that far into the future.'

His chest rose and fell in a steady rhythm at her back. Such iron control this man had, though she was pretty sure the bulge in his tight-fitting pantaloons had increased in size when she had leaned against him and his arm had come around her to rest on her hip.

She sipped at her tea while she awaited his answer.

He remained silent. Brooding. Angry? 'Has something happened?' she asked.

'I beg your pardon. I was thinking of something else.'

'A high compliment indeed.' She tried to sound annoyed, but then she laughed. Men did not like to be criticised. They liked a female to accept their moods and tempers. She'd had a lot of practice of such things with her husband and his acquaintances.

His warm lips pressed against her temple. 'Forgive me?'

She put down her cup and placed a hand on his chest, toyed with the pearl buttons on his grey silk waistcoat. 'How could I not?' she whispered huskily.

He tipped her face up with one finger and took her lips in a kiss. A gentle tender kiss at first. Infinitely sweet and wooing. Her heart picked up an unsteady rhythm of longing.

The kiss deepened with wicked passion and she could hear his heart now, beating hard and strong, his breathing growing ragged.

Her insides tightened, her own stupid heart picked up speed, her breathing increased tenfold, her skin warmed. Never before had she felt such desire for any man. It was as if her body controlled her, not the other way around. She turned in his arms and he settled her across his lap, his arousal making itself known beneath her buttocks. One hand slid down to caress the curve of her hip and the length of her thigh, the other to palm her breast. Meantime, tiny, sensual, drugging kisses landed at the corner of her mouth and across her bottom lip.

Deep inside, her body hummed with pleasure and desire.

He broke away on a rumble deep in his chest. As he gazed down into her face, his eyes were slumberous, his lids drooping and heavy. 'See what do you do to me, Nicky,' he murmured.

'What do I do to you?' she whispered, stroking his lean cheek with her fingertips, burying her other hand in his silky hair while hanging on to her mental abilities by no more than a fingernail. Terrified he would know what he did to her too, yet wishing with all her heart she could let down her guard and be herself. Forget all about the war. About what he was and who she had become.

'You drive me to madness,' he muttered

In a quick move, he flipped her over and laid her on the sofa, one knee pressing between her thighs. He dipped his head and captured her startled gasp in his mouth, plundering her mouth with his tongue. Ferociously. Fiercely. Punishing her for what she made him feel. A heavenly assault on her senses.

Once more he pulled away from her. There was vulnerability in the bright blue eyes staring down into her face. And regret? Her heart tripped a warning. 'Gabe?'

He gave her that heartbreakingly angelic smile of his. The one he used to keep females at a distance and she found she didn't like being its recipient. But this was a game and she had to play by the rules. He sat back on his heels, his gaze raking her body. 'Take down your hair, love.'

Only two pins held the knot at her nape in place. So easy. So carefully designed to come loose. She shook the tresses free and smiled up at him, pleased by the pleasure she saw in his face. He slipped the shoulders of her gown down her arms with a look of sensual intensity that drove a spear of lust deep into her woman's core, sweetly painful, incredibly arousing. His gaze flicked back to her face. She prepared to help him lower the gown the rest of the way. 'There is a tie at the back,' she murmured.

He nodded and leaned forward to press his hot dry lips to the rise of her breast, sending a breathless shiver through her body while his hands stroked her calves. She tried to lift her hand to stroke his hair and realised her arms were trapped. A flicker of disquiet caught her breath. 'Gabe?'

But he seemed oblivious to her voice, too absorbed in pushing her skirts to her waist, his whole attention now on what his hands were doing. Cool air drifted over the naked flesh above her stocking, then his hands were stroking and caressing. Her insides turned hot and melting, her breathing shallow as she watched his expression turn from softly sensual to stark with lust. She raised herself up on her elbows and breathed into his ear, and heard the hiss of his indrawn breath. 'Undo the gown, silly.'

A press of his hand against her shoulder pushed her back against the cushioned arm. His gaze drifted down her length to the juncture of her thighs with an expression of such wickedness on his face, her insides tightened unbearably. Warm hands went to her hips and with a swift jerk he pulled her to lie flat on the sofa. She read his intention on his face as his gaze once more returned to her core. 'Yes,' she said, knowing he was not asking for permission, because he already knew he had it. A man of his expertise would bring her great pleasure with his mouth.

One hand beneath her buttocks, he lifted her, draping her thighs over his shoulders, moving closer so she was open to his gaze. And gaze he did. Anticipation flooded through her in a wave of desire. Unbearable in the length of time it took him to touch his tongue to her centre. He stroked and licked and nibbled at the little nub deep within her cleft. Her eyes drifted closed against the insidious weakness. Her limbs felt like warm honey.

Mindless, she moaned with relief as his tongue plunged deep within her and with agony as the incredible tension of passion drew tighter.

So close now. She could feel the darkness beckon. And the bliss building. And building.

And then he stopped.

Her eyes shot open. He gazed into her eyes,

his face etched with the strain of holding back his lust.

'Please, Gabe,' she whispered. 'Now.'

'I want the name of your contact,' he ground out between gritted teeth.

Blank-minded, she stared at him.

'I need a name, Nicky.'

'Gabe?' She could hear the lust in the throaty sound of her voice, and the confusion. 'What are you saying?'

'I want to know who is stupid enough to send a woman against me.' His voice was full of regret.

But his expression showed anger. Hard. And hot. How could she have missed it? She, who prided herself on being able to read a man like an open book?

Not this man.

Fury rose up in her at the way he had used her. 'You think your powers of seduction are so great, I will tell you anything for the pleasure of using your body?' She made a sound of derision.

'Won't you?' He bent his head to torture her again with his tongue. She twisted and writhed, but with her arms trapped by her sides by the gown, she could not do any damage. His hands clamped hard on her hips, making movement nigh on impossible. He proceeded to circle his tongue around the heart of her pleasure, scraping gently with his teeth, bringing her to hover at the peak of orgasm once more.

'Damn you,' she said. 'Please. Finish it.'

He raised his head and blew on the sensitive nub, making her twitch and convulse with the delectable sensations. 'Tell me, Nicky.'

She wanted to scream out Paul's name. Tears leaked into her eyes and spilled down her cheeks. 'Names are not given.'

'Tell me, *chérie*, and we can both relax. Just one name.'

And one name would lead to another. 'I can't help you.'

'Can't or won't?'

When she remained silent, he stood up, dropping her legs on to the cushions with a sigh. He looked down at her, his eyes hard, his expression remote. 'Your choice.'

Her body thrummed and ached. With disbelief

she watched him make for the door. 'Don't you dare. You can't leave now.'

'Watch me,' he threw back over his shoulder.

'Gabe!' She could not keep the plea from her voice. The need.

He stopped and turned around. 'Give me what I want and I'll come back and most willingly. Or you'll have to deal with it the same way I will.'

Fury overcame passion. 'Go to hell.'

He gave a short laugh. 'Make no mistake, Nicky, you will tell me. Next time my methods won't be quite so pleasurable for either of us.' He frowned. 'By the way, there is no white knight riding to your rescue.' He dipped a finger and thumb into his fob pocket and pulled out a folded piece of paper.

Nicky recognised it instantly and fought to keep back her groan of despair. It was the note she'd sent to Paul. No wonder he was angry. He must have intercepted it. He stared at her. 'No one is coming, Nicky. So you might as well tell me what I want to know.' There was some raw emotion in his voice she didn't recognise.

A band tightened around her chest. It sounded

like…like betrayal. As if her treachery had caused him pain. She fought with the sleeves binding her arms and with his weight gone, she managed to slide first one, then the other up her arms and onto her shoulders. She sat up and pulled her skirts down. She gave him a haughty stare. 'I have no idea what you are talking about. That is simply a letter to my companion. You would not let me tell her I was unharmed.'

'A message that tells her you went west.'

She fought to maintain her stiff posture of outrage. 'Nonsense.'

'I recognise the quote, Nicky.' He began to read. '"And now it is about the very hour, That Silvia, at Friar Patrick's cell, should meet me."

'If I recall correctly, it begins: "The sun begins to gild the western sky".' He gave her a hard look. 'Does it not? Tell me everything or suffer the consequences.'

She must not give in. She must stick to her story. 'I was worried. It is a note to my companion, nothing more.'

He stared at her, long and hard. 'Tell me, Nicky, or I cannot be responsible for what happens.'

The sorrow in his voice was only too real. Her stomach roiled. Numb, panicked for the first time in a very long time, she could only stare back.

He walked out.

She collapsed back against the sofa.

So much for her power of seduction.

He was right. Someone would pay for this. But it would be the people of England unless she could find a way to get another message to Paul. One that would not be so easily found.

Chapter Eight

Never had Gabe hated himself so much as he did at the moment. His fist clenched. He wanted to hit something. Anything. He was disgusting. Despicable. He deserved to be hanged for what he had done to Nicky. Something he'd never done before. Used his body as a weapon.

But it was either that or something worse.

It was better she told him what he wanted to know than he hand her over to Sceptre. The thought of what would happen if he did made him feel ill. If it went that far, there would be nothing he could do to stop it. He already had one woman's death on his conscience, albeit it had happened without his knowledge. He would not allow another. Especially not this one.

Damn it all. Such a weakness could destroy

him and everything else that he'd worked for all these years.

Which meant he had to do anything—anything short of hurting her—to get her to tell him the truth. What he needed was her primary contact. Her chain of command. What secrets she had already unearthed and passed on. And he feared that the time to handle her with finesse was swiftly running out.

He stormed into his chamber.

Freddy looked up and winced. 'No go?'

He took a deep shuddering breath and got a grip on his emotions. 'Not yet.'

Freddy's eyes filled with concern. 'Time is running out. The order to leave could come at any moment.'

Gabe paced the chamber. 'I know. We were lucky Barge discovered the message before his idiot son sent it off.'

'Do you think she has tried again?'

'Nothing can get in or out of this house without my knowing.'

'You hope.'

His body was slowly coming to heel, his lust

subsiding, giving his brain a chance to think clearly. He shook his head. 'I know so. She looked pretty devastated when she saw the note.'

'You have to tell Sceptre. If it is discovered by chance that you are risking our mission for the sake of a tumble, I wouldn't want to be in your shoes.'

Gabe gave him a sharp look. 'Planning on telling them?'

'Of course not,' Freddy said hotly. 'But—'

Gabe put up a hand. 'Let me think.'

He had to find a way out of this. Freddy was right. Too much rested on them fooling the French into divulging their secrets for him to risk exposure by Nicky. He couldn't let her go. And if he sent her to Sceptre she'd likely be found in the Thames in a day or so.

'You are hatching a plot.' Freddy said. 'I don't like it.'

'Hear it first. Look, I know she said she worked for the French, but it came out of her mouth so glibly, I had trouble believing her.'

'Let Sceptre figure it out.'

'But if she *is* telling the truth, then that leaves

me going blind into whatever the French have planned. I need the truth. One more day is all I require.'

Freddy glared at him. 'Whoever she works for, she'll make every effort to escape.'

'She won't escape.'

Freddy's mouth tightened. 'I hope you are not going soft on me, Gabe. They got very close to killing you once because of her. Don't expect to be lucky a second time.'

Gabe let go a breath. 'She also saved my life.' A bit of an exaggeration, but men had been known to die of lesser wounds when left untreated.

'So you owe her one.' Freddy sounded resigned.

Honour among spies. It was accepted. At least by the gentlemen among them. It was something Freddy understood, even if he did not like it in this particular case. 'Perhaps we'll find a way to send her back from whence she came. In the meantime, get yourself to the drop point and pick up our delivery.'

'Damn you, Gabe,' Freddy grumbled. 'Don't let her get you killed trying to get her back to France.'

* * *

Nicky sat beside the hearth in her room, listening. Earlier, she'd heard some sounds from the chamber above. Men talking. Even a chuckle or two. She gripped her hands in her lap. It wouldn't be the slightest bit of good to lose her temper. Gabe must be feeling just as frustrated as she was. His blood would also be singing in his veins, his body aching for fulfilment. And, yes, she could take care of it. To a certain extent. But it wouldn't be the same. Nowhere near as fulfilling. Or as pleasurable. No. It was better to suffer because it left her irritated and angry and unable to fall asleep. Because she wanted to look for that book. It might well give her the means to escape and report her findings to Paul. They needed to know what Gabe was even if the thought of telling them made her feel sick to her stomach.

She glanced upwards. There hadn't been any sounds from above for about an hour.

The hands on the clock slowly circled, ticking off the numerals. Every time Nicky looked at it, it didn't seem to have moved. But she wasn't wasting her time watching it. She was putting down on paper everything she could about what had happened, about the layout of the house and its relation to the cliffs and what little she'd learned about Mooreshead. It felt better to think of him by his title, than his name. Less personal. She returned to her notes. Paul had to know about the caves beneath the house, the reason Mooreshead used Beresford Abbey for his nefarious undertakings.

Getting the message out to him was another matter. One would normally expect to find someone in need of funds who could be talked into taking a message, like the boy at the inn. But apparently his father was far more loyal than most. She needed another way to get her message out. But if Gabe caught her out again, his anger tonight would look like a pleasant drive in Hyde Park compared to what he might do next. He'd probably kill her and toss her body in the sea. And no one would be any the wiser. Or care. Apart from Paul.

She couldn't risk it. She had to get back to France and learn the truth once and for all. The reason she had entered into this dangerous world of espionage in the first place. If she died, and Minette was alive, the child would have no one who cared. And Nicky knew only too well what that felt like.

She shivered, then drew in a deep calming breath. She could do this.

Hopefully, Gabe wouldn't think about doing away with her until he had the information he wanted. And she would not be bullied into telling him anything. In the meantime, she would find a way to escape his clutches.

She stared at the diagram she'd made of the house and the detailed notes of her suspicions. Where could she hide it so it could be found if something happened to her? The wardrobe? Beneath a board in its floor, perhaps? She grimaced. A bit too obvious. The first place Gabe would look. He had probably given her this time alone for the purpose of tricking her into making such a mistake.

She glanced around the room. A chink in the window frame might work. She got up and ran her fingers around its edges. Nothing loose. She gazed around the room. Up the chimney? Again, too obvious. What she needed was… The wall sconces. They had a concave wrought-iron disc, the edge of which fit tight to the wall. She might be able to wedge the paper behind it. Even if she was…gone by the time Paul's men arrived, they would strip everything back to the bare walls looking for the note they would know she would have left. It was all part of her instructions.

Careful to make no sound that would alert Gabe in the chamber above, she went to her door, turned the key and opened it. To her surprise, there was no one outside. Nor anyone further down the corridor. Likely it was a trap. He would be expecting her to try to leave after what happened tonight. She didn't dare risk venturing forth until after she had hidden her note in case she didn't get another chance. Once it was safe, she'd take a late-night walk to the library and look for the little book. After all, it was not unusual to read when sleep evaded. She relocked the door, picked up the paper and tried to slide the note between the disc and the wall.

The space wasn't wide enough to slip the folded sheet behind the metal disc. She twisted the sconce to see if it would loosen. The wall moved. Startled, she leaped back. And stared. There was an odd glimmer running vertically down the wall. The sort of glimmer one notices when a door to a well-lit room is ajar. A cool breeze stirred her hair, lifting up the fine strands around her face. The low, steady grumble of the sea was louder than before. She stepped closer, putting her hands to the crack in the wall.

Oh. It wasn't a wall at all. It was a secret door. She had her way out.

Her throat dried. As long as Gabe hadn't heard that terrible creak. She stood stock-still, listening with every nerve in her body. No sound came from above. No footsteps on the stone steps outside. A glance at the clock told her it was half past two in the morning. Everyone in the house must be asleep. Holding her breath, she gave the sconce another twist, harder this time. The wall moved a good two inches and no longer made any sound at all. Hand on the sconce, ready to close the opening, she waited for a hue and cry. Nothing.

She'd been right. The house did hold secrets

from the days of religious persecution. Of course, the door might lead only to a priest's hole. A hiding place with only this one entrance and exit. The breeze said otherwise. Still no sound came from above. Nothing to suggest anyone had heard anything suspicious.

Well, then. She went to the sconce on the other wall. It behaved exactly as it should, giving just enough for her to slide her note behind it. Luck was with her for once. If she had chosen this sconce for her note first, she would never have discovered the secret entrance. She lifted her gaze to the ceiling. Did Gabe know about this? How could he not? But if so, why had he left it open, easy for her to find. Was it a trap?

For what purpose? No, if it didn't make sense then it likely wasn't true. It was pure blind luck.

Trembling with a healthy dose of dread about what she might find behind the wall, she dressed quickly in her riding habit, which had been returned while she was at dinner. If she did find a way out, she would need its warmth on the long walk to the nearest town. With a deep breath, she ventured into the passage.

It ran both right and left, lanterns casting small circles of light at distant intervals to the left until the tunnel made a turn. Moving carefully and quietly, she went right. Not very far. The passage ended at a set of spiral stone stairs leading upwards similar to the stairs outside her chamber door, only narrower. Leading up to the chamber above hers, the steps rough blocks of stone. So this was where Gabe had appeared from. Was that why he had…? Of course. Her stomach sank. He'd used her desire to distract her from wondering how he had arrived. And she'd fallen for it. Her body heated. Anger, not lust, at the memory. Definitely not that. And the foosteps she'd heard earlier must have been Gabe leaving by way of these stairs.

Her throat dried. Was it possible he was down here somewhere? Lying in wait. Or up to something nefarious? Or was he fast asleep in his bed, looking forward to their next encounter, when he would torture her some more? Blasted man.

She couldn't afford to let her fears stop her from exploring further. The French were massing on the coast behind Boulogne, waiting for their chance to invade Britain, the way they had run over so many countries in Europe. She had to discover what Mooreshead was up to. Britain's future depended upon her. If Bonaparte conquered England, there would never be any hope for her sister.

She shivered and wished she had her pistol. But what excuse would she have had for carrying such a weapon when out for an innocent ride?

Taking a deep breath of damp, musty air, she turned around and glided along the tunnel to the next splash of light. The lanterns were barely more than a glimmer, intended for guidance rather than light. At the turn, she stopped and listened.

The rhythmic sound of waves crashing against cliffs and retreating made it hard to hear anything apart from the thud of her own heart. Slowly, she edged around the corner. Nothing. Apart from another lantern in the distance. The ground was rough under her feet and she tested each step before she moved forward, making sure she made as little sound as possible, yet moving at a steady pace, ready to hug tight to the shadows of the rough stone wall, should anyone appear. She glanced over her shoulder from time to time to make sure she was not followed. At the next lantern, she stopped at a fork in the tunnel. In one direction, the passage turned back towards where she thought the house must be. In the other, the floor sloped downwards into pitch-black darkness towards the sound of the sea. She headed for the sea. If there was anyone down there, they would not be able to hear her any more than she could hear them. Comforting. Somewhat. With no light ahead to guide her way, she pressed a hand to the wall and began walking as quickly as the rough terrain would allow. Another curve in the rock wall. And beyond it, a small speck of light casting shadows on the rocky walls and glimmering off rough surging water.

For a long time she remained still, breath held.

Gradually, her eyes adjusted to the gloom. A man's shape took form, sitting on the edge of the rough-hewn quay. A dark shape. He was too far from the lantern to make out his features. But she knew him. Gabe. Alone. Apparently waiting. She settled in to watch.

From out of nowhere, a small boat rode a wave up to the jetty. Gabe leaped to his feet and caught a line thrown from the vessel. Not a movement was wasted. In a matter of moments the boat was fastened securely and the two men were unloading boxes from the bottom of the boat. They talked as they worked, the sounds echoing in the large chamber, making it impossible to make out individual words. What on earth could they be doing unloading cargo at this time of night?

Smuggling?

She had to see what was in those boxes. The sense that they were vital to understand what was going on here, what Gabe was about, had her creeping closer. One hand against the wall as a guide, she moved closer, straining her eyes to see. They piled the boxes against the wall of the jetty—some of them were long and narrow, others square. She needed to see inside them.

Her hand hit empty air. She gasped and almost lost her balance. The wall had somehow disappeared. She stepped back to where she had felt it last and shuffled along without lifting her hand from the rough surface. It took a sharp left turn.

An alcove? She followed the wall and her view of the men below disappeared. This was not the way she wanted to go, but it was good to know there was a place she might hide in should it be needful. She took a chance and stepped away from the wall. Two steps and she reached the other side of the crevasse, if that was what it was. Slowly, carefully, she stepped back into the main cave.

They had finished unloading the boat and were now opening one of the square crates. They peered inside, talking as they did so. The other man pulled the lantern down from the wall and held it high. The light cast their faces into sharp relief. Gabe and his valet, Freddy. Oh, if only she could see inside the box. Could know what they were so intent on. Perhaps it was nothing. Perhaps they were smugglers after all. It would be a relief. But she could not let them see her.

The air around Nicky turned to ice, a cutting wind blowing from somewhere behind her, as if someone had opened a door. She glanced over her shoulder. A misty light glowed from the crevasse behind her. Light, but not light, her mind said. Another lantern? It had shape and form. It flowed and moved like the fabric of a gown. The form of a woman, but not the shadow she had seen in the garden, a thing of light. *'Go down,'* a mournful voice said. *'Down. Down.'*

Her blood ran cold. Her skin prickled. Go down? *'Trust.'*

The word echoed and re-echoed. Icy fingers touched the back of her neck, the draught increasing in strength. The sloping floor pitched her irresistibly forward. Off balance, she grabbed for the wall. The ground fell away at her next step. She was falling backwards. She shrieked in alarm. And black descended.

Gabe cursed as he crouched beside the still figure sprawled on the ground. What the hell was she doing down here? She should have been busy in the library, looking for the little history book. He'd given her a clear run at it. Anger surged through him. How on earth had she found her way into these tunnels?

'Oh, hell.' Freddy leaned over him and gave a soft whistle. It turned into a chorus of ear-splitting echoes. 'Is she dead?'

Nicky groaned.

'Apparently not.'

'Too bad,' Freddy said. 'It might have saved us a lot of trouble.'

Gabe swallowed the urge to grab Freddy by the throat and part his body from his breath. 'Shut up and go away.' He began chafing Nicky's cold hand. 'Nicky?'

Freddy put the lantern down. 'I'll see you back at the house, then.'

Nicky moaned and struggled to sit up. *'Ce qui s'est passé?'* Then she seemed to realise where she was. She pressed a hand to her temple. 'Oh, my head.'

'You fell.' Gabe raised the lantern. There were no marks on her face.

'I was pushed.' She moved her fingers to the back of her head. 'Ouch. There's a lump the size of an egg.'

He probed it gently. A lump indeed.

She winced.

He looked at his fingertips. 'No blood. What do you mean you were pushed?'

She glowered. *'Il n'est pas difficile.* Someone pushed me.'

The fall must have affected her mind in some way. 'There is no one down here but Freddy and me. And you,' he added. 'What are you doing here?'

She shrugged. 'I found a secret door in my room. I wanted to see where it led.'

He cursed softly. He knew about the door, but it was impossible to find it unless you knew where to look, surely? 'And now you know. What did you see, Nicky?'

Apprehension filled her eyes. 'I saw you unloading boxes.' She closed her eyes briefly as if trying to recoup her senses. 'What is it you do here? Smuggling?'

It would be easy to follow her lead. But she was too clever to be fooled. He rubbed his thumb across her palm. 'You know I do not.'

Her gaze became misty. She blinked the moisture away. 'Oh, why do you have to be a French spy?'

She sounded…sad. Everything inside him said he should take a chance on this woman. Logic and past experience told him it was the last thing he should do. He remembered Sceptre's last sentence of the instructions. Words he had not passed on to Freddy. Cold filled his chest. 'I do not, *chérie*. I work for the British.'

'But—'

'I will put all my cards on the table. And so will you. Come. I will show you what is in the boxes.' He helped her to her feet. 'Can you walk?'

She looked around anxiously as if expecting to see someone.

'Freddy has gone back to the house,' he said.

'It isn't that,' she said with a shiver. 'There is someone else.' She looked up at him. 'Did you feel a strong breeze? Just before you found me.'

She looked almost panicked. 'I felt nothing out of the ordinary.'

She looked towards the tunnel that came down from the ruins. 'It came from up there.'

'The door to the outside is locked and bolted, I assure you.'

Confusion filled her face. 'I don't understand. There was a light. A cold wind. I felt a touch on the back of my neck.' The blood leached from her face. A shudder rippled through her body.

'You are behaving as if you saw a ghost,' he joked, trying to ease her fears.

Her eyes widened. 'The White Lady.'

'I am joking. There is no one else. You stumbled and fell.'

She touched her temple. 'Yes,' she said uncertainly, then spoke more strongly 'Yes, that must be it. I remember I was trying to see what was in the crate you opened.'

'And that is just what you will do.' If his instincts were wrong about this, a lot of people were going to lose their lives. Himself included. 'Are you sure you can make it on your own, or shall I carry you?'

She took a breath and steadied herself. 'It will be easier now there is a light.'

He held the lantern high and put an arm around her waist to give her support. 'You were lucky. The path drops off steeply, you could have fallen to your death.'

The path was little more than a narrow ledge along the top of a cliff. 'Lucky indeed.'

He could not help but admire her courage. Most women would be having fits of the vapours. That was at the very heart of what held him in thrall. Her bravery along with her wit. He just wished she'd tell him the truth. But she would never be fool enough to trust him completely. In that she'd be right. No matter whom she worked for.

At the bottom of the slope the going became easier and he took her hand. He glanced down at her face. She was still pale. Even in the light of the lantern he could see she wasn't quite herself.

The lid of the box Freddy had pried open lay on the ground where he'd flung it when he heard her cry out. He picked it up and leaned it against the cave wall. Held the light over the box to reveal its contents.

She reached inside and lifted one of the coats. She gasped. 'British uniforms?' She raised her gaze to his face.

'Yes.'

She frowned. 'Why—?' She stepped back, comprehension in her face.

He grabbed her. 'Careful. You'll go off the edge. I'm in no mood for swimming.'

'You are going to put French soldiers in British uniforms.'

'It seems so. The other boxes contain muskets.'
This was the watershed. Her next reaction would dictate everything that followed

'This is how they plan to invade?' She jerked her arm free of his hold. 'Someone has to be told. You know what they did in France, surely you cannot want that here?' She swung around. 'I don't care what you say. I have to let Paul know.'

Relief rushed though him. He caught her around the waist. 'Wait.'

She fought against him. 'You'll have to kill me if you want to stop me.'

If he was wrong about her, a lot of people were going to pay with their lives. 'Think, Nicky. Use your brain. There are a dozen uniforms here. Nowhere near enough for an invasion force.'

She stilled in his arms. 'What are you saying?'

'I'm saying there is a plan afoot, but we don't know what it is.'

She shivered violently. 'You are trying to keep me here. To stop me from telling the British government.'

'There are a lot more sure ways of stopping you, than trying to get you to listen to reason.'

Her teeth started to chatter.

'You are freezing.'

She put a hand to her head. 'I feel a little dizzy.'

The blow to the head. Blast it. He caught her behind the knees and she rested her head on his shoulder. It felt good to hold her like this, as if she trusted him to protect her. It would be nice if she did. He cursed his stupidity. He didn't deserve her trust. While he was pretty sure they were both working on the same side, that didn't mean she wasn't at risk in his company.

He travelled swiftly up the tunnel. There were several entrances from the caves into the house, one in the library, two in the tower where he had his rooms and another from outside. The one into the library was barred as was the one emerging in the ruins. He should have had Freddy bar the one in her room, where he usually slept, but he'd assumed it impossible to find without knowledge of its existence. Didn't he know better than to make assumptions?

* * *

Gabe laid her down on the bed. A wave of dizziness made her close her eyes against the nauseating sensation of the room spinning about her head.

'Nicky,' Gabe said urgently. He massaged her hand. His skin felt deliciously warm. 'Nicky,' he repeated. 'Look at me.'

She opened her eyes. The room seemed to have settled into its normal orientation. 'I have to get up,' she whispered. 'We must go to London. Warn them.'

'You are not going anywhere until I am sure you feel better.'

'Really, Gabe. I'm fine. A blow to the head, that is all. Please, don't make a fuss. All I have is a bit of a headache.'

'Rest now. In the morning we'll decide what to do next.' He leaned over her and looked into her eyes. 'How many of me do you see?'

'One. And that is one too many.'

The grimness in his face eased a little. 'You are sure?'

'This is a question you have to ask? *Mon Dieu.*

Are you sadistic? De Sade was also a marquess, if I recall correctly.' It annoyed her that she sounded quite so plaintive, but her headache had grown worse.

'I'm going to ring for Manners and see if he has something that will help with the pain.'

'Gabe, no. The poor man must be asleep. I would love a glass of water,' she said, suddenly aware of her parched mouth.

He reached over and picked up a glass from the night table, raising her up with his hand at her nape and holding it to her lips. 'Just a sip. Until we see how it settles in your stomach.'

The water tasted deliciously cold. She took a careful swallow and he laid her back down.

'Better?' he asked.

'Better. Or I would be if it wasn't for the lump on the back of my skull.'

'How did on earth did you find the secret door?'

She certainly didn't want to tell him about her note. Not until she was sure she believed his story about working for the British. 'The candle in the sconce was flickering. I was holding it while trimming the wick and it opened.'

He looked puzzled. 'Just like that?'

'Just like that. I was exceedingly surprised, I may say.'

'You were fully dressed.'

'I had thought to go to the library. For a book, you understand. Since I could not sleep. But when I saw the tunnel behind the wall I could not resist taking a peek.'

He frowned. 'I wish you had gone to the library.'

'You wish I hadn't discovered your secret.'

'That too. But I really hate to see you hurt.'

The words made her feel warm inside. 'It wasn't your fault.'

His grim expression eased somewhat. 'Who is this Paul you mentioned down in the caves?'

She swallowed. She should not have blurted out his name like that, but it was too late now. If she was going to convince him to trust her, she would have to tell him everything in the hopes he would reveal all of his plans. If she was wrong about him, if he really was working for the French… She forced the terrifying thought aside. 'I only know that he works for the Home Office.'

'The Home Office.' He sounded oddly bitter.

'Why not? Why should a woman not help in the fight against Napoleon?'

He frowned. 'Even the Home Office would be more circumspect than to recruit a woman. What does he look like, this Paul of yours? What is his full name?'

'He gave his name as Paul Moreau. He is of average height and build. Fair-skinned. Sandy brown hair and moustache.' She closed her eyes, remembering. 'His eyes are hazel. He speaks as you do. Very English. He sounds like a gentleman.'

'So how do you contact him?'

'Through Mrs Featherstone.'

'So it is your contention that the Home Office suspects me of treason and you are here to learn the truth.'

'*Exactement, mon cher* Mooreshead. What do we do now?'

'You rest. And I will decide what to do in the morning.'

'Gabe. It is important we let someone know what is afoot. I must tell Paul.'

'We don't yet know what is afoot. Until we do, we must wait.'

He leaned over her and pressed a kiss to her lips. A light velvety brush of his lips. Shivers rippled down her spine. She put her hands on his shoulders and pulled him towards her, opening her mouth, kissing him deeply.

A groan rumbled up from his chest and he pulled away. 'Sleep, Nicky.'

He went out and locked the door behind him.

A prisoner. She pressed a hand to her forehead. Her headache was the least of her worries. What if she had made a terrible mistake by trusting him?

Chapter Nine

She was a prisoner. Once more she was trapped. At the mercy of a man who would use her for his own purposes. For two days she'd been shepherded from her chamber to the library or the breakfast room by the cheerful footman, John, who seemed embarrassed by his role, or by a silent and watchful Freddy, who did not. Gabe had joined her for dinner last night and had been charming and pleasant company, yet beneath the polite veneer, he seemed withdrawn. Remote. It had been quite a shock when he had escorted her back to her room and locked her in from the outside. Clearly, now she had confessed the truth, she was no longer of interest. The pain of her disappointment had shocked her badly.

In the night, she had been awoken by movements above her head. The footsteps of comings and goings, voices. Try as she might, she could make out nothing of what was said. Plans were underway, though, of that she had no doubt.

Why, oh, why had she told him everything? Instead of giving her his trust, he'd shut her out.

And left her feeling anxious.

The *accident* in the cave must have shattered her guard. More than that. Every time she thought about it, an icy fear trickled down her spine. Someone, or something—she shivered— had pushed her from behind in the dark. And whispered what? *'Trust.'* Was that really what she had heard? Or was it simply wishful thinking on her part? And if not, if she was correct, trust what? Trust who? Gabe? Her heart wanted to believe him, to trust in him. Every instinct suggested that she should. Trust. A word whispered in the cold and dark. Logic, cool reason, said she would be a fool to trust a man of secrets who clearly didn't trust her. She had given up everything she was when she had trusted her uncle to know what was best for her, to provide her with a husband. Look where that had led.

Gabe was nothing like Vilandry. No one could be as manipulative and amoral as her husband with his avuncular manner and kind promises. The truth of the man had been utterly different. She was no longer young or innocent, yet something inside her told her that Gabe had told her the truth.

Her heart twisted painfully. Why, then, could he not see that she had done the same? What could she say that would convince him?

Nicky gazed out of the breakfast-room window where she was taking luncheon on her own. Small, fluffy clouds drifted across a pretty blue sky. The door opened and she turned her head, expecting to see Manners.

Gabe stood on the threshold, looking incredibly handsome in a dark blue coat of superfine, riding breeches and top boots. 'Good afternoon, Countess.'

A strange sense of shyness swept through her. With difficulty, she pulled the Countess close, afraid to let him see her vulnerability to his smile. 'So formal, my lord? Good afternoon. Are you going somewhere?'

'I wondered if you would care to take a stroll with me, around the grounds?'

Surprised, she stared at him.

He raised a brow. 'No?'

Anything to get out of the house. Also this would be her chance to discover his intentions regarding her future. At least that was what she told herself. There was also a sneaking gladness that he hadn't abandoned her completely after all. She rose from the table and picked up her shawl. 'It sounds delightful.'

He took her arm and walked her outside through the front door.

Fresh tangy air filled her lungs. Gulls cried overhead and the sea sparkled in the distance. They meandered through the ruins. The old broken walls threw dark shadows on a tangle of weeds. None of the sense of dread that had overtaken her in the tunnel beneath the house lingered here. Today there was no one skulking about. She took in the view and filled her lungs with salt-laden air that tasted of freedom. The freedom to be herself, if she dared. The scared child inside her felt exposed, raw and terribly hopeful.

Trust, a voice whispered in her mind.

'It is a beautiful place,' she said tentatively, feeling a blush heat her cheeks.

He glanced down at her with a slight smile on his lips. 'I thought you preferred town life.'

Her heart tumbled over. Her insides trembled like that of a young girl meeting a boy she'd admired from a distance. He had listened. She reached for her familiar shield, but it slipped from her grasp. Her heart raced at the risk she was taking. 'I grew up on my parents' country estate. I loved the freedom it gave me.'

He looked puzzled. 'Freedom?'

She ducked her head, unwilling to meet his gaze in case she saw condemnation. 'It was safe. I was free to wander the grounds at will.' Free to dream her own dreams of the future. She smiled at the memory. 'There was a grotto on the other side of the lake. My sister and I would go there in the summer. Legend had it that if you tossed a coin in the pool and made a wish it would come true. There are many silver coins of mine in the bottom of that pool.'

'What did you wish for?'

She risked a brief peek at his face. His expression was one of interest, but darkness rolled in the depths of his icy blue eyes. Not mockery, more like pain, as if he too knew the futility of childish dreams.

Immediately on guard, the Countess counselled discretion, suggested some witty remark to change the tone of the conversation. Nicky, the Nicky who had thrown her little hoard of coins so hopefully in the still water beneath the trees, felt the need to answer his question honestly. 'Like all young girls on the threshold of becoming a woman, I wished for true love.'

She felt his body tense, but his tone was calm when he answered. 'And did your wishes come true?'

'My parents died when I was fourteen. My Uncle Charles, the husband of my father's sister, became guardian to my sister and me.' She stopped and looked towards the sea, lifting a hand to shield her eyes from the glare and from his too-sharp gaze as the memories intruded. 'He did his best, but the revolution made things difficult. Terror stalked around every corner. People were being carted off to prison on a whisper. No one was safe. Count Vilandry, a man who moved in high political circles, who seemed so securely placed, must have seemed the answer to all of his fears when he arrived in the district looking for a wife.'

A brief swallow and she started walking again. 'I was fifteen when I met him the first time. He was older than my uncle and so very kindly.' Kind or not, there had been something about him she hadn't liked that first time. Or any time thereafter.

Gabe took her hand in his, threading his fingers through hers, as if sensing her disquiet. 'You don't have to tell me this if you don't wish to.'

She looked up at him and couldn't help but smile at the concern in his eyes. A deep longing filled her heart. 'I would like to. If you would not mind?' Her voice caught in her throat, but she forced herself to continue. 'You see, I have never told anyone else.'

He made a soft sound and pulled her close against his side. 'Go on.'

She took a shaky breath. 'When my aunt saw my distaste for the match—after all, what girl of fifteen would be drawn to so old a man?—she took me aside. She explained the realities of life. Without the Count's protection our family would likely find our way to the guillotine very soon. My father had been a known royalist, whereas the Count had supported the revolution. He was well thought of in Paris. She asked me if I would like to see my sister in prison. Or worse.'

He cursed softly. 'Blackmail.'

'In a way. But my aunt wasn't wrong. The royalists were rising up against the new government throughout the region. Our family was in real danger. Even I understood that much. She told me that I wouldn't be the first woman to marry a man she did not care for to help her family. One must simply pretend to be someone else. Play the part of the wife.'

She recalled her aunt's face when she'd said the words and the anger in her voice. 'I don't believe hers was a happy marriage. It was very clear to me, that she was right, though. It was my duty to help my family. For Minette's sake, I agreed.'

'Minette is your sister?'

She nodded. 'Much later, I learned Vilandry had paid my uncle a large sum of money. He wanted our lands and my person along with guardianship of my sister. My uncle and aunt used the money to help them flee the country.'

'Leaving you to pay the price for their freedom.'

And Minette too. 'While Vilandry never took me to Paris, he brought his friends back to our estate for their amusement. I took my aunt's advice, I followed the example of the women who came with his friends and buried myself in the role of Vilandry's countess. He proved to be not as kind as I thought him at first, and if I balked at his friends' loose manners, he would threaten my sister's innocence. He liked younger girls, you see. She was eleven.' She shuddered. 'I became his marionette. I lived in a cage of my own making. But Minette was free to be a child. It was all that mattered.'

'How did your husband die?' The suppressed

violence in Gabe's voice was balm to the fifteen-year-old who had been so rudely stripped of her innocence.

'When the Vendée erupted in flames, Vilandry thought he was inviolable. He had proved his loyalty to those in power over and over again. But he misjudged the ego of a young, ambitious soldier.' A face swam before her eyes, lit by flames, a cold smile on his lips. 'Captain Chiroux had recently been assigned to the directorate. The gossip among the local people was that he had burned down an orphanage with the children still inside. When my husband invited him for dinner, he had clearly heard rumours about me.' She recalled the feeling of Chiroux's hand on her thigh, the fingers rubbing over her flesh. 'I told my husband I would have nothing to do with him. Henri agreed. He had larger fish to net.' She swallowed. 'The soldiers had already burned and pillaged several of the great estates in the area. Henri had been assured by their general that we were safe. I should have known a man like Chiroux would not take kindly to rejection. They came to our house when I was gone to visit a tenant who was ill. I came back to see the house in flames and his men shooting any who tried to escape. He must have thought I was inside along with Henri.'

'Then you are free of them both.'

He believed her. She hadn't been sure he would. The tension left her shoulders, her stomach. She let herself lean into his side. But how could she ever truly be free? The Countess was so much more than a mask; she was woven into her fabric. And in the end she had failed to protect her sister. She swallowed hard, trying not to choke on the lump in her throat and yet determined to finish. 'Minette was also inside the house. I wanted to go to her. Our coachman held me back. Dragged me away.' She stopped walking and buried her face in her hands. 'It was my fault. If I had given Chiroux what he wanted…'

He swung her around to face him, tipping her chin up, looking down into her eyes, his full of sympathy. 'No. You must not say that. The blame is all his.' His expression darkened. 'What he did was unconscionable.'

'My mind knows you are right.' She pressed a

hand to her chest. 'My heart—' She couldn't go on for the pain.

'And so you decided you wanted to help defeat Bonaparte?'

She felt empty, drained, as if relieved of a great burden. 'Free to choose, I wanted to do what was right, instead of always dancing to someone else's tune. Then, months after I arrived in England, I heard that my sister might have escaped the fire.' She swallowed. 'I couldn't believe it, but the hope… Paul promised to help me find her in exchange for gathering information.'

'About me,' he said grimly.

'Yes,' she said softly. 'You don't know how happy I am to discover you are not working for the French. I will be glad to tell him so.'

'You believe me?'

'I do.' It was the reason she felt so different, as if for once in her life she could be herself. It was such a relief to know they were not enemies, but friends. Perhaps even more than that, though she didn't dare voice the need. It wasn't because she didn't trust him; it was just that she had spent so long as the pawn of her husband, she wasn't sure she could risk putting herself in another man's power.

He brushed his mouth against hers, the softest whisper of a caress. 'Thank you.'

'For what?'

'For telling me your story.' He released her arms and took a step back with a quick breath as if he had come to some sort of decision. 'There is something you ought to know.'

Her senses went on alert. 'What is it?'

His mouth flattened. 'I made enquiries with regard to this man Paul.'

'And?'

'It is too soon for a reply. But, Nicky, I know of no one in the Home Office who fits his description. And nor does Freddy.'

'It is hardly likely that you would, if he works in secret.'

His firm lips pressed together. 'Perhaps.'

A warning tightened her insides. 'Surely you can't think I work for the French?'

He didn't answer.

Her throat dried. 'Do you?'

'I have had a lot of practice listening to the lies

of others, as well as making up my own. I believe you are telling me the truth as you know it.'

An odd feeling swept over her, a numbness, yet her mind was racing to keep up. 'You think I do not know the truth?'

His body tensed. 'Do you trust me, Nicky?'

She blinked and realised this was vitally important. 'I— Yes. Yes, I do,' she said firmly.

He let go a long breath. 'We received our instructions early this morning. They know you are here and require that we bring you along.'

'Instructions from whom?'

'The French.'

The breath left her body in a rush. 'Wh-what? I don't understand.'

His jaw flexed. 'Nor do I. But we go tonight.'

'And I am to go with you?'

'As Freddy and I see it, we don't have a choice.'

Gabe had learned how to contain his emotions, but the anger at what Nicky had endured at the hands of men was a beast struggling to be free. He had absolutely no doubt that she was telling him the truth. And that she had not given voice to the worst of it. If her husband had still lived, he would have strangled him with his own hands. And as for this Chiroux fellow... But he would not lose control and give free rein to the violent rage surging in his gut. If he did, it would make his mission impossible to complete. Instinct also told him that if he in any way appeared to disapprove of what she had been forced to do, she would break.

The woman gazing up at him was not the countess who traded barbs and sent him mad with lust, this was a girl whose hopes and dreams had been crushed by those who should have protected her. He could not help but admire her pluck. He swallowed his anger until it sat like a lump of molten lead on his chest.

And he despised himself for what she had yet to understand from what he had told her. He prayed it would not be the final blow to a brave spirit that had survived despite the cruelty she had suffered. He prayed that when the truth finally sank in, she would be strong enough to accept the final betrayal. Gently he took her by the hand and led her up to the cliff edge. Out on the sea, ships and small boats plied along the coast, white sails and red, large and small. Some close in. Some little more than vague shapes on the horizon. 'The view is magnificent from up here,' he said calmly as the breeze caught at her skirts, pressing them against her slender legs and form. A form he'd been avoiding these past two days.

It had been two days of hell.

A hell he no doubt deserved. By bringing her to Cornwall he'd served her a very bad turn. Sceptre had killed one woman to save his skin—he was not going to let it happen to Nicky. The only way to keep her safe was to send her away the moment the mission was over. And if his body still yearned for her then that was his cross to bear. She said she trusted him and now he had to try to live up to that trust. Somehow.

They halted a few yards from the place where the sea had carved out a small cove and he gazed down into its depths.

'Gabe?' Nicky said as she stared at the sea rushing up the sandy beach far below. 'How do the French know I am here?'

There. Either she was very clever and had

worked out that this was the question he would expect her to ask, or she genuinely didn't know. Freddy and he had wagered on it before he'd come to have this talk. Nothing she would say would ever allay Freddy's suspicions. But his friend didn't know Nicky as Gabe did. Didn't know her courage and her heart.

'No one here told them,' he said, gazing at her profile, at the way wisps of hair played around her face and the way she narrowed her eyes against the glitter of the sea. Daylight or candlelight, she was perfectly lovely. A sinful temptation. And one he must resist.

She glanced up at him, caught his gaze and coloured. She must have seen something of his thoughts on his face and wondered why he'd been avoiding her. She frowned. 'But they couldn't know unless...'

'Unless?'

Her expression turned to one of horror. 'If Paul is not working for the English but for the French, they would know.' She stepped backwards, wrapping her hands around her waist. 'That is what you think, isn't it?' She started to walk away from him, clearly distraught.

He caught her up, walked alongside her, hesitating to touch her in case she ran. 'We won't know for certain until tonight.'

She stopped and faced him. 'But…if that is indeed the case…' She pressed her fingertips against her lips. 'Minette.' She spun away from him, but not before he glimpsed the well of tears in her eyes. 'What have I done?'

He hesitated, but couldn't stand to see her so upset. He put an arm around her shoulders and pulled her close. If they couldn't be lovers, he could be her friend. For a while. 'It is not your fault. And besides, we don't know if he has even tried to find your sister.'

If he was asked to guess, he would assume the French would do everything in their power to locate the girl. It would be a way of making sure Nicky followed orders. It was what Sceptre would do. And given her history, the way she'd protected her sister in the past… He felt physically ill.

She drew in a breath. 'I've been such a fool.'

'You weren't to know.'

'I should have gone to the Home Office. Asked someone. All I thought of was finding Minette.'

'We'll find her.' Damn it. Why was he making a promise he didn't know he could keep?

Her fingers gripped his lapel. She gazed up at him, her eyes moist, her expression full of trust that was a sword blade between his ribs. 'Thank you.'

He was sunk. He could not let her down. Not when she trusted him. There were few in his life who gave him their trust. His father never had, for some reason. 'Once the mission is over, I'll do my best.' Even if he had to go rogue to do it.

'You'll take me with you.'

He almost groaned out loud. 'We'll see.'

'No. That is not good enough. You must promise me.'

He wanted to kiss her determined mouth and make her forget her demands. He wanted far more than that. He closed his eyes briefly in a plea for resolve. 'I promise to discuss it with you when the mission is over. We have more urgent things to deal with right now. We must plan for tonight. Nothing must go wrong. And you must follow my orders. Do you understand?'

She straightened and moved away from him. Her gaze became steady. Determined. And something welled in his chest. Admiration for her bravery. Tenderness. Neither emotion could he afford. But he would do his level best to discover news of her sister if it took him the rest of his life.

'I understand,' she said.

'Very well. Freddy is waiting for us in the library. Please do not mention anything we have spoken of out here to him.'

'You do not trust him?'

'I trust him with my life.' He didn't trust him with hers, if it proved true that she had been fooled into working for the French. That part of it was not something he'd actually discussed with his closest comrade, choosing instead to blame Armande for the leak about her presence here. A small lie. Guilt twisted in his gut. It was the first time he'd ever lied to his friend.

Clearly Nicky was a weakness Sceptre must never learn of.

* * *

Dinner proved to be a brief and rather tense affair. They were both dressed ready for travel, she in her riding habit, he in breeches and riding boots. Gabe answered when she spoke to him, but seemed lost in his own thoughts. She would have liked to question him more about how a marquess became involved in spying, but found the shyness she'd experienced when they'd walked outside encumbered her ability to maintain her role as the countess.

He had pierced the armour she'd so carefully constructed. She wasn't sure she could ever completely rebuild it.

Neither one of them ate very much. Gabe finally put down his knife and fork and glanced at the clock. 'It is time.'

Her throat dried. Her heart beat a little harder and a whole lot faster. 'I am ready.'

'Freddy will meet us in the caves.' He escorted her up to the chamber above hers. The secret door lay ajar. He closed it behind them.

Again the cool, damp chill of the tunnel made her shiver.

'Don't be scared, Countess,' he said, linking his arm through hers. 'I will keep you safe.'

She knew better than to believe such a promise. Vilandry was supposed to keep her and Minette safe and then she'd spent most of her marriage trying to keep Minette safe from Vilandry. To keep him too thoroughly content to turn his gaze on her younger sibling. Her uncle must have known the sort of man he was, what tastes he had, and still he had pressed her into the marriage. For money. No, the only person she could truly rely on was herself. The urge to trust him was some leftover naivety the Countess had failed to eradicate.

'I'm not scared.'

He gave her a look of approval and her heart gave an odd little clench. *Nom d'un nom*. Every time she thought she had managed to put him at a distance, he somehow disarmed her.

They passed the offshoot to the left she remembered from last time. 'Where does that go?' Her voice bounced off the rock walls.

'To the library,' he murmured low in her ear, so there was no echo.

They continued until they reached the crevasse where she had hidden. A breeze picked up. Icy cold. It pushed at her, like someone trying to make themselves known. Her fingers clutched at Gabe's sleeve. 'Do you feel it. The wind?'

He frowned down at her. 'I feel nothing. The path narrows here, we must go in single file. I will go ahead with the light.'

Unable to resist, she glanced up the other fork. A glow emanated from around the first turn as if someone was walking towards them. The wind picked up, tossing her cloak. Then she saw her— the shimmery figure of a woman. The same figure she had seen in the gardens, but surrounded by light. *'Trust,'* a voice whispered, repeating again and again. She grabbed at Gabe's coat. 'There,' she said, pointing.

Gabe swung around and looked where she had pointed, but the figure was gone. Nothing. There was nothing to see. Had the blow to her head addled her brain?

He stared at her in puzzlement. 'Are you all right? Having a change of heart?'

'No. I am perfectly well. I thought I saw something. Some sort of light.' She shook her head. 'It must have been the reflection of your lantern.' But if so, why wasn't she seeing it now? 'Please. Continue.'

A prickling sensation tickled the back of her neck. As if someone was watching. She resisted the urge to look back. She didn't believe in ghosts. And if it was one, then it seemed to be encouraging her to go this way. As if she had a choice.

She quelled a shiver. Wasn't it bad enough that she was heading out to meet the French, without adding the spirit of a woman long dead waving her farewell?

Chapter Ten

The deck of the *Phoenix* creaked and rocked beneath Gabe's feet. He held Nicky steady against his side, aware of the erratic beat of her heart against his ribs as they waited for the rendezvous. Despite her outer stillness, that rapid flutter gave her away. She should be afraid. Of him. What sort of man involved a woman in war? His sort of man. Men without honour. Without feeling. Yet he felt something now. His own brand of fear. Fear that along with failing his father and Marianne he would fail her too. And of everything he had failed at, that would be the worst.

All his life he had tried to live up to his father's expectations. Tried to be the son his father thought he deserved. And yet in the end his father had found him unworthy. A blot on the family name. True blue-blooded Englishmen didn't sit around philosophising, they charged ahead and protected what was theirs. Built on it. They didn't seek to tear down all that had gone before.

His radical tendencies in his youth had driven a wedge between him and his father. He'd said too many things, done too much and driven his father to take extraordinary measures to defend the family name and wealth.

Yet it was his brain, his ability to see the other side of a question that made him so good at what he did. And he was good at it. Even if no one would ever know of his role in this war. Indeed, if the *ton* ever discovered the way he skulked around in the dark, lying through his teeth, pretending to be what he was not, he would be reviled more than he was already.

He forced the bitter thoughts aside. He had chosen this path. Made it his own years ago. Regrets about the past were useless. The future depended on what happened next. The future of Britain. And equally worrying, Nicky's life.

Despite the lack of a moon, the night was clear

and the breeze perfect for sailing. The light wind stung his cheeks and he tasted salt on his tongue. He tucked Nicky closer into his side. He would not fail. He must not.

'Run up the light,' he said to Brice, his captain. He buried the rise of anticipation in cold stillness.

A sailor ran to do the captain's bidding. Cornish seamen were the best in the world. Hard men, courageous men, who took pride in cocking a snook at the King's excise men. Smuggling was a way of life in Cornwall. Smuggling and wrecking. Even so, they would likely part him from his breath if they had any hint of his real activities. Or at least, what the French thought he was up to.

He glanced to the top of the mast, waiting for the signal. Sail Ho! would not be yelled out, but the man in the shrouds would drop to the deck. Off the rail, stars twinkled, and was that…? Yes, a shadow winking out the glimmers between him and the horizon. He tensed. Everyone on board stiffened, ready to run should it not be the ship they expected.

A lantern flickered to life, showing a mast and a gleam of sails.

A thud beside him on the deck had everyone grinning.

'You are sure?' he said to the lookout.

The man nodded. 'Coming up nice and slow.'

'Make the signal, then, and lower the boat.'

He glanced down at Nicky. 'Are you ready?'

She nodded tersely.

He glanced over to where Freddy, dressed as a common seaman and hiding behind a set of full whiskers, was helping lower the boat that would take them to the other vessel. He would board with them and disappear into the crew.

Gabe cupped Nicky's cheek in his hand, tilting her face up so he could look into her eyes. 'You swear you will do exactly as I or Freddy says, no matter what? I am trusting you in this, Nicky.'

'I will.'

He had no choice but to believe her. He picked up his valise.

The time for talk was ended. Now they each had their roles to play.

Gabe helped her up and over the side of the ship. It was a small coastal vessel. The kind used to transport goods and passengers up and down the coast and was therefore unlikely to draw the attention of the British fleet.

A man in the uniform of a French infantry officer stepped forward to greet them. 'You are Colonel D'Arcy?' Light from the lamp hanging from the mast illuminated his face. 'Major Chiroux, *à votre service.*'

Nicky jerked. She could not contain her gasp as images of the look on his face as he watched her home burn battered her mind.

Gabe's hand tightened on her shoulder, a gesture of warning as much as support. 'I am. Where is Major Taloise?'

'Dead, I'm afraid. I am in charge of this mission.' He put out a hand. 'I am sure we will work equally well together.'

Gabe took his hand and shook it.

Chiroux turned his gaze on Nicky, his expression heated. 'We meet again, Countess.'

She took a deep breath. And another. She had to remain calm. In control. 'Indeed. Congratulations on your advancement.'

'You two have met before?' Gabe asked, his

voice dispassionate, as if he had never heard her story. The man was a master at dissembling.

Or did he really not care?

Chiroux's smile broadened. 'We have indeed. Her husband was an acquaintance. I am very much looking forward to renewing our friendship.' There was no mistaking the leer in his voice.

Gabe stiffened, his fingers digging into her upper arm. 'I think not, Major.' He pulled her closer and pressed his lips tenderly against her forehead. The gesture made her feel like purring and she showed it on her face, glad she had finally managed to call the Countess forth.

Surprise filled Chiroux's eyes. A sly smile curved his lips. 'Like that, is it? I cannot say I am surprised.' His voice hardened. 'It is a good thing you did not fail to bring her with you.'

'I had no intention of leaving such a tasty morsel behind,' Gabe said, his voice silky soft and full of innuendo. 'I assume you have a cabin set aside for us?'

Chiroux's lip curled. 'I see you haven't changed, Countess. The lieutenant will see you to your cabin. Make sure to never leave her alone, Colonel. Women on a ship are trouble.'

A threat if ever she'd heard one. And Chiroux was a man capable of anything. A shudder ran through her body. Gabe pulled her closer against him.

'Good advice,' Gabe said.

'There is a briefing in my cabin in five minutes,' Chiroux said sharply. 'For both of you.'

Gabe stiffened. 'Both?'

'Why do you think we insisted you bring her along?'

'We'll be there,' Gabe rapped out. They followed the lieutenant down a companionway.

The moment they were alone in their assigned cabin, Gabe pushed her down to sit on the single bunk in the tiny space. 'Are you all right?'

Trembling inside from shock, she nodded. 'I—Yes.' She took a shaky breath.

He looked pale. 'This is bad.'

She forced herself to think. Clearly. Logically 'Maybe not. My husband was a known supporter of the revolution. He was despised by many of our neighbours. Chiroux may think I hold to my husband's opinions.' She'd certainly done nothing to make him think otherwise. 'He does not seem particularly suspicious. Perhaps you are wrong about Paul.'

Gabe grimaced. 'Then how in the devil do the French know about you?' He paced the small space for a minute, a frown creasing his forehead, then stopped and looked down at her. 'We will have to see how it plays out, but I don't like it. You have the pistol I gave you?'

Freddy hadn't liked him giving her a weapon. She'd appreciated the gesture of trust. She patted her reticule. 'I do.'

He took her hand and raised it to his mouth, his lips velvety soft and warm. 'Then let us go. It wouldn't do to keep the major waiting. We have one thing in our favour. I outrank him.' He looked at her gravely. 'Whatever you do, follow my lead and we'll come out of this all right.'

Were they? How could she be sure? He grinned and looked suddenly boyish. 'We're in this together, whatever may come.'

She frowned, but he grasped her hand and led her out of the room. She drew in a long breath and sank into the Countess. It was all that would save them from this moment on.

A waiting sailor outside the cabin door directed them to the small captain's cabin at the aft of the ship. A few deep breaths and Nicky stepped inside with a seductive smile pasted on her lips. Only Chiroux awaited them.

'What is the plan, Major?' Gabe said briskly.

Nicky perched herself on the bunk while the two men bristled at each other like dogs with a juicy bone set between them. The major's eyes dropped first. Gabe was right, it was a good thing he outranked the Frenchman.

'You have guessed our target, no doubt,' Chiroux said, picking up a sheaf of papers from the desk.

'King George,' Gabe rapped out. 'How? There are four thousand troops centred around Weymouth.'

Nicky hid her surprise that he would relay such explicit information. *Trust.* It was all she had to cling to.

Chiroux thrust one of the papers at Gabe. 'We will land further up the coast, with some of my men dressed in the uniforms you brought. We will ride to the beach where he swims each morning at seven. No one will question us and, if they do, we will have a British officer in command who will smooth the path.'

'You kill him, while he is bathing,' Gabe said. 'A forlorn hope, then.'

Chiroux raised a questioning brow.

'English soldiers call it a forlorn hope when everyone in an assault expects to die,' Gabe said tersely. 'Volunteers only.'

A chill ran down Nicky's spine at Chiroux's triumphant expression. 'No, no, *mon Colonel*, you have it all wrong. It is only the countess who will die.'

Gabe tensed. 'Your meaning?'

The Frenchman shrugged. 'We will deliver her to the beach. The king is known to have an eye for a pretty lady. And a lady in wet petticoats fawning all over him, well, who would suspect? All she has to do is get close enough to shoot him. She is the only one who will die. Unless Moreau was wrong and she does not care about her sister.'

'He has found her?' Nicky asked, feeling the blood leach from her face.

'What the devil?' Gabe said, his fists clenching.

'Don't tell me she fooled you,' Chiroux said. 'She is a British spy, according to a man named Paul Moreau. It is why we hold her sister.' His eyes narrowed. 'Or are we wrong about your loyalties, Colonel?'

Heart pounding, Nicky rose to her feet. 'No. You are wrong about me. I am loyal to France. To the revolution. As is Citizen D'Arcy.' She pressed a hand to her heart. 'I admit, I offered to help the English, for my sister's sake. But I gave them nothing of importance. I would never betray my country. You must remember how my husband and I supported General Napoleon.'

'Moreau said you offered to help defeat our country,' Chiroux snarled.

'It sounds as if Moreau lied to her,' Gabe put in swiftly. 'Had he told her he worked for the French, she would have been better pleased.'

'I cannot trust her,' Chiroux shot back.

Gabe scrubbed at the back of his neck. 'Why not? I do.'

Despite the fears churning in her stomach, Nicky wanted to smooth his ruffled hair. Instead, she gave Chiroux a teasing smile. 'Moreau is a bumbling fool. Unlike you, Major. I sincerely regretted my husband's antipathy. You and I would have done very well together.'

Chiroux's shoulders relaxed. 'We would have.' He gave a small shake of his head. 'I have to say I was not unhappy when I learned you had escaped the fire. I was sorry you did not think to come to me.'

'I was afraid. And badly advised. A woman alone…' She let the sentence hang. Let him imagine what he would.

He gazed down at the papers in his hand. 'The plan is agreed. You are to kill the king or your sister dies.'

'Very well,' Gabe said, musingly. 'It is a good plan. It requires only a few changes.'

Nicky tried not to swallow against the dryness in her throat. Hopefully Gabe knew what he was about.

By the time Gabe had convinced Chiroux that he and his men would not survive if he stayed with his original course and had laid out his own plan, the ship's captain had come to tell them they must prepare to disembark. They did so with silent efficiency. Gabe, standing on shore, could not help but marvel at the slackness of the English coastguard. Not one challenge had been issued as the ship had made its way along the Cornish coast and then that of Dorset. Had no one spotted them? Or had they assumed they were just what they appeared to be?

'Your ship is well known in these parts?' he said to Chiroux, who was now dressed in the uniform of a Hanoverian Captain, as they made their way up the beach. With some difficulty, Gabe had convinced the Frenchman to leave the rest of his men on board ship.

'*Bien sûr, mon ami,*' Chiroux said as if it was obvious to even the most obtuse of dullards. 'Ever since the King arrived in Weymouth.'

Freddy had also been left on board the *Regina*. If he and Nicky did not return with Chiroux as planned, he would have to make his escape as best he could. If they were successful then their next stop was France, but not in the manner Chiroux expected.

'Are you ready?' the Frenchman asked.

Gabe glanced down at Nicky, dressed only in her shift beneath her borrowed seaman's cloak. She gave him a smile full of bravado. 'Absolutely.'

'Vive la France,' Chiroux whispered.

They marched up the beach to an inn where Gabe hired three horses while Chiroux kept out of sight. The cove they had landed at was seven miles from the town of Weymouth, a distance they accomplished in under an hour while eliciting little notice from the few country people on the road, a milkmaid and a goose girl off to sell their wares. All passed with a wave and a smile.

When they reached the edge of the town a clock chimed. They were half an hour ahead of the King.

Several bathing machines waited in a row along the beach. Gabe and Nicky picked their way over the sand to the one closest to that used by the King, while Chiroux made his way to one at the far end, carrying a valise containing their change of clothes.

'The lady wishes to swim?' the large woman with the forearms of a navvy asked as they reached her.

'Both of us, if we may,' Gabe said, winking at the woman. 'My wife is fearful. And I would like to be the one to introduce her to the pleasures of sea bathing.'

The woman chuckled knowingly. 'Very healthy, sir. Climb aboard and I'll push you out. The tide is on the way in, but I'll have you out of there before it gets too deep, don't you worry.'

Gabe helped Nicky into the gaily painted wooden-and-canvas structure on two wheels. They sat on the benches each side of a square hole in the floor. It allowed bathers to dip in complete privacy should they so wish. They listened to the wheels creak and the woman puff and blow as she pushed them into the waves.

'The poor *madame*,' Nicky said. 'Pushing a strapping young fellow like you.' She giggled.

As always her courage left him feeling utterly

astounded. He briefly kissed her lips. 'It will work.'

She nodded, but looked as if her teeth might chatter if she relaxed her jaw.

The machine came to a halt. 'Open the seaward door when you are ready,' the woman called out to them. 'Four steps down. You cannot be seen from the beach if you stay right in front.'

Something Gabe's plan hinged on.

He checked the pistol Nicky had been carrying in her reticule. He rewrapped it in the oilskin to keep it dry and placed it inside a small waterproof bag, which he slung across his back. By the time he was done, Nicky had removed her cloak and stood ready in her shift. Gabe stripped naked. He turned to find her watching him with an appreciative look in her eye. 'Stop it,' he grumbled as he hardened. 'You will embarrass me before my King.'

'The cold water will solve that little problem.'

'Not so much of the little.'

She closed the distance between them and cupped his balls, gently squeezing. 'Not little at all.'

His blood rushed south. 'You, my sweet,' he said hoarsely, 'are one wicked woman.'

'Only with you,' she said softly.

There might be enough time. He pulled her close and kissed her deeply, feeling her beaded nipples against his chest as he rocked his hips into her hand. He slid one hand up to her breast, the heavy weight so very enticing.

Sounds outside on the sands, an order to halt, stopped him cold. 'Damnation,' he murmured.

'Later,' Nicky whispered. 'If there is a later.'

'Don't worry, Nicky. I won't let anything happen to you.'

She didn't look convinced, but reluctantly moved away from him. 'Don't forget, I can't swim.'

Gabe opened the door to the sea and prayed she would keep her head. If she panicked, it could very well mean death for them both.

Hidden within the machine, Gabe watched her battle for balance against the incoming waves. She was so very brave.

He was taking a huge risk putting his trust in a woman he knew to have been working as a

French spy. Risking not only himself, but his country.

Damn it all. He wasn't wrong. Not this time.

Chapter Eleven

Achingly aware of Gabe's intense gaze, Nicky splashed in water that was surprisingly refreshing once she became acclimatised. The sand shifted under her feet. She tasted salt on her tongue. The cool water certainly did nothing to cool her ardour. He was right. She was a wicked woman. But she had meant it when she said 'only with you'. She felt deliciously, uncontrollably wicked around him. All her previous encounters had been cold-blooded. Necessary. This desire for him controlled her. It was inconceivable, when all her focus should be on saving the King without losing her life. One look at Gabe's beautiful body and she'd become wanton and foolish, like the schoolgirl she'd been before her marriage. She could not afford to be foolish, or read more into his obvious desire than animal lust. She didn't want more. She wanted her sister home, and she wanted the freedom to be herself.

Even if he did want her after this was over, a man as virile as Gabe would expect an obedient wife. He would want to attach strings that would jerk her hither and yon. She could not do it again. Could she?

She risked a glance at the machine being pushed into the sea a yard or so away. Could Gabe really swim that far underwater? A soldier in the same uniform as Chiroux was wearing marched stolidly into the water in advance of the bathing machine. He frowned at Nicky for a long moment, warning her not to come any closer with his expression, then turned his back, all his attention fixed on the door through which the King would emerge.

A band tightened around her throat. She couldn't breathe. She was shaking so hard, she felt as if she might fall over. She took one deep breath, then another, and dipped shoulder-deep into the water, watching for the King's appearance from the corner of her eye. A naked, very corpulent figure lurched down the steps and wallowed in the water. Then another gentleman, this one still in his shirt, carrying the King's towel. This was her cue. Casually, Nicky turned her head to look back at her machine as if to check that she had not strayed too far and saw Gabe acknowledge her signal with a lift of one hand. When the King spluttered to his feet, Nicky looked over, made an exclamation of surprise. As soon as she knew she had the King's attention, she made a deep curtsy. 'Your Majesty.'

'No need, my dear lady. What! What!'

The soldier and the King's gentlemen both gazed at her in rapt astonishment. Her shift was now wet to the neck.

A soft splash and Gabe was gone.

'Oh!' Nicky said, crossing her arms in front of her, at the same time allowing herself to be knocked over by a wave and coming up floundering, arms flailing, crying out.

'Gentlemen, avert your eyes,' the King said crossly, striding towards her.

The two men turned their gaze seaward.

'There, there, young lady.' He caught her by

the arm and stood her on her feet. 'My daughters are always the same. Always falling. You must brace your feet.'

'Your Majesty is too kind.'

He frowned, his bulbous eyes looking at her sharply. 'French, what?'

'Yes, your Majesty. I am not used to bathing in the sea.' She saw Gabe slip into the King's little hut like a wraith with a sigh of relief.

'Hah!' the King said. 'If the French were more at home on the waves, I dare say they would be better able to give us a trouncing.'

Nicky flopped in his direction and banged against one of the wheels of his machine. 'I can't seem to keep my balance.'

'Brace. What?'

Using the structure to hold her up, she staggered to his steps and sat down hard.

'Your Majesty!' his gentleman said in disgusted accents. 'Shall I have her removed?'

Nicky gave him a wide-eyed look, then smiled at the King. 'Do you want me to go, your Majesty? I would love to see how you swim.'

The King puffed up his chest. 'Nothing to it.

The water keeps you afloat.' He demonstrated floating on his back, his large belly rising above the waves like a pallid island.

'It is time to go, sire,' the gentleman said after the King had not only demonstrated his own skills, but had held her under her middle while she splashed her arms and legs. The man held out the towel.

Nicky snatched it. 'Allow me, sire.' She gave him an arch smile. 'Or perhaps your Majesty would prefer to dry off inside?'

The King hesitated. His loyalty to his wife was well known and thus the weakest part of their plan, but she could see he was tempted. She smiled as only the Countess could smile and fluttered her lashes. 'I have gentle hands and a massage after sea bathing is excellent for the circulation.'

'Your Majesty!' his gentleman said, sounding scandalised.

'Poppycock,' the King said, glaring fiercely at the man.

Nicky took her chance and climbed the steps into the machine. The King followed with alacrity.

Gabe shut the door in the other man's face and bolted it.

'What! What!' the King said, as he realised there was someone else crowded into his space, a male wearing nothing but a towel. 'We did not invite you, sir.' He lowered his head like a bull about to charge and stared at Gabe. 'I know you.'

'Yes, sire,' Gabe said. 'Mooreshead. I met you at a levee at St James some time ago. I am surprised you remember.'

'You have the look of your father,' the King said. 'Good man. Good man. In his way. You are with Sceptre.'

'Yes, sire.'

The King turned his fishy eyes on Nicky. 'And you, *madame*?'

'In a way, your Majesty,' Nicky said, handing the King his towel. She wrapped another she found on the bench around herself.

'What is this all about, hey?' the King asked. 'Trouble? What!'

'Trouble indeed,' Gabe said. 'We are required to kill you.'

* * *

'Gabe.' Nicky's scandalised face was a picture Gabe would never forget.

The King clearly saw the funny side of it, because he broke out in a roar of laughter.

A knock sounded at the door. 'Are you all right, your Majesty?' a rather hesitant voice said.

'Go away,' the King said. 'We will call when you are needed.' He lowered his voice. 'What are you up to, young fellow?'

In broad brush strokes, Gabe laid out the plot and the reason they needed Chiroux to believe in its success.

'Your sister,' the King said stroking his chin while looking intently at Nicky.

'The last of my family, your Majesty,' Nicky said well aware how much the King treasured his family—apart from his eldest son, that was.

'As well as the rest of their conspirators,' Gabe added. 'We need to net them all.'

'And so you will shoot the pistol and escape through the floor. While my people try to gain access, you swim off. What!'

'That is it in a nutshell, sire.' Gabe unwrapped the pistol.

The King eyed it askance. 'We'll jolly well serve that Bonaparte fellow a turn.'

Gabe let go his breath in a sigh of relief. The old fellow was as game as a cockerel. 'Thank you, your Majesty. You have to stop your men from killing us, though it would be good if they attempt to give chase for a while. We'll do the rest.' He carefully aimed the muzzle of the pistol towards the hole in the floor. 'Ready, sire?'

The King nodded. 'When this is over, we will talk.' He and Nicky covered their ears.

Gabe fired.

Fists hammered on the door.

'We are coming,' the King said, watching with sparkling eyes as Gabe lowered Nicky into the water and followed her in. 'Patience,' he called out to another round of knocking.

Nicky clung to Gabe's back like a limpet. 'Deep breath,' he said. He dived beneath the bottom of the equipage and swam underwater parallel to the beach until he was sure her lungs must be near to bursting. He broke the surface. She gasped for air.

Nicky looked back over her shoulder. 'The soldier. He's coming after us.'

The King's guard had seen them and was wading through the waves.

A cry came from the King's bathing machine. The King's gentleman, calling the soldier back. The man hesitated, looking at them and then back. Another shout and he turned back, plunging towards his King.

'Good old Farmer George,' Gabe said.

Other soldiers were hurrying down the beach, their focus on the King's bathing machine. Gabe dived beneath the waves, only coming up for air when absolutely necessary. The hardest thing now would be convincing Chiroux they had completed the task.

'Well?' Chiroux asked the moment they popped up through the floor in the machine he had rented. 'I heard the shot.'

'The King is dead,' Gabe said, hauling Nicky up beside him.

'You are sure?'

'Positive.'

'We must hurry.' Chiroux rang the bell for the machine to be hauled back to dry land. To Gabe's surprise, the man seemed anxious to accept their word without proof. Worried about his own neck now the beach was a hive of activity. Gabe and Nicky dried off and were dressed by the time they had reached the sand.

'Here!' the woman shouted, when the three of them emerged. 'What's going on? You only paid for one.'

Chiroux threw several coins at her feet and she scrabbled about in the sand.

They ran for their horses.

A shout behind them said they'd been seen. Gabe looked back. A troop of Hanoverians were headed down the beach at a run. Hopefully it was the King trying to make the pursuit look realistic after explaining they weren't to be caught.

They galloped out of the town to curses and fist waving. There was still no sign of the Hanoverians as their boat pulled for the *Regina* a half hour later.

* * *

Their arrival on board the *Regina* was surrounded by hastily raised sails and a speedy escape while everyone watched for ships of the Royal Navy. Nicky stood at the rail beside Gabe. 'I can't believe we actually did it,' she said softly. Or that finally she would get to see Minette.

'Nor I.'

Chiroux clapped him on the back. 'There will be great rewards for this day's work for us all.'

A broad smile crossed Gabe's face as he looked down at Nicky, his eyes twinkling. 'I certainly hope so.'

She shook her head at him, knowing full well the kinds of reward he had in mind.

'We go at once to Boulogne to report our success, so the next stage of the plan can go forward.'

'You don't think Parliament will simply put the Prince of Wales in the King's place without missing a step?' Gabe asked, wondering how much Chiroux knew or would be prepared to say.

'The Prince is disliked. Others will deal with him. He will become our puppet.'

With effort, Nicky retained her calm expression as did Gabe, though it was hard not to steal a conspiratorial glance. Gabe's eyes held a warning to be careful. The *Regina* heeled over, catching the wind and speeding over the waves heading for France. The disreputable-looking Freddy walked past, whistling.

Gabe looked up at the sails. 'A fair wind.' He smiled down at Nicky. 'Time for a little relaxation, I think.'

Nicky felt her insides quiver at the sensual note in his voice.

Chiroux glared at him, but remained silent.

Gabe put a proprietary hand on the small of Nicky's back.

Her skin jumped to life under his touch. A delicious shiver ran down her spine. Her breath caught. Was he planning to make good on her promise of earlier?

'Let us know when we arrive,' Gabe ordered Chiroux before hurrying her down the companionway. Inside the cabin, he stood, his head cocked to one side, listening.

'Is something wrong?'

'Hold on to something.' He gestured to the edge of the bunk.

Frowning, she did as he bid. *'Qu'est-ce que c'est?'*

A loud crack. The ship bucked, then tilted to port. It pitched and rolled uncomfortably.

'What was that?'

'Freddy,' Gabe said. 'If all goes well—'

A cannon shot rang out.

'What is going on?' she said, raising her voice.

He grinned. 'The *Phoenix*. She found us exactly where Freddy said she would.'

And here she was thinking she was the reason they had come below, even when she knew Gabe was the greatest dissembler alive. 'You knew this was about to occur?'

'Freddy told me.'

'When he whistled.'

'Right. We planned it before we left. But I wasn't sure we could pull it off.' He retrieved a pistol from the bag he had left in the cabin when they boarded the first time. 'Wait here.'

'You brought me down here, so you could

go back up there alone, didn't you? I'm coming with you.'

He looked as if he planned to argue. 'It isn't safe.'

'I am not staying down here when the ship is sinking.'

'It won't sink.'

'I'm coming. And don't think you are going to fetch Minette without me.'

He heaved a sigh. 'All right. But stay close. And stay away from Chiroux until we have him safely under guard.'

Was that a note of jealousy she heard? If it was, it certainly made her feel a whole lot less disappointed. Madness. She had lost her reason.

She followed up the steps to the deck.

Up on deck, Gabe saw with satisfaction the jib sail dragging in the sea and the *Phoenix* closing in on them at a rate of knots. He strode across the deck to Chiroux with Nicky at his side. 'What the deuce is going on?' he said to Chiroux. 'This is a disaster.'

Chiroux looked thoroughly shocked as he

stared over the rail. 'Isn't that your ship? Why is she firing at us?'

'My captain probably wonders what the hell is going on. He knows what is at risk. He'll put some men aboard to help get this mess cleared away and get us on our way France.'

'I was lucky not to be killed,' Chiroux grumbled.

'That would not have been good,' Gabe agreed. They needed him alive, for his information.

Freddy moved to stand in the vicinity of the *Regina's* captain, a hand in his coat pocket. They were ready.

Captain Brice brought the *Phoenix* sharply alongside. Men climbed aboard.

Gabe pulled his pistol and placed it at the back of Chiroux's neck. 'One move and you are a dead man.'

Freddy did the same with the *Regina's* captain.

Within minutes they had the crew in custody in the hold.

Chiroux glared at Gabe. 'Traitor. Liar.'

Gabe smiled and squared off. The Frenchman took a half-step back. Too late to prevent Gabe's fist from a flush hit. Chiroux staggered back, rubbing his chin.

'That's for what you did to Nicky's family. There is much more to come.'

The British sailors chuckled as they went about their work cleaning up the tangle of rigging.

'I was just doing my job,' Chiroux pleaded.

'You took a bit too much pleasure in it, old fellow. But tell me what I and my government need to know and you'll spend the rest of the war in a British prison and not feeding the fishes.'

Chiroux's eyes turned wild. 'You can't kill me. I am an officer. There are rules.'

'Not in my army.'

Chiroux cursed. 'What can I tell you? They give me orders. They don't tell me anything about their plans.'

'Tell me about Minette.'

'Who?'

'Countess Vilandry's sister. Tell me exactly where she is.'

He hesitated.

'Freddy, find our cat o' nine tails, would you?' Gabe said coldly.

Chiroux blanched. 'Moreau will kill me.'

'I'll do worse than that. Or, if you co-operate fully, I could arrange for you to be taken to a prison in, say, Scotland, and kept under a different name.'

Chiroux swallowed.

'Here,' Freddy said, coming up from behind him.

One look at the vicious-looking whip in Freddy's hand and Chiroux spilled everything he knew and the *Regina* was headed back for England, sailed by part of the *Phoenix's* crew with a chastened Major Chiroux under guard.

Nicky came up to him with a smile of gratitude. Gabe placed his hands on her shoulders. He felt a great well of tenderness for the woman gazing up at him. It put him all abeam. He wanted to hold and protect her for the rest of his life. But he couldn't.

Their affair was over. Born of the need for information, they had nothing left to learn from each other. Once they had rescued her sister that would be an end to it. There was no room for a woman in his life. Not when either side would exploit such a weakness.

'Now we go for your sister.'

Chapter Twelve

Once they were done with Chiroux and his men, Nicky was surprised to see that they were sailing west, into the setting sun. 'What is happening? I thought we were sailing to France.'

'So you want us to land in broad daylight?'

Heat scalded her face. 'Oh, I didn't think of that.'

'It is a good thing one of us did,' Gabe said drily. He frowned. 'It is not going to be easy. The garrison at Boulogne is on high alert. Your friend Colonel Moreau will have Minette under guard.'

She groaned softly. 'After the way he spoke of his hatred of Napoleon, I still have trouble believing he is an officer in the French army.' She could not keep the bitterness from her voice

Gabe gave her waist a reassuring squeeze. The

contact was warming, comforting, it restored her equanimity. Something that should not be happening. She should be in control of her emotions.

'Fortunately my rank of colonel comes with a uniform and free movement around France. With Chiroux in chains there is no one to tell Moreau the truth of what happened today.'

'What is our plan?'

'As I said. I am an officer in the French army.'

'You are going into the garrison to get her.' She looked at Freddy. 'He goes with you.'

Freddy shook his head. 'I don't have a uniform. And there are other reasons...' He looked at Gabe, whose return glance stopped him mid-sentence. 'Family obligations,' Freddy mumbled.

A buzz started up in her ears. 'You can't possibly go alone.'

'Countess—'

'No. I won't allow it. And anyway, she doesn't know you. She will be afraid. She might refuse to go with you.'

'There is that,' he admitted.

Because he'd already thought of it.

'I thought if you wrote to her...' he said. 'She would recognise your hand?'

'I meant what I said earlier. I am going with you.'

He shook his head. 'It is too dangerous. This Moreau fellow knows you.'

'And he might know you too,' Freddy said. 'But a drunken officer bringing his doxy back to his bed might be less noticeable than a man alone. We can give you a moustache and an eye-patch. Put your arm in a sling, so you can hide a weapon.'

Nicky stared at Freddy, who had always been so unfriendly in the past. Was he jesting, or was he really on her side in this? Seemingly the latter from the way he was looking intently at Gabe.

Gabe's jaw worked as if he was trying to swallow something unpleasant and it wouldn't go down. 'Damn you, Freddy. I can do that without her.'

'But not so convincingly,' Freddy said quietly. He glanced at Nicky. 'He needs someone there to make sure he doesn't get himself killed. He has a death wish, you know.'

'I do not have a death wish.'

'I'm going,' Nicky said. 'Even if I have to swim to France.' Not that she could, but she could see he understood her determination.

Gabe let go a breath. 'All right. Freddy's suggestion will indeed improve the plan. We just need to refine the details.'

Nicky put her hand through his arm and smiled. 'I knew you would finally see reason.'

'It feels more like madness,' he said gruffly, pulling away.

She closed her eyes against the pain of rejection. Right. He didn't want her that way any longer. He'd become more and more remote since this mission had started.

'Come below,' Freddy said. 'I have everything we need.'

Nicky blinked. 'You have done this before.'

'Many times,' Gabe said. He cursed softly. 'But never with a woman.'

Entering the garrison after the curfew hour had been ridiculously easy. Especially with Nicky flirting with every male she met along the way.

The girl was an incredible actress. Whereas he hadn't needed to pretend he was jealous of her attempts to seduce anything passing in breeches—and, no, he was not going to think about how easily shc'd seduced him. The Nicky he cared for was not the woman on his arm flirting and exuding sensuality. The girl he— He cut the thought off. Women had no place in his life. And if he managed to get this one killed, he wasn't sure he would care to go on.

As they approached the officers' quarters, the general noises faded into the background. He glanced around. There were no guards and no officers either. Well, it was after midnight. Anyone on duty in the morning would be in bed and those on duty tonight were at their posts.

He slipped his arm out of its sling and freed the pistol lodged inside the linen.

'It was very kind of that corporal to tell you where you could find Colonel Moreau's quarters,' Nicky said softly.

'Very obliging.'

'Thank goodness the dear Colonel is not at home.'

'We hope.' They had guessed that Moreau would be waiting for news of the assassination. Either at the harbour here in Boulogne, whither the *Regina* had been bound, or in England, where he would be needed to put the next stage of his plan into play, though Chiroux hadn't known what it was. Both he and Freddy had agreed it was the latter. If they were right, Moreau would be their next and final target in this mission, though Sceptre would likely be furious about this little detour.

It was the reason he hadn't wanted Freddy along. He could claim he knew nothing about Gabe's plans. And if they failed...he could go after Moreau and no harm would be done.

'There,' Nicky said. 'The officers' barracks.'

It was an old château the army had commandeered. The rest of the garrison were using outbuilding and tents. The officers liked their comfort.

They strolled in through the front door. The soldier on duty saluted as they passed. Nicky blew him a saucy kiss. Gabe pulled her close to his side and she giggled.

Sloppy guard work. But then the French were great believers in *amour*. War or no war, apparently.

Once inside the grand hall, they headed for the stairs. Colonel Moreau had his room on the second floor, at the far end. Nicky had been furious to learn that he had kept her sister in his chamber. And beneath her anger there had been fear, despite the fact that they had all agreed that if Paul intended to use Minette to control Nicky, he would not have harmed her. Clearly Nicky believed it logically, but not in her heart.

Because she'd been used very badly.

Somehow Gabe had to get her out of this safely and make sure she was never in danger again.

'This way,' he said when they reached the top of the stairs. The room they were looking for was at the end. Each door had the name of its occupant nailed to it. Very efficient.

'Moreau,' Nicky murmured, stopping at the last door.

There was no guard outside.

Gabe put his arm back in the sling. He winced. His arm still pained him occasionally. He could only hope Nicky didn't notice or she'd be wanting to take charge. The thought made him smile a little. He willed himself to concentrate.

Nicky turned the handle. The door swung inward and they barrelled in like a couple of drunks, laughing uproariously. They stopped short at the sight of the young woman sitting on the bed, a rope around her neck attached to the rail and a young soldier sitting opposite. They were playing cards. The young woman seemed to have all the money on her side of the table.

The soldier leaped to his feet, sending cards and money flying. 'Halt,' he said, struggling to get his pistol free.

'A bit late for that, my fine fellow.' Gabe said. He drew his arm free of the sling and struck the lad on the temple with his pistol grip.

'Nicky?' the young woman said.

Nicky stood stock still, staring at her sister. 'Minette,' she said in a soft, pained voice. 'Is it you? You look so grown up.'

Gabe cut the rope and the young woman flung

herself into Nicky's arms. 'That horrid man said you would come.'

'Horrid man?' Nicky choked out. 'Did he hurt you?'

'No. I hurt him. He took me from the nuns. You remember Sister Therese? She and some of the other nuns were hiding in a barn. Then Colonel Moreau came and threatened them. Someone had given me away. So I had to give myself up. I couldn't let them hurt the sisters. But I got him back. I kicked him in the *couilles* when he put me up on his horse.'

'Minette!'

'If you are going to kick a man, it might as well be there,' Gabe said, amused by the chatter and the bravado. Nicky would have been like that once. Innocent. Passionate. He tied the unconscious young soldier in Minette's place and shoved the lad's handkerchief in his mouth. By rights he should kill him. One less soldier to fight against the Crown. But not in front of the ladies. The boy groaned. He was coming to his senses. 'You two can catch up on the news later. Right now we have to go.'

They locked the young soldier in and took the key with them. They reached the front door without incident. 'The guard might not be so friendly on the way out,' Gabe murmured.

'Leave him to me,' Nicky said. 'Give me your pistol.'

Gabe didn't like it, but he didn't see an alternative. If they could get out of the garrison without raising the alarm, it would be the best of all possible worlds. He handed over his weapon. 'No noise,' he said.

A quick wave of acknowledgement and Nicky sauntered out of the door. He could hear her talking to the soldier outside, but not the words. The voices faded. Then he heard something that sounded like a grunt. He gritted his teeth and stopped himself from following and causing a scene.

'Now,' he said to Minette. Arm in arm they strolled out of the door.

A second later and Nicky joined them, looping her arm through his on the other side.

He cocked a brow.

'He's asleep and dreaming,' she said, laughing. 'I did to him what you did to the soldier in Minette's room.'

'David,' Minette supplied. 'I'm glad you didn't kill him. He is a nice boy. He never once realised I was cheating.'

The two women hung on Gabe's arm and they weaved a bit as they made their way to the guard post at the gate.

'Having a good night, are you, Colonel?' the corporal asked as he opened up.

'Excellent,' Gabe slurred. 'Except we've run out of wine. Tell Colonel Moreau I'll bring his little ladybird back safe and sound in the morning.'

Nicky pinched his arm. Gabe grinned down at her. 'Now, now, *chérie*, no need to be jealous, I will see to both of you equally.'

The guard laughed while Nicky glowered at him. And that was it. They were out in the lane leading away from the garrison and hurrying towards the town where a rowboat was waiting to take them out to the *Phoenix*.

It was over. Almost over. He had to find a way to hide Nicky and her sister from Sceptre. False names. False papers. A new country. America?

Her whereabouts unknown even to him, in case Sceptre decided to question him closely.

He wasn't going to let what happened to Marianne happen to Nicky, even if it meant he would never see her again.

The residual pain in his arm was nothing compared to the pain in his heart.

Dear God, he'd done what he always said he would not.

He'd fallen in love.

Not with the seductress, but with the woman beneath. The brave, unselfish, lovely woman who'd given everything she had to save her sister. Her fierce loyalty was a thing of beauty. Men had used her and abused her because of that loyalty, because of the love she'd kept bright and sharp in her heart, and he'd been no different.

This time, he would not be the one to put her life in danger.

In the stern of the *Phoenix*, sitting on the window seat, Nicky and Gabe watched Freddy and Minette play cards while the ship tossed and plunged. The weather had turned for the worse, the winds beating them back from England's shores. Captain Brice had insisted they ride the storm out instead of attempting a landing anywhere along the south coast of England.

Freddy threw down his cards. 'Stop cheating.'

'I'm not.'

Freddy grabbed those she held in her hand. They both started as if stung. With a glower at her, Freddy fanned eight cards on the table whereas there should only have been five.

Minette's brown eyes sparked with fury. 'I wouldn't have to cheat if you'd let me win.'

'You little brat,' Freddy said. 'You are spoiled rotten. You either win or you lose. You don't cheat.'

Minette sent Nicky a look of appeal.

Nicky pushed to her feet, but Gabe's strong arm captured her around the waist. He hauled her back against his chest. 'Leave the children to their quarrel,' he murmured in her ear. 'They will work it out.'

At the moment, they looked as if they might come to blows. The two of them had seemed to dislike each other on sight. Nicky had never seen her sister act so badly. But then she hadn't seen her for a long while. She'd done a lot of growing up in the meantime. Nicky had the feeling she had seen a lot more than any young, gently reared girl ought to have seen, but when she'd asked her sister about the past few years, Minette had simply shrugged. 'We did what we had to do to survive' was the only comment she would make.

When Nicky had asked who she meant by 'we', Minette had turned sullen. Later. Her sister would tell her later.

Freddy gathered up all of the coins on the table and divided them equally. 'Start again. And this time no cheating. You can't pull the wool over my eyes, so don't bother trying.'

Minette thrust her bottom lip forward and glowered at him. *'Cochon.'*

Freddy cracked a hard, somewhat bitter laugh. 'You'll have to do better than that. I've been called far worse.'

Minette looked at him, an odd expression on her face. Then the sullen look returned. 'You no doubt deserved it.'

'No doubt,' Freddy said wryly.

'I need to talk to you,' Gabe said in a low voice for Nicky's ears only.

She dragged her gaze away from her sister and met Gabe's eyes. They were dark with shadows that made her think of pain. 'Does your arm trouble you still?'

'No. At least not much. There is something I need to tell you.' He shot the other pair a sideways glance. 'Come to my cabin.'

This was the captain's cabin they were using as a drawing room while they waited out the storm. Gabe had his own cabin, she had learned earlier, when he went to change out of his French uniform and into something more befitting an English marquess. She, on the other hand, had nothing but the riding habit she'd worn when leaving Beresford Abbey. Goodness, she really was looking forward to regaining her own wardrobe.

'We'll be back in a moment,' Gabe said to Freddy, who acknowledged his words with a slight nod as he watched with narrowed eyes as Minette dealt another hand.

Gabe closed the cabin door and opened a door on the right-hand side. He ushered her in.

Polished wood and brass and a large bed scattered with cushions. The bed took up most of the space between the bulkheads.

He gestured for her to sit on the bed, while he took the chair.

She looked about her in admiration as the sheer luxury. '*Tiens.* I might have guessed you would have a cabin like this.'

He looked a little shamefaced. 'The yacht was a gift.'

Her insides tightened. 'From a woman?'

He nodded.

She wanted to hit him.

He grinned. 'My aunt. It belonged to her husband. When he died she gave it to me. Said I might as well continue in his footsteps, since I seemed bent on going to hell.'

The heat of her anger dissipated. 'She is the aunt who left you Meak.'

'She did. For some reason she liked me. Or she did it to annoy my father, who didn't.'

She frowned. 'Your father didn't like you?'

'No.'

While he tried to disguise it, she could hear the pain in his voice. 'Why?'

'He thought me a traitor to my country and my name.'

'You didn't tell him you were a spy for the British government?'

'It was long before that.' He pressed his lips together, then shrugged. 'In a way I don't blame him. I turned idealistic when I went to university. Beresford and I were fired up by the American revolution. Mesmerised by the ideals of Locke and Montesquieu and Rousseau. About the governed being free to choose those that govern them.'

His voice was full of irony.

'What made you change your mind?'

'I didn't. Or not entirely. Of course I went home at half-term after reading a speech given by Fox, spouting idealistic sentiments and demanding my father change things.' He cracked a hard laugh. 'My father, a dyed-in-the-wool Tory, was apoplectic. We argued. And the more intransigent he got, the more revolutionary I became, until he believed I was a turncoat and a traitor. According to him I didn't deserve to inherit the title and he was going to do everything he could to make sure I never got the chance.'

She blinked. 'Can he do that?'

'He came pretty close. When he died, I discovered he'd put all the money in trust for my heir.'

'Oh.'

'That came later. I was so angry at his lack of trust, and his inability to see the truth—' he shrugged '—I went to France to be a part of the way the world should be. I met a woman who was an avid revolutionary. Marianne Martin. She was amazing. Brilliant. The fact that she chose me over a legion of men who admired her was heady stuff.'

A twinge of jealousy twisted in her chest. 'You fell for her.'

'Hard. And she put me to work, drafting manifestos, taking notes at meetings, running errands. I felt as if I was really doing something.'

The edge in his voice said the memories were not happy ones. 'What happened?'

'Slowly, too slowly, I became aware of the killings. Of women and children. I couldn't see how it helped. When I spoke of my worries to Marianne, she listened. I thought she agreed with me. When a friend approached me to help get his family out of the city, I did. It was a bit of a lark, really, fooling the gendarmes. But I discovered there were others doing the same. And soon I was involved up to my neck.'

'I heard that many of the aristos escaped because of such people,' she said, feeling glad about what he had done, but beginning to wonder why he was telling her all of this.

'Something made Marianne suspicious. Likely my absences at night.' He shook his head. 'First she accused me of having an affair with another woman. I came home one day after delivering a letter for her and discovered that she'd gone through my papers. Looking for love letters, no doubt.' He sounded bitter. 'What she learned instead was that I was an English nobleman. You would think I was poison the way she turned on me. She didn't care about my beliefs, or the work I had done in advancing the cause. My title meant I was no longer worthy of her trust.'

'She hurt you.'

He leaned forward, and gazed at his hands loosely clasped between his knees. 'I honestly thought she loved me.' He looked up. 'Sounds a little egotistical now, but I would have given my life for her love. I needed someone to believe in me. I was very young. When she wouldn't listen, I left. And out of her sphere of influence I truly saw the direction the revolution was taking. It was not one I was prepared to follow. I became involved with a group trying to save the Queen's life.'

She swallowed. 'Risky indeed.'

'Yes. And Marianne wasn't yet done with me. She followed me one evening, determined to catch me out so she could denounce me.' He stood up and went to the porthole to look out, his shoulders tense. 'I never dreamed she would betray me. She followed me to one of our secret meetings. One of the others saw her and watched her write a note in a coffee shop. When she left, he grabbed her. The note, addressed to a police inspector, listed not only me, but everyone at the meeting.'

'She intended to have you arrested.'

He nodded tersely. 'I learned later that she had been killed in order to save my life. So I could continue working against what she believed in.' Bitterness twisted his lips.

'Gabe.'

He turned and faced her, shoulders square. 'That is who I am, Nicky. What I am.' He spoke matter of factly, but the pain in his voice was like a blade.

'Why are you telling me this?'

His expression darkened. 'You know too much. You could well suffer the same fate as Marianne.'

She put a hand to her throat. 'You think the English will kill me.'

'I know they will. The moment we land in England, you have to disappear. Freddy will help. But the Countess Vilandry must be no more. We can never see each other again.'

'Never?' The word was a knife to her heart, but the look in his eyes said he meant it. 'But—'

'They won't trust you, Nicky. They know you were working for Moreau. They already made one attempt to kill you. In Hyde Park. My most recent orders are to end your life.'

'Are you saying I am the target of the English?'

He nodded. 'Yes. It was them who fired that shot in Hyde Park. It was meant for you, not me. By rearing up, Bacchus saved your life. But they won't miss next time. They have proof you are a spy.'

'It was all a mistake.'

His expression hardened. 'Britain can't afford mistakes. They won't hesitate. And don't forget Minette.'

Her heart stopped beating. 'She is only a child.'

'She's a woman. Full-grown. The only way to protect her is for you to get as far from me as possible. America would be best.'

He knew she would do anything to protect her sister. If he was right, what choice did she have? 'You really think they would harm her?'

'Yes.' The implacability in his voice told her he believed what he was saying.

'Then you are saying this must be *au revoir*.'

He paced the small space between the bed and

the bulkhead. When he finally faced her his expression was deathly calm. Determined. 'Yes.'

She wasn't sure she could bear it, yet she could see he would not have it any other way.

She held out her arms to him. 'Oh, Gabe.'

Gabe stared into her eyes, consumed by a need he hadn't expected and didn't want. It held him in thrall. Not just desire, but something deeper and stronger and, if the pounding of his heart was anything to go by, far more dangerous.

Something he would never dare speak of. Not when he had so little to give to this beautiful, brave woman. Yet he could not resist her offer of one last kiss, but that must be all it was. He caged her small face in his hands, felt the silk of her skin against the pads of his fingers and looked deep into her eyes, willing her to be sensible. 'We should not do this.' Not when he had to give up all hope of happiness to ensure she was safe. Give up his love.

How it had happened in so short a time, he didn't know. Perhaps it was her courage. Or her quick wit, or those damned freckles. Or everything together. It didn't matter how, or why. It just was.

She lifted her face and gave him a kiss so tender it caused what felt like an enormous fissure in the shield around his lonely heart. The sweet ache rocked him.

He loved her. His heart stuttered. The words hovered on the tip of his tongue. But he didn't dare speak them. Not now he had decided she must go.

She was far more important to him than anyone in his life had ever been. To admit that to anyone, even her, in his line of work, might well mean her death. If anyone, friend or foe, suspected just how much she meant, they would move heaven and earth to use her against him.

He made a sound, like a soft groan—half anger, half laughter—and pulled her into his arms. He shouldn't do this. But it would be a memory and he'd take whatever he could get. He kissed her.

Her heart thudded wildly against his chest. She kissed him back with fervour and he sank into the wonder of her lips, her soft body pressed against his, the way everything else fell away, leaving nothing but them. He pulled her to her feet and turned her around, dealing swiftly with her fastenings and her buttons and the laces of her stays until all but her shift were heaped on the floor. He pulled the pins from her glorious mane of hair.

'My,' she said, smiling over her shoulder as he swept her hair aside and pressed kisses to the freckles on her nape, 'you are quicker than any maid.'

'I have reason to be.' He was aching to be inside her. His arms aching to hold her one let time. His lips longing to taste every inch of her.

She turned and sat on the bed, her expression gentle and misty. So lovely. So delicate. So fragile. Yet the heat of her own desire glowed in her eyes. He swallowed against the dryness in his throat.

Leaning back on her elbows, the swell of her breasts, the hard little points of her nipples, pulling the fine fabric tight, she arched a dark brow. 'Do you need my help?'

Hell, he'd been standing stock still, staring at her like a randy schoolboy. 'It will be quicker if

I do it myself.' To prove it, he removed his boots and stripped out of his clothes, unable to take his gaze from the lovely vision on the bed as he did so.

She licked her lips, gazing unashamedly at his hard, naked body.

He grew even harder.

'Tease,' he said, smiling.

'Not at all. You know I always keep my promises.'

The image of her between his knees in the carriage flashed into his mind. A breath left his lungs in a hiss of pleasure.

'You honour me,' he said hoarsely. Yes, he wanted that and from the way she was looking at him, she wanted it too. But he wanted more. He wanted to give as well as take and they had so little time.

He leaned over and took her lovely, lush mouth in a long, drugging kiss, his hands stroking her slim, soft shoulders, her arms, while he climbed up to lie beside her.

He raised his head to look down her length. 'You are lovely,' he whispered. 'Beyond words.'

She smiled and sighed. 'Oh Gabe, you do know how to flatter—'

He pressed a finger to her lips. 'No flattery. No pretence. No lies. Not here. Not now. Forget the war. There is only us. Together. '

Her eyes widened.

He held his breath. Could she let it all go, for this brief moment of time?

A sheen of moisture glimmered in her eyes. She blinked it away. 'Yes,' she said softly. 'Us. Together.'

'Just this last time' hung in the air.

The recognition of that truth gutted him, but he needed her far too much to analyse what it might mean.

He dipped his head to kiss her and she twined her arms around his neck, rising to meet him halfway. His match. His love. Inwardly, he smiled at the pleasure of that word. With tender lingering kisses he dragged himself from her lips to her jaw, to her ear. She gasped at the touch of his tongue and he teased and tormented while she mewled and twisted her hips beneath the weight of his thigh. So sensual. So enticing.

Freckles stood out against her pale skin, a mirror image of scattered stars in a night sky. They beckoned his lips and his tongue. He followed their trail to the swell of her high breasts and nuzzled at her nipple. She arched her back, pressing against his mouth. He suckled.

The deep groan of approval left him in no doubt of her pleasure. This she liked. Greatly. He devoted himself to the task, giving each delicious peak equal attention until her nails were digging into his back in mindless tension. He moved over her. Her thighs parted in welcome.

His welcome. His woman. A bone-deep shudder of possession rippled through his body.

'Now?' he asked, gazing down into her face.

'Now,' she urged, lifting her hips.

He eased into her. So tight. So hot.

Her eyes glazed with real pleasure. As if the mask she wore to keep out the world she lowered just for him. That look hit him hard. Made him feel powerful and humble at one and the same time. A strangely heartbreaking combination.

For years, he'd never doubted his prowess. But this time was different. The urge to please her more than any other man ever had was paramount.

He drove forward.

Her sigh was music to his ears.

'Tell me what you like,' he rasped from a throat that seemed to have swallowed a cartload of gravel.

The dreamy expression sharpened, her eyes widened. Apparently no man had ever asked. He did not mask his smile of satisfaction and she giggled.

'Tell me,' he insisted, smiling down at her. 'Anything you want.'

'Slow,' she said softly, her lashes fluttering shyly as if she were a virgin. 'And deep.' She lifted her legs and wrapped them high around his waist. 'So I can reach the top, tip over and then go higher still.'

His body jerked at the honesty of her words. No virginal miss, this woman. But incredibly sweet. And as wicked as hell. And his. He kissed her mouth. 'As many times as you want, *ma belle*. I promise.'

A promise he would keep.

He drove long and slow, deep into her body, over and over again, watching the play of expressions over her face, and feeling in the subtle movements of her hips and the stroking of her inner muscles, which movement brought the most pleasure. The internal flutters grew stronger, more frequent, and he watched in awe as she tipped over into bliss while he fought his climax, the tickle at the head of his shaft, the drawing up of his balls.

Before she had a chance to drift into total bliss, he moved again.

The third time she came, the look of abandon on her face undid him. Her skin was slick with sweat beneath his fingers, her forehead and upper lip bedewed and tasted salty on his tongue. He had nothing left to give.

He drove into her hard and fast.

'Yes,' she said. 'That.'

The word sent a rush of heat that took him hard. His body took control and his mind went blank. And beneath him he was aware that as he hit the peak she also shuddered to her own climax.

He collapsed, barely able to move to the side so

as not to crush her with his weight. He lay panting, weightless, mindless and for ever enslaved.

'It's all right,' she said.

He blinked at what seemed like a mist distorting his vision.

'Don't cry.' she whispered, smoothing a palm across his cheeks.

He rolled on his back and covered his eyes with his forearm. 'Sweat,' he mumbled.

'No lies, remember, Gabe,' her soft voice with its pretty accent admonished gently.

'Tears of joy,' he admitted.

Heaven help him, he was ruined. He loved her. Love had always been his downfall.

He had to let her go. He could not cage such a free spirit and there would be no other way to keep her safe.

The ship creaked and heeled over. A change in the wind. He felt the ship leap forward, heading for England, and saw emptiness stretched out before him.

Gabe brought them to his London town house where he could be sure of his servants' discretion. He'd left her here with Minette and gone first to report to his superiors with Freddy, and then to the docks to arrange for their passages to America. He'd left them shortly after breakfast.

Minette looked up from her book. 'Should Mooreshead not have returned by now?'

Nicky glanced at the clock. Almost two. She'd expected him before this. Though he'd gone to great pains to disguise his worry, he'd clearly been concerned about the meeting. The few words she'd managed alone with Freddy had made it plain that by going to France, he had committed a grave sin. She could not prevent the tremor building inside her. Her fear for him. 'He will return when he has completed his business.'

Minette got up and went to the window, looking down into the street, but careful not to be seen from below. Dark-haired, dark eyes, she was beautiful. So much like the mother they had lost. Nicky had the constant urge to touch her, just to make sure she was real.

'Gabe won't let us down,' she said.

Minette spun around, her hands clasped at the waist. 'How can you bear it?'

Startled, she stared at her sister. 'Bear what?'

'Leaving him. You love him.'

Nicky flushed. She hadn't realised she had been wearing her heart on her sleeve. 'It is for our safety. And besides, I am not sure he feels the same way.' She gave a small laugh that came out false and brittle despite her efforts to keep it carefree. 'His work for the government is more important than I am.'

'Spying, you mean.'

'Minette!' she gasped. 'How can you say such a thing?'

'I should think it is obvious.'

'What is obvious?'

Nicky started at the sound of Gabe's voice outside of the room. Coloured up as he sauntered in with Freddy and the two men made their bows.

'What is obvious?' Gabe asked again, looking at her with eyes full of regret, his shoulders set square and determined.

'That you don't want us here because we are inconveniently French,' Minette said.

'I had heard that French manners were impeccable,' Freddy muttered. 'It seems the rumours are wrong.'

Gabe raised his brows in question. Nicky shook her head. She had no idea why her sister was acting this way. The years had changed her. 'Did you find a ship?'

'Your passages are booked for tomorrow.'

So soon. The realisation made her heart shrivel a little more, but she kept her face calm. 'Thank you.'

'The necessary introductions and a draft on my bank will arrive before it is time to depart, along with your effects from Golden Square.'

'Mrs Featherstone?'

Anger filled his expressions. 'Gone. With your jewels, I'm afraid.'

'They were nothing but paste. I am glad she left my wardrobe. She could have sold everything.'

'She left in too much of a hurry from what I gather. Your groom, Reggie, wants to know what he should do about your mare. It seems that he has every intention of following you to America. Seems to think it's his duty to stand by you. I for one am glad of it. I hope you don't mind, I bought a ticket for him and the horse.'

Her heart ached at his thoughtfulness. 'I fear I am putting you to a terrible expense.'

He brushed her protest aside with a sharp gesture. 'It is the least I can do.'

A loud hammering on the front door echoed through the house. 'What the devil?' Gabe said.

Freddy beat him to the window and his face was a frozen mask when he glanced at Gabe, who had reached his side.

'Sceptre?'

'Damn it,' Gabe said. 'How did they find out?'

'What is going on?' Minette asked. 'You are talking in riddles.'

'It seems that despite my best efforts to keep your presence here a secret, we are discovered.'

'They know about me. That I worked for Moreau,' Nicky said. 'Am I to be arrested?' She rose to her feet. 'None of this is to do with Minette.'

The hammering increased in volume. 'If we delay any longer, they are going to break down the door,' Freddy said. 'Tell me what you want me to do, but you know they will find you eventually.'

Gabe's expression darkened as he looked at her. 'I should never have brought you here.' The pain in the depth of his gaze was palpable. 'We can try running. But Nicky, you'll never be free.' He took a deep breath. 'There has to be some sort of trade-off.'

'What do you mean by a trade-off? Trade-off with who?' Nicky asked, terrified by the resolution in his face. 'What are you thinking of doing?'

'Sceptre,' Freddy said. 'They've been after Gabe to go to France. To find a way to get on Napoleon's staff.'

'No,' Nicky said. 'It is too dangerous.'

'Perhaps it won't come to that,' Gabe said. 'What I am not going to do is let them force you into hiding for the rest of your life. You've had enough of that. You should have the chance to live as you please.'

'Not if it means putting you in danger,' she said softly.

The sound of shattering wood silenced all conversation. Heavy footsteps ran up the stairs and then a cavalry captain stood on the threshold.

His gaze swept the room. 'Mooreshead?' he rapped out.

Gabe stepped forward. 'Yes.'

The man looked relieved as if he had expected Gabe to have somehow evaded him. 'Your presence is requested at the Queen's House.'

Gabe returned Nicky's puzzled glance. Clearly this was not what he had expected.

'Along with the Countess Vilandry,' the captain added.

Gabe shook his head. 'The countess has nothing to do with this.'

'I'm sorry, my lord. Those are my orders. I would prefer it if you came of your own free will.'

The threat was clear.

'Minette,' Nicky said, her heart racing.

'She'll be safe with me,' Freddy said. 'No matter what happens.'

Despite the fearful thumping in her chest, Nicky believed him. 'Then it seems we must obey the summons.'

Gabe escorted Nicky down to the waiting carriage where a troop of light horse waited to escort them. Their captain opened the carriage door.

'Are we under arrest?' Nicky asked him.

'If you would be so good as to get in, my lady?' he said without inflection. He looked at Gabe. 'Please leave the blinds down.'

Gabe helped her in and the soldier shut the door.

'What is happening, Gabe?'

The grim expression on his face did not bode well. 'Follow my lead. Whatever you do, don't argue. Promise me?'

She nodded and tried not to show the fear that had her so firmly in its grip her mind was blank. It must be like this for those taken by tumbril to the guillotine, this empty feeling, but at least they were not to be paraded through the streets, the target of the public. Also, rather strangely, the soldiers had surrounded them in such a way as to hide them from the curious stares of those gathering outside the house.

The Queen's House was located at the end of the Mall only a short ride away. Nicky's legs felt as stiff as boards when she climbed down at the palace door and they were finally ushered into an imposing drawing room.

A small grey-haired woman sat in a high-backed chair.

Gabe looked stunned for a moment, then bowed elegantly. 'Your Majesty.'

Startled, Nicky gasped. This was the Queen. Gathering her wits, she curtsied deeply.

When she rose, she discovered the Queen had raised a lorgnette and was studying Gabe closely. 'So you are Mooreshead. You don't look like a revolutionary.'

The Queen had a heavy Germanic accent and there was a severe edge to her expression.

'Your Majesty, I assure you I am a loyal British subject.'

'So we have been led to believe.'

Gabe gestured towards Nicky. 'May I introduce Countess Nicoletta Vilandry, your Majesty, a loyal subject of France?'

'Ah, yes. We have heard reports of you,' the Queen said. 'But which France?'

Beside her, Gabe stiffened 'Your Majesty—'

'King Louis's France,' Nicky said proudly.

The Queen gestured for silence.

Gabe pressed his lips together.

'We asked you here today to personally extend our thanks for your timely intervention last week.'

A stunned look crossed Gabe's face. 'It was my duty, ma'am.'

'Hmmph. The King's talked of nothing else for days. His health—' She shook her head. 'We did not bring you hear to discuss that. Your father served you a bad turn, Mooreshead, but you have proved your loyalty over and over again. We do not agree with this trusteeship your father set up.'

Gabe's jaw dropped. 'No, your Majesty.'

'Our opinion is that the terms of your father's will are insupportable. It will be dissolved.' She frowned at Nicky. 'And you, *madame*, we gather it is your wish to depart our country?'

Nicky looked at Gabe, but his face remained blank. He'd made it very clear he feared for her and Minette's life if she remained and she wasn't sure that this interview had changed his opinion.

But the Queen had asked her a question. 'I do

not want to leave, your Majesty, but I am told that it is not safe for me to remain.'

'This is true, Mooreshead?'

'Your Majesty, my work...'

'That work is finished. You have other matters we require of you. Your estates. Your seat in our Parliament. And should the countess wish to remain, we will have no objection. Do we make ourselves clear? We need your support in the halls of government at this critical time.'

Astonishment on his face, he bowed. 'Indeed, your Majesty.'

She waved a hand. 'Very good.'

The equerry signalled for them to leave and they backed out.

Outside the closed door, Gabe looked stunned. 'I gather I've been relieved from duty.'

She frowned. 'Are you saying she is part of this spy organisation you work for?'

'Lord, I don't know. But it is a good political move to bring a man as Whiggish as I am presumed to be into government circles.' He took her hand and kissed the back of it. 'It seems you are free to stay or go. It is your choice, Nicky.'

Even though it would hurt him, he was prepared to let her go, so she could be free. She could see it in his face. In his eyes. He would not make her his puppet.

'Do you want me to stay?' she asked, just to be sure, because the Nicky of old had been so uncertain and apparently she was pushing the countess aside.

Gabe groaned. 'I have never wanted anything so much in all my life.'

She smiled. 'Then I will stay.'

He glanced around them and then dropped to one knee. 'I know this is hardly the time or the place, but, Nicky, I have to take this chance. Will you marry me?'

Her eyes felt as if they might pop out of her head. She glanced at the footman a few feet away. 'Gabe? Are you mad?'

'Nicky, I love you. I want you to be my wife. Will you marry me? Only say yes if you truly want this too.'

Her gaze went all misty. 'Are you sure?'

'I have never been so certain of anything in my life. But the last thing I want is for you to feel forced into something because you are too soft-hearted to say no. Whatever you decide, I will make sure you and Minette never want for anything. I want you to be happy. Nothing else.'

'Oh, Gabe, yes. I love you so much. I thought you didn't want me any more and that was why you were sending us away.'

He rose to his feet and cradled her face in his hands, kissing her lips so tenderly. 'It was breaking my heart to let you go. I can't believe...' He glanced at the closed door. 'As I said, this is neither the time or the place, my darling, darling, brave, loyal girl, but you have made me the happiest man alive.'

The nearby footman applauded, the sound muffled by his gloves, but there was no mistaking his grin.

They left the palace, giggling like children.

Epilogue

Not only had the Queen insisted that the Marquess of Mooreshead be permitted to marry his French bride, she'd insisted that the Prince of Wales give her away. Much to Nicky's surprise, the whole St George's church thing became the wedding of the year. The support of royalty made them the most popular of couples among the *ton*.

With the matter of his father's will in the hands of the lawyers, they had come to Meak at the beginning of October. The Earl of Beresford and his wife had called in to take afternoon tea on their way to a brief sojourn at the Abbey.

While the two men discussed the progress of the war, Lady Beresford, Mary as she had asked Nicky to call her, was relaying the latest *on dit* from town while they waited for Minette to return from her afternoon ride.

With a quick glance at her husband, Mary leaned closer. 'Beresford said you visited the Abbey before you wed.'

Nicky knew Gabe trusted his friend and if he had imparted the knowledge of her sojourn in Cornwall, she wasn't going to deny it to the man's wife. 'A few days.'

'Did you meet our resident ghost?'

Nicky frowned. 'Surely you do not believe—'

Mary nodded. 'I do. She saved my life on at least one occasion. Possibly two.'

A coincidence, surely? Or perhaps not? Her face must have given her thoughts away.

'You did see her,' Mary said gleefully.

'I think I saw something. A sort of shimmery light.' She frowned.

Mary nodded eagerly. 'She brought me and Bane together.' She slid a glance towards Gabe. 'Did she do the same for you?

If Nicky had not fallen in the tunnel, would she and Gabe ever have trusted each other? 'Perhaps,' she said cautiously. 'If it is so, I will be for ever grateful.'

'Me too,' Mary said softly, looking over at her tall stern-looking husband and placing her hand on her stomach. She was in the last stages of pregnancy. Nicky had quickly learned that the earl's gruff manner hid a kindly heart.

The door opened. Walter stood framed between the jambs, looking as proud as a peacock in his new butler's livery. He wasn't a very good butler, but he tried very hard and it was easy to forgive his little foibles.

'A guest for you, my lord,' he announced carefully.

Gabe looked up sharply. He'd been looking as if he was expecting someone for the last few days, glancing out of the window at odd moments and cocking his head at the sound of wheels on the drive, even if it was nothing more interesting that the local butcher making a delivery. 'Who is it, Walter?'

'A friend of yours, he said, my lord. He'll be right along.'

Mary covered a smile with her hand at this rather unconventional announcement.

They all turned to face the door as Walter stepped back and waved the newcomer in.

'Freddy?' Nicky said.

The young man looked travel-stained and his eyes held exhaustion.

'Good to see you back safe,' Gabe said, getting up and going to the table, which held a decanter of brandy. He handed Freddy a glass.

So this was who he had been expecting. She might have guessed. Gabe had been having some difficulty adjusting to the role of idle nobleman about town, as he called it. Not that he had been all that idle. There were a great many matters of business required of the Marquess of Moores-head, now that he was to be afforded all the rights and privileges of the title.

'Sit down and tell us your news,' Gabe said.

Freddy hesitated, looking around the room, then took a deep breath. 'You'll hear about it sooner or later, but keep it under your hats for now.'

'Bad news?' Beresford asked.

'It was an utter *débâcle*,' Freddy said. 'Not one French ship did we damage.'

'Fulton's toys did not work?' Gabe said.

'What are these toys you speak of?' Nicky asked. 'And who is this Fulton?'

'An American inventor,' Gabe said.

'I had the pleasure of trying to use what he calls a torpedo catamaran,' Freddy said. 'I paddled the damn thing all the way across Boulogne harbour. The French saw us coming and I barely escaped with my life. The damned thing was so low in the water the powder was wet before I got anywhere near one of their ships. Not even the fire ships reached their targets.'

'So the invasion threat continues,' Bane said.

Freddy looked grim. 'So it appears.' He glanced up as Minette strode into the room, her expression stormy.

She glared back at him. 'What are you doing here?'

'Freddy is my guest,' Gabe said sternly. 'It would behove you to treat him as such.'

'Pah,' Minette said, then dipped a curtsy, looking as if butter wouldn't melt in her mouth. 'Welcome to Meak, *milor'*.'

Colour stained Freddy's cheekbones. 'How many stable boys have you cheated out of their wages this week, brat?'

Minette lifted her chin. 'I do not cheat, do I, Nicky?'

'If you do, it is not terribly successful,' Nicky said frowning. 'This morning I had to reclaim the brooch Gabe gave you for your birthday for the sum of one shilling. I wish you would not gamble with the servants.'

Minette shrugged. 'Can I help it if I am bored?'

Gabe's mouth tightened, but he did not say anything. For Nicky's sake, he was doing his best to be gentle with Minette. She had refused to talk about what had happened during the three years she had been required to survive on her own in France.

'As pleasant as this scene of domesticity is, I cannot stay,' Freddy said tersely, putting his glass down with a snap and rising to his feet. 'I have to be in London tonight, but I knew you would want to hear how it went, Gabe.'

'Thank you. I did.' Gabe rose to shake the young man's hand. 'Be careful.'

'Why don't I see you out?' Minette said. 'It is always a pleasure to bid you *au revoir*.'

'The feeling is mutual,' Freddy said.

Minette flounced out of the door.

Freddy made his bows and followed her out.

'My goodness,' Mary said. 'Young love does not go smoothly.'

Surprised, Nicky stared at her. 'I assure you, it is quite the opposite, they disliked each other on sight.'

'It is often the way of it,' Mary said mysteriously. 'And it is also time we departed if we are to reach our inn in time for dinner.'

The earl shot to his feet with a fond look at his wife. 'We are making the journey in easy stages. Mary has decided that our child should be born at the Abbey.'

'Hopefully Walter ordered your carriage brought round as requested,' Nicky said.

Gabe glanced out of the window. 'He did.'

Together they walked to the front door. To Nicky's surprise, Freddy and Minette were nowhere to be seen. She and Gabe watched the Beresfords' carriage disappear down the drive at a slow and sedate pace. Gabe put his arms around her shoulders and bent to kiss her cheek. 'Happy?'

He never took her happiness for granted, no matter how often she assured him her life was perfect as long as they were together. The soft feeling in her heart expanded and she smiled at him through her own tears. 'I love you, husband.'

'As I love you,' he said, his voice hoarse with emotion, his eyes tender.

She couldn't put what she felt into words at that moment. It was deep, it was wide and it was full of contentment. Her cup runneth over.

Yes. That described it exactly. Her cup was full and overflowing. With love.

* * * * *

MILLS & BOON®

Why shop at millsandboon.co.uk?

Each year, thousands of romance readers find their perfect read at millsandboon.co.uk. That's because we're passionate about bringing you the very best romantic fiction. Here are some of the advantages of shopping at www.millsandboon.co.uk:

* **Get new books first**—you'll be able to buy your favourite books one month before they hit the shops

* **Get exclusive discounts**—you'll also be able to buy our specially created monthly collections, with up to 50% off the RRP

* **Find your favourite authors**—latest news, interviews and new releases for all your favourite authors and series on our website, plus ideas for what to try next

* **Join in**—once you've bought your favourite books, don't forget to register with us to rate, review and join in the discussions

Visit **www.millsandboon.co.uk**
for all this and more today!